TOVE DITLEVSEN

The Faces

Tove Ditlevsen was born in 1917 in a working-class neighborhood in Copenhagen. Her first volume of poetry was published when she was in her early twenties and was followed by many more books, including the three volumes of *The Copenhagen Trilogy: Childhood* (1967), *Youth* (1967), and *Dependency* (1971). She died in 1976.

ALSO BY TOVE DITLEVSEN

FICTION

The Trouble with Happiness

NONFICTION

The Copenhagen Trilogy

   Childhood

   Youth

   Dependency

The Faces

The Faces

TOVE DITLEVSEN

Translated from the Danish by TIINA NUNNALLY

PICADOR   NEW YORK

Picador
120 Broadway, New York 10271

Copyright © 1968 by Tove Ditlevsen & Hasselbalch, Copenhagen
Translation copyright © 1991 by Tiina Nunnally
All rights reserved
Printed in the United States of America
Originally published in Danish in 1968 by Hasselbalch, Denmark, as *Ansigterne*
English translation first published in 1991 in the United States by Fjord Press
English translation published in 2020 by Penguin Random House, Great Britain
First American edition, 2022

Library of Congress Cataloging-in-Publication Data
Names: Ditlevsen, Tove Irma Margit, 1917–1976, author. | Nunnally, Tiina,
    translator.
Title: The faces / Tove Ditlevsen ; Translated from the Danish by Tiina
    Nunnally.
Other titles: Ansigterne. English
Description: First American edition. | New York : Picador, 2022.
Identifiers: LCCN 2021050353 | ISBN 9781250838193 (paperback)
Classification: LCC PT8176.14.I58 A5713 2022 | DDC 839.8/1372—dc23
LC record available at https://lccn.loc.gov/2021050353

Our books may be purchased in bulk for promotional, educational, or business
use. Please contact your local bookseller or the Macmillan Corporate and
Premium Sales Department at 1-800-221-7945, extension 5442, or by email at
MacmillanSpecialMarkets@macmillan.com.

Picador® is a U.S. registered trademark and is used by Macmillan Publishing
Group, LLC, under license from Pan Books Limited.

For book club information, please visit facebook.com/picadorbookclub or email
marketing@picadorusa.com.

picadorusa.com • instagram.com/picador
twitter.com/picadorusa • facebook.com/picadorusa

10 9 8 7 6 5 4 3 2 1

The Faces

In the evening it was a little better. She could smooth it out and look at it, cautiously, hoping that someday she would have a full view of it, as if it were an unfinished, multi-colored Gobelin tapestry whose pattern would perhaps be revealed one day. The voices came back to her; with a little patience, they could be unraveled from each other like the strands of a tangled ball of yarn. She could think about the words in peace, without fearing that new ones would appear before the night was over. During this time the night held the days apart only with difficulty, and if she happened to breathe a hole into the darkness, like on a frost-covered windowpane, the morning might shine into her eyes hours ahead of time.

They were all asleep except Gert, who hadn't come home yet, even though it was almost midnight. They slept, and their faces were blank and peaceful and didn't have to be used again until morning. Maybe they had even taken off their faces and placed them prudently on top of their clothes, to give them a rest; they weren't absolutely necessary while they were sleeping. In the daytime the faces were constantly changing, as if she saw them reflected in flowing water. Eyes, nose, mouth – that simple triangle – and yet how could it contain such an infinite number of variations? For a long time she had avoided going out on the street because the crowd of faces frightened her. She didn't dare take on any new ones, and she was afraid of meeting the old ones again. They didn't match her memory of them at all – in her memory they had lain down next to the dead, whom she was protected from in a different way. When she met people she hadn't seen in years, their faces had changed, aged, turned strange, and no one had tried to prevent it. She hadn't taken care of them, they had slipped out of her protective hands, which should have held them up above the surface of the water like people drowning.

Preoccupied with other things, she hadn't taken care of the face, and at the very last moment it was replaced by a new one, stolen from a dead or sleeping person, who then had to make do as best he could. It was either too big or too small, and it bore traces of a life that didn't belong to the new owner. And yet, when you got used to it, glimpses of the original face would appear, just the way old wallpaper will crack and reveal patches of the hidden layer underneath, still fresh and well-preserved and filled with memories of the former tenants of the house.

But some people, out of impatience or a need to keep up with fashion, would take on a new face long before the old one was worn out, just as people buy new clothes even though the ones they have on have hardly been worn. Many young girls were like that, and sometimes they would even trade individual features with a girlfriend, if they were going out in the evening and wanted to dress up with eyes that were bigger and brighter than their own, or with a nose that was more slender. This made their skin tighten up, of course, but it felt no worse than wearing shoes that pinched because they were a size too small.

But it was most apparent in children who were still growing. You couldn't fix them with your gaze; it would reflect off them, as empty as a mirror that you've stared at for a long time. Children wore their faces like something they had to grow into, which wouldn't fit them for many years. The face was almost always put on too high, and they had to stand on tiptoe and make a tremendous effort just to see the images on the inside of their eyelids.

Some of them, especially girls, had had to live out their mother's childhood while their own lay hidden in a secret drawer. Those kinds of girls had the most trouble. Their voices would break out of them like pus from a sore, and the sound would frighten them, just like when they discovered that someone had been reading their diary, even though it was locked up among the junk and old toys from the time they had worn the discarded face of a four-year-old. That face would stare up at them from among the tops and crippled dolls with innocent, astonished glass eyes. They slept lightly; their sleep smelled of terror. Every evening when they cleaned up their rooms they had to gather their thoughts for the night like birds that have to be coaxed into their cages. Sometimes one of them didn't belong to the girls, and then they wouldn't know what to do with it. Hurriedly, since they were always tired, they would stuff it in the back of a cupboard or in between two books on the shelf. But when these girls woke up, their thoughts didn't suit their faces anymore; the faces had dissolved during sleep – Halloween masks whose stiff cardboard had become torn and soggy from their warm breath. With difficulty they would put on the new faces like destiny, and they would get dizzy looking down at their feet, the distance had grown so great overnight.

She looked out into the room, out of the corner of her eye, without moving her head. There was a dressing table, a nightstand, and two chairs. The room seemed bare as a grave with no headstone or cross. It resembled the rented rooms of her youth where she had written her first books, and this was the only place where she found that fragile sense of security which is nothing more than the absence of change. She was lying on her back on her made-up bed with her hands behind her head.

It was essential to remain completely still and avoid sudden movements so that whatever was inside the built-in cupboards, those disturbing cavities, would not come tumbling out with all the compressed terror of her entire childhood.

Slowly she reached out her hand for the sleeping pills. She shook out two of them and washed them down with water. She had gotten them from Gitte, who gave all of them whatever she thought they needed. Gitte required more alertness than the others. You had to stifle certain words before they crossed her lips, at any cost and by any means. It was a disadvantage, thought Lise, that they were on a first-name basis. She and Gert had had a few drinks with Gitte on one of the first evenings after she had started working for them, and since she was not without a certain junior-college 'sophistication', they had felt they couldn't treat her like an ordinary housekeeper, whose personal life was none of the family's business.

Gitte was a result of Lise's sudden fame two years ago, when she had been awarded the Academy's prize for children's literature for a book that she herself had considered no better or worse than her other books. Aside from a virtually ignored collection of poetry, she had never written anything except children's books. They had been nicely reviewed in the women's pages, had sold well, and had been reassuringly overlooked by the world that was preoccupied with literature for adults. Fame had brutally ripped away the veil that had always separated her from reality. She had given a thank-you speech that Gert had written for her, and during the speech she had been seized by her childhood fear of being unmasked, fear that someone would discover that she was putting on an act and pretending to be someone she was not.

That fear had never really left her since. Whenever she was interviewed, it was always Gert's or Asger's opinions she repeated, as if she had never possessed an independent thought.

When Asger left her ten years ago, he had left behind a storehouse of words and ideas inside her, like a forgotten suitcase in the left-luggage room at the train station. When she had used them up, she drew on Gert's opinions, which changed with his mood. Only when she wrote did she express her own self, and she had no other talent.

Gert had taken her fame as a personal affront. He maintained that he couldn't go to bed with a piece of literature, and he cheated on her with great diligence, keeping her meticulously informed of his conquests. She had felt as if her soul were sinking down into a hole in the ice because, at the time, she still loved him and was gripped by the fear of losing him too.

Nadia, her best friend, who was a child psychologist, had sent her to a psychiatrist, who had explained to her that she attracted men with complex emotional lives and assertive personalities, filled with doubt about their own abilities. She had been a clever patient and had discovered certain similarities between Asger and Gert. Except that Asger, rather late in life, had been seized by that career ambition which requires the absolute, tireless cooperation of the family; and a wife who wrote something as ridiculous as children's books was suddenly a liability, a weakness in himself that his enemies might pounce on at any moment. On the other hand, Dr Jørgensen explained to her, Gert's infidelities would never lead to divorce, since they were committed primarily on her behalf. It was merely an act of spite, just as two-year-old children spatter their porridge. Gert was bound to her by virtue of his own neurotic entanglements, and it was hardly likely that he would relinquish his identity again to something that only resembled love.

The sleeping pills were starting to work, and because she wasn't on her guard, a face tore itself loose from all the others and began to stare at her with that old, undisguised malice. It

7

was the face of a dwarf she had turned around to look at as a child; at the same instant he had turned his head and looked at her. To the end of her days she would carry that face with her like an ancient guilt that no remorse could expiate.

The key was turned in the front door and the sound reached her as if through many layers of wool blankets. It was Gert coming home. She heard him walk through the dining room and thought he was going out to the kitchen for a beer or into the maid's room to see Gitte. Then the door opened and he was standing in the doorway of her room.

'Are you asleep?'

'No.'

She raised herself on her elbows and looked at his shoes. They came closer, getting bigger and bigger, like in an absurd drama where mushrooms grow up between the floorboards and getting rid of them every day is the only meaningful act in the world. He came closer and, panic-stricken, she thought that it was just too much to be married to a whole person all at once.

She awakened some of the few words they still had between them; stiff and uncomfortable, they stretched themselves on her lips, like children being yanked out of sleep.

'Sit down,' she said. 'Is something wrong?'

He sat down in the chair on the other side of the nightstand. The light from the lamp fell on his hands, which were clenching and unclenching nervously. His face was hidden by the darkness, and she pulled it out of her memory: delicate and haggard, with small, regular features.

'Yes,' he said. 'Grete has committed suicide.'

She felt his gaze on her face and turned toward the wall. Her heart was pounding rapidly. What were you supposed to feel or say when your husband's lover has taken her own life? There was no precedent. She had grown accustomed to using her old, worn-out feelings on him, just as the blind man orients himself with the aid of more and more distant visual impressions from the time before he was blind. Certain words and tones of voice belonged to these feelings, and it was as dangerous as walking through a minefield to move outside this familiar terrain.

'I'm sorry,' she said with idiotic politeness, 'but weren't you through with her? I thought you told me that.'

Suddenly the green curtains looked as if they were made of crêpe paper. That must be because of the sleeping pills. She noticed how they dulled her alertness.

He moved the lamp in order to reach the cigarettes. Now the light fell on his face, but she had to avoid looking at it.

'Yes,' he sighed. 'But she stayed home from the office without calling in. And they knew, presumably from her, that I had a key to her apartment. Josefsen asked me to go over and see what was wrong. And there she was, lying on the bed with the empty pill bottle in her hand. It was a real shock. Not that it could damage my position, but you can see it's damned embarrassing. They stared at me as if I had murdered her.'

His hands were shaking as he lit a cigarette.

'I knew from the start that it was stupid to choose one of the girls at the office. And someone that age too. When single women reach their mid-thirties, it's risky just to show them a little sympathy.'

'I'm forty,' she said absentmindedly. She regretted it at once. It was part of their exhausting game that she never drew attention to herself. She felt his gaze like a burning searchlight.

'That's different,' he said, annoyed. 'It's hard to take you seriously as a human being anymore. It's like when we see your ex-husband in a magazine as one of the ten best-dressed men in the country. Even you think it's ridiculous.'

'Gert,' she said with that gentleness in her voice that she used to hide her lack of love. 'You don't know that she did it because of you. Nadia says that some people may have a low suicide threshold. Once she told me about a girl who took her own life because her bicycle had been stolen.'

'I know that,' he said. 'I'm not one to overestimate my own importance. But I take my work seriously. And something like this throws it all off.'

For the first time in the conversation, she looked at his face. There was something wrong with it. All his features seemed to be dissociated from each other, like furniture from successive marriages. Two little round pouches had formed under his eyes, as if he were carrying in them the bitter memories from a failed life. Something resembling empathy swept over her for a second, like the beam of a lighthouse over distant waves. Then she caught sight of his ears, which were enormous and overgrown with hair like an animal's. That couldn't be right. She closed her eyes and sank back on the pillow.

'It'll all be forgotten in a few days,' she said. 'Go to your own room now, Gert. I need to sleep.'

'Excuse me,' he said, offended. 'I forgot for a moment that your time is precious.'

He stood up with more noise than was necessary and left the room without saying goodnight.

She turned off the lamp, but the dark brought her no solace. What did he mean, her time was precious? Did he assume that she didn't have long to live?

Someone was running water out in the kitchen, and a boy's rough laughter penetrated into her room. She turned on the light again. It was Mogens who was laughing. He had no idea that she knew he was sleeping with Gitte. Gitte was sleeping with Gert too; she said that it was good for their marriage, which she had set her mind on saving. Over by the wall was a pair of Hanne's shoes, and she hadn't noticed them before. They were red, with pointed toes, and Gert had given them to her. Gitte said it was a shame for the boys that Gert spoiled Hanne like that. Lise had never thought about it until Gitte drew her attention to it. For some reason the sight of the shoes bothered her, and she got up and put them outside her door, before she lay down again and turned off the light.

2

Daylight filled the room with a guileless virginity that for a moment made the events of the night more distant than any random childhood day, preserved in her mind like a thousand-year-old insect encased in a lump of amber.

She pulled back the curtains and looked out on the enclosed courtyard. A thaw had set in, and steam rose up from the oily pavement as if from a wet rag. In the pale, cold February sun a cat was sitting on the lid of a garbage can, licking its paws. She listened to the reassuring murmur of voices from the dining room, where Gitte was eating breakfast with the children. Gitte was protective of Lise's writing time, as if she were a Goethe or a Shakespeare. And in spite of the fact that for two years she hadn't written a line. There was something touching, she said to herself, about that motherless orphan girl who had burned all her bridges to bring order to the existence of total strangers. It dulled her fear to think like that, it made something or other easier, just as when children appear to yield to grownups.

She put on her bathrobe and sat down at the dressing table, making as little noise as possible. In the mirror her face seemed to her tired and used, like an old glove. Her mouth was set in brackets by two faint, sketchy lines that stopped a little before the slope of her chin, as if the unknown artist had been called away in the middle of his work. Her eyes had the same open, sincere expression as in children who are telling a lie. Three delicate wrinkles lay like a pearl necklace around her neck, and they would dig deeper day by day. Would this face last out her time, this face that bore traces of so many things the world must know nothing about? Did it turn toward her with hostility whenever she wasn't looking? And what would be underneath, when it fell apart one fine day? She thought about the much-too-large dresses and shoes that she had worn as a child, always bought to grow into, always designed to fit her just when they were worn out.

Whenever Hanne saw pictures of her in the newspapers, she said: 'Oh, you're so photogenic, Mother.' Søren said: 'You're the most beautiful mother in my class.' Mogens didn't say anything. Gitte said that it was difficult to have a famous mother. She quoted Graham Greene: 'Success is a mutilation of the natural human being.' Gitte used world literature and the newspapers as if they were kitchen appliances that were supposed to make her daily work easier.

The door opened, and she turned her head with a start, as if she had been caught at some secret vice. It was Søren, with a milk mustache over his mouth and a knapsack on his back.

'Goodbye, Mother,' he said uncertainly. 'Gitte said I could come in and see if you were asleep.'

'No, I'm not. Goodbye, Søren. Won't you give me a kiss?'

She leaned down and kissed him on the mouth. He put his arms around her neck, and a smell of interrupted sleep, of school dust and childish guilt, fell over both of them for a moment like a protective cape wrapped mercifully around a fallen foe. She held him by the shoulders and, full of dark sympathy, regarded the exhausted little face.

'You need a haircut,' she said with false cheerfulness and stroked his blond, silky hair.

'No,' he said vehemently and wriggled out of her hands.

'Gitte says that long hair looks good on me. The other kids laugh at me when I've been to the barber.'

'I see.'

She straightened up quickly, and at the same moment Gitte stepped in between them. She took the little boy by the wrist.

'Get going,' she said with authority. 'It's two minutes to eight.'

She strode through the room with the expression of someone who has a goal in life, and stopped as suddenly as a car that brakes before an unexpected roadblock. She picked up the bottle of pills and stared at Lise with an expression of moral intensity in her nearsighted eyes.

'Gert has asked me to keep them,' she said, 'This thing with Grete has given him a shock. He doesn't ever want to go through that again.'

'Oh,' said Lise and sat down on the bed with a feeling of transparency, as if she were clipped out of paper. 'Did he tell you about that?'

'It's your own fault.'

Gitte stuck the bottle carelessly in the pocket of her jeans and sat down next to her. She was fascinatingly ugly, and she smelled of sweat. Lise smiled broadly. Fear filled the room like a liquid. The clock in the dining room struck eight.

'He came in to my room looking for comfort last night. He wanted to make up, Lise. He was ready to come back to you, he wanted to give up all thought of being unfaithful to you. He wanted to go to bed with you. But you were too tired, you wanted to sleep, you didn't understand a thing.'

Her voice resounded with bursting impatience. She put her elbows on her knees and rested her face in the cradle of her hands.

'Gitte,' said Lise, 'don't I get any morning coffee?'

'Oh God, yes. Then we can talk.'

Lise took off her bathrobe and crept down under the comforter again. There was no more sleep to be found in its familiar folds. Nadia, she thought, I'll call her today. She leaned toward the gentle, unwavering image that Nadia had of her. Nadia found her to be impressively tolerant, but she mistook tolerance for indifference. To be intolerant you had to be involved. Candor, she thought, that's all that Gitte is asking for right now, a little corner of my soul, an expression of something human. Then one more day would pass before the hatred broke loose.

'Now eat something, you need it, I've just baked some bread.'

Gitte placed herself in the chair where Gert had sat during the night, and she poured coffee into two cups.

'You have to understand,' she said earnestly, 'that it was awful for him. He had to call the police and an ambulance, and he was questioned like a criminal.'

'Yes, I know that. But it's as if it happened to someone I don't know anymore, if you know what I mean.'

'Yes, I do, but you missed the right moment. And then he came in to see me, but I'm only a substitute for you, like so many things are. He said that it had all just been revenge against you.'

'What have I ever done to him?'

Lise stirred her coffee while she saw her daughter Hanne's closed, enigmatic face in front of her. Whenever she went past Hanne – they had avoided touching each other for a long time – she noticed the smell of warm milk and wet rubber boots from her own childhood and knew, full of dark guilt, that Hanne's own nostrils were filled with a completely different smell that her maternal senses were too full of memory to pick up. And Hanne's face trembled and blew away in a terrible state of non-being between the abandoned face of yesterday and the one she would wear tomorrow. When you took everything into consideration, she thought, it wasn't strange that in the evening, when he was deeply preoccupied with other things, Gert had acquired animal ears – after all, wasn't it common to see a dog staring at you through the eyes of a close relative? In such cases, you had to pretend tactfully that there was nothing unusual, and take down all the mirrors in the house until the mistake was corrected. If you made those around you aware of this kind of negligence and oversight, you would expose their vulnerability and arouse their anger, just as if you openly informed a tuxedo-clad gentleman at a party that he had forgotten to button his trousers.

'Nothing,' said Gitte, 'you haven't done anything to him. It's like in Strindberg. All his characters – they hate each other for no reason.'

'Because they stay together, even though the love is gone,' said Lise slyly, as she eased Gitte onto the old, safe track. 'Because you can't love just one person and forget all the rest of humanity.'

'Yes, that's why,' said Gitte, satisfied. 'Love your neighbor – the other way is totally anti-social. That's why I don't feel sorry for Grete either. It was an egotistical act.'

She sniffed as if she had a stuffy nose; exhausted, Lise felt that this time the danger had passed.

'Some of the things you learned in junior college were OK,' she said with a feeling of sick gratitude.

'That's right.' Gitte stood up and collected the dishes on the tray. 'The family has died out. We don't want to get married or bring children into the world either. But if you've done it, the way you and Gert did, you have to stay together. We don't care for divorces. You should have taken him in last night. That would have been smart.'

The last remark came breathlessly, as she pressed down the door handle with her elbow.

Lise got out of bed and opened the door to her study. She took a deep breath and stared at her typewriter standing there dusty and untouched, sprawling accusingly on the desk, which was in the kind of depressing order that results when no one ever does any work at it. There was a neat stack of her award-winning book. It was called *The Deviant*. It was about a sex criminal. Suspicion was directed at a poor bachelor who was afraid of women and who invited the little girls in the neighborhood down to his basement shop for soda pop and cookies. The murderer was the homicide detective who was the most zealous during the investigation. The resolution had come as a surprise even to her. After she had created her characters, they decided for themselves what they wanted to do. Writing had always been like a game, a pleasant task that allowed her to forget everything else in the world. She thought: If I start to write again, this whole nightmare will be over. Hanne had come running home from school every day. 'Have you written a new chapter, Mother?' she would ask excitedly. And she would read it with shining eyes. 'Oh, this is so good. I can't wait for the next part.'

Hanne ran in and out of her mind like a ray of sunlight in a darkened room. The first child, the miracle, a girl. All her books were written for Hanne: fairy tales, short stories for little children, short novels about a childish girl's fantasy world. It had astonished her that she could give birth to boys. She had been disappointed and had then resigned herself to it. Gitte said that both Mogens and Søren knew that she had wanted girls. Gitte gave them the love Lise had denied them. Lise was fond of them, but they knew, said Gitte, that she loved Hanne more than them.

She lifted one of the books in her hand. The dust jacket was brilliantly colored and dramatic. Gitte had read the book in junior college. The whole LSD clique had been enthusiastic about it. They saw it as a revolt against the authorities, a weapon in their fight against conformity and those in power. Gitte had read her ad for a housekeeper and grabbed it like a drowning person grabs the rescue plank. She wanted to escape her addiction because she could see where it was leading. She wanted to be healthy and independent and serve an artist, for only in art were you a free person, raised above the deadliness that created all the unhappiness in the world.

She sat down at the desk in her modest cotton nightgown, with her bare feet on the cold parquet floor. She hadn't been alone with Hanne for a long time. She didn't know who was preventing her from this. No doubt it was just difficult to be alone with someone in an apartment that housed six people.

'I'm scared,' she whispered aloud. Why had he told Gitte about the suicide? What was it that was getting closer day by day, as inescapable as time? She saw Gert's big, furry ears before her and knew that she must not tell anyone about it. And she saw the dead woman. How many pills did it take? Fifty – a hundred? Gitte had taken them away. But she would have to give Lise two every evening or she wouldn't be able to sleep. She gave all of them something that they couldn't do without. She went to bed with Gert; she went to bed with Mogens; she gave Søren desserts with whipped cream; but what did she really give to Hanne? Hanne treated her with a kind of guarded reserve, and Lise couldn't figure out why.

She pulled herself together and went out to the bathroom. The hot water in the bathtub caressed her gently, and she heard Gert come out of his room and call Gitte. He wanted coffee and at 10 he was going over to the ministry. Had he really wanted to sleep with her last night? But that had become just as impossible as if an ocean separated them. Gitte said that all men had some kind of perversity. At the junior college, in the course of six months, she had slept with 49 men, and none of them had been normal. One man could only do it if he was wearing rubber boots. Another one got off on hitting her hard in the face. Gert wanted to have his nipples pinched, and Lise had been married to him for ten years without finding that out. You had to dig in with your nails, said Gitte, then he would come with wild ecstasy.

There was a rushing in the hot-water pipe that ran along the edge of the bathtub. Someone was apparently taking a bath upstairs. Gitte almost never took baths. She had a black line under her chin because she would just rub the sponge across her face. Dirt was part of her view of life. You have to remember, she said, that penicillin is made from mold.

The rushing noise in the pipe continued, and suddenly there was the sound of triumphant laughter. She rinsed off the soap from her armpits and stared at the rusty pipe, which ended at the grating under the tiles. A different pipe extended from the ceiling to the floor and connected the apartments to each other. When Gitte pressed her ear to her radiator, she could hear what they were saying down below. It was a basement apartment where an old deaf woman lived with her two middle-aged children. Right in front of her they would discuss when she was going to die, because she had purchased some life insurance with them as beneficiaries. The laughter grew louder and louder, and Lise stared at the water pipe as if it were a cupboard from her childhood, containing something horrible that would come darting out when sleep and darkness had overwhelmed her. Someone was talking to someone else, interrupted by fits of laughter. It sounded like Mogens talking through the nylon stocking he pulled over his head when he wanted to scare his little brother. She took off her shower cap and pressed her ear against the pipe.

'It's worse when she smiles. Her front teeth are the wrong color.'

She touched her two porcelain crowns with her finger and heard Gitte's voice again:

'She only sees things that you can touch or hold.'

'We'll manage to break her if we're patient. Leave the pills on your dresser. Then one day she'll take them, just like Grete. She's already thinking about it.'

That was Gert's voice.

Anger made the blood race hotly through Lise's body. She got up out of the bathtub and pulled on her bathrobe without drying off. In the kitchen Gitte was pouring water into a coffee filter. Gert was standing next to her with his hands in the pockets of his blue bathrobe.

'I can hear everything you say,' Lise said sharply. 'But you'd better be careful. I've got friends too. I'll tell them what's going on in this house.'

They both stared at her with well-feigned astonishment.

'What on earth do you mean?' asked Gert.

'You know very well what I mean.'

She gathered her bathrobe at her throat with a shaking hand.

'You must have fallen asleep in the bathtub,' said Gitte calmly as she continued making coffee. 'I know how that is. You're totally confused when you wake up.'

The anger disappeared like water that dripped onto the floor and formed a little puddle at her feet. Doubt and confusion took its place.

'Do you think so?' she asked. 'I thought I could hear your voices through the hot-water pipe.'

'What did we say?' Gert smiled at her and sat down at the kitchen table. Deep in his eyes flickered a malicious little flame.

'Nothing special,' she said slowly. 'I can't really remember. I probably did fall asleep.'

She took a glass out of the cupboard and went over to the

sink to get some water. The door to Gitte's room was open, as usual. It was a declaration that she had no private life, that you could enter her room as freely as you did the rest of the apartment. Lise stared through the open door, and it was as if a wet rag were twisting around her heart.

The sleeping pills were on the dresser.

She turned around quickly to face them while she drank the water. She thought they were avoiding her glance.

'I was thinking of inviting Nadia to lunch today,' she said in a light tone of voice. 'I haven't talked to her for such a long time.'

'Yes,' said Gitte as she sat down at the table across from Gert, 'you do need to see some other people besides us.'

'That's right.' Gert turned a page of his newspaper. 'You get a little strange if you isolate yourself too much.'

They both smiled kindly and reassuringly at her like a couple of parents who think it's about time for their teenage daughter to go out a little and have some fun.

3

Later in the morning the light had already grown old. It had a yellowed, withered cast to it, like fading snapshots left in a drawer that no one opens anymore. The sun was hidden behind gray, floating clouds, and the sky gave off a flat, stale smell like the breath of people who don't eat.

Lise closed the window. Out on the wide boulevard the cars were driving along, without the least thought of each other. The man from the warehouse below the living room was standing there arguing with a truck driver whose vehicle had stopped the traffic for a moment. He threw up his hands in excitement and looked like a person who, for the first time in his life, was confronted with a selfishness greater than his own. Maybe all this had happened millennia ago, the way that light from long-dead stars reaches the earth.

She sat down again at the low enameled table between the two London sofas and continued her meticulous manicure. She had lost Asger because of her nails. Shortly after he was appointed to the Foreign Ministry as the Minister's right-hand man, they had been invited to a government dinner. With Nadia's help she had picked out a new evening gown, which had cost a small fortune, and had gone through a beauty treatment that changed her so much that her own mother wouldn't have recognized her. Her face stiff with makeup, she had carried on an exhausting conversation with the gentleman seated next to her, a member of Parliament who had recently had a cerebral hemorrhage. 'Have you actually written something since *Princess Sibyl*?' he babbled. He mistook her for the wife of a counselor at the Foreign Ministry, who had really only written that one book. She had endured many hours of suffering only to hear that remark.

The dinner was over by eleven, and it had been filled with the same inconsolable endlessness as her childhood Sundays. 'I was so ashamed,' said Asger when they got home, 'about your nails. I noticed them during coffee. You probably don't realize it, but a man can't make a career as a diplomat if he has a wife who doesn't bother to clean her fingernails.'

At the beauty salon they hadn't been able to remove completely the traces of her intimate relationship with carbon paper and typewriter ribbons. If they *had* been able to, maybe she would still be married to him. Life consisted of a series of minute, imperceptible events, and you could lose control if you overlooked a single one of them.

She waved her hands to make the nail polish dry. Through the open French door she saw Gitte moving along the book-shelves in her study. Every day she sniffed at the books the same way a dog sniffs at trees and stones to find the smells that will prompt him to lift his leg. With self-assured instinct and exquisite economy Gitte greedily sucked in the juice and spat out the peels. Rilke, Proust, Joyce, Virginia Woolf – they were hers, and Gitte had no intention of letting them go again now that she had discovered what they were all about. She sipped at them fastidiously, let them slide over her tongue like a confident wine connoisseur, tore them out of context and drenched them with her shameless understanding.

She stood there, thin and bent as a question mark, as she pulled out a book from one of the lower shelves. She stood there a little too long, like a marionette whose string you've forgotten to pull. You have to watch over them all the time, thought Lise, full of anxiety, and make them play their roles: one step forward, two to the side, and a little clap with the puppet hands. They noticed if you neglected them for a moment and thought your own thoughts, which were dangerous and different and threatened their whole borrowed existence. Then they would take revenge and start to live for themselves, just as that unknown woman, Grete, had done.

Quickly she slipped in under Gitte's skin, which was slovenly and badly stitched together because there had been too many people working on it.

'Gitte,' she said in that cajoling tone of voice you use with children who refuse to eat, 'don't you think Hanne's dress would fit you, the pleated blue one? She's grown out of it and I think it would look good on you.'

'Oh, yes,' said Gitte, 'I'd love to have it.'

Her skinny body unfolded like a jackknife and she looked happy – as if there were nothing wrong – with the sudden, simple joy of a young girl at an unexpected gift. Lise recalled what it meant to be poor. You would skip a meal so you could buy a book you'd wanted for a long time. It was a catastrophe if you got a run in your only pair of stockings. You walked from one end of town to the other to save the streetcar fare. Poverty clung to you like an unpleasant odor.

Lise's award-winning book had been translated into eleven languages, but she felt that affluence paralyzed her just as much as poverty once had.

'*Lolita*,' said Gitte, lifting the book triumphantly in her hand. 'I haven't read it since I was in the orphanage. We read it in secret, as if it were pornographic.'

'Yes,' said Lise as her courage sank within her like sand in an hourglass. 'The most touching thing about it is his empathy with the girl. He sees her loneliness, he knows that he is separating her from all of her friends.'

She pulled her upper lip down so it covered her teeth, which Gitte found so repulsive, because she thought there was something about every face that offended and challenged the world in the same way as a doctor's illegible handwriting offends the self-esteem of the pharmacist.

She allowed a quiet, disheartened thought to slip in between the pages of the book. It fell out again and hung onto the edge of the dust jacket for a moment, before it dripped toward the floor like a tear from her eyelashes. The book was Gitte's, as if this was the only copy in the whole world and there was only one possible interpretation of it.

'I read an article by Simone de Beauvoir in some magazine the other day,' said Gitte as she sat down on the arm of the sofa; an expression of simple complacency slid over her face. 'It was called the Lolita Syndrome. She says that immature, infantile men are behind it. They think that grownup women can see right through them. Gert is infantile too. He doesn't want an equal partner. It reassures him that, when all is said and done, I'm just his housekeeper.'

Gitte's legs were dangling loosely and insolently like the legs of a ventriloquist's dummy who has taken control from her owner and is expressing his most secret thoughts before a cheering auditorium. Gleeful laughter slipped free from her tightly closed lips, and she had grown so clever, Lise noticed with a sidelong, stolen glance, that her larynx wasn't moving at all.

'Yes,' she said and continued quickly, diverting attention, postponing the inevitable for a moment longer. 'Make a few sandwiches for Nadia and me. And please let us be alone. She canceled a patient in order to visit me. She only has about an hour and a half.'

'I'll take care of it, no problem.'

Gitte jumped up and stood for a moment in front of her, while a glimmer of cruel mirth showed in her green, close-set eyes, above which her eyebrows grew together like a couple of girlfriends who can't tear themselves away from each other.

'It'll be good for you,' Gitte said meaningfully, 'to talk to a sensible person. Gert doesn't think you're very well. He was really alarmed when you came into the kitchen this morning. You have to watch out not to mix up dream and reality.'

Lise stared at her narrow back as she left the room. There was a quivering in the air like the stripes you see before your eyes after a sleepless night – a thought torn loose from her self which she could no longer call back.

'You don't really think that Gert and Gitte want you to kill yourself like Grete did, do you?' said Nadia with her mouth full of food, giving her a slow, piercing look as if she were an untrained stenographer.

Her gentle, heavy Slavic face suddenly collapsed into a turkey-like wattle under her chin, as if seeking refuge there for a moment, incapable of keeping itself in place any longer. So that it wouldn't completely slide off – they had always supported each other in hard times – Lise said quickly, 'No, Nadia, I don't think so.'

Lise grasped for what people call 'common sense', which she possessed as if it were an artificial language with a few, crude words that could only be used to exchange remarks about the weather, the evening meal, or the train schedule.

'I know full well,' she babbled on, 'that for Gert she's just someone who is easy and close at hand. He doesn't have to mobilize any emotional apparatus to go to bed with her, that's all it is. And she doesn't dream about love or marriage. In fact, I think you're right, that I was just out of it for a minute in the bathtub, and then my imagination ran away with me. You know I've always daydreamed about writing a horror story for adults. Hanne's seventeen, and she's through with children's books.'

'That's right. How is she? I haven't seen her in ages.'

Nadia's face slid back into place, and her eyes were so pure and shining, as if they had just come from the cleaners. She had always been neat and meticulous with her things, and nothing in her possession was ever allowed to decay.

'Fine. But there still don't seem to be any boys in her life. And she's old enough for it, you know.'

'It'll come. She's always been a family girl.'

Nadia took a gulp of her beer while her eyes grew long and narrow like wet watercolors that are about to run into each other. It gave her face a cunning, shifty expression. Lise would have liked to know what Gitte had said to Nadia when she let her in. She stared at her friend as a feeling of total desolation slipped through her, as if she were drifting away on an ice floe without a single living person hearing her cries for help. She searched behind many secret veils for Nadia's face from twenty years ago, when they would meet each other at the Royal Library, where so many young girls go to escape the homes that have become too confining for them, like last year's dress. Nadia had shared her circle of friends with her, and since nothing was holding her back, she had slipped in, as if into a ballroom that was decorated for someone else, just as all the presents she had given Hanne had always been meant for some other child. Nadia's friends were students from the provinces, and one of them was Asger. If she hadn't met Nadia, she might have married a mechanic and lived in Nørrebro, a few blocks from her childhood home.

A deafening noise broke the silence so abruptly that Nadia dropped her fork on the floor in fright. She stared at the door to the dining room.

'What in God's name is that?' she asked.

'That's Gitte. She's put on a record,' Lise replied indifferently. 'She and Mogens can't live without loud noise. He must have come home early from school.'

'Why don't you throw her out?' asked Nadia point-blank. 'You can't stand her.'

'She gives me sleeping pills,' said Lise guardedly. 'And it's not true that I can't stand her.'

She raised her voice to drown out the noise, and fear swooped down on her again like hawk wings over a chicken yard.

'She's very intelligent; it's amazing how many books she's read. And she's fond of me, as if I were her mother.'

Her heart was pounding violently as she fixed her gaze on Nadia's face so that it wouldn't float away again.

'You can get sleeping pills from any doctor,' said Nadia slowly, 'if you need them. You shouldn't make yourself dependent on Gitte that way. It would be much better for you if you were still able to feel jealousy.'

'Dr Jørgensen removed that feeling from me,' Lise explained in a tone of voice as if they were talking about a ruptured appendix.

'Yes, but there's something unnatural about that. By the way, you should go see him again. I think you need it. To be perfectly honest, you don't seem as though you're very well.'

Those were the words Gitte had used. It couldn't be a coincidence. The danger was approaching from many directions at once, and she couldn't imagine what it was all about.

Nadia stood up and brushed off the crumbs from her smooth skirt.

'I have to go now,' she said. 'It was nice to see you. Every time I've called lately, Gitte has kept me away, as if there were a corpse in the house. She said you were working and must not be disturbed.'

'That's a lie,' said Lise as they both went over to the door. 'But for some reason she didn't have anything against your coming over today.'

In an impulsive gesture, Nadia gave her a hug and kissed her on the cheek.

'Promise me,' she said earnestly, 'that you'll talk to Dr Jørgensen one of these days. He has helped you before, and you know that he's your friend.'

Out in the dining room Gitte and Mogens were performing a wriggling dance in time to the music. They let go of each other and Mogens gave his mother a hostile look.

'Gitte and I,' he said, 'are going to the demonstration at the American Embassy against the war in Vietnam.'

'Then stay on the outskirts,' said Nadia cheerfully, 'or you're liable to get a club in the head. Aren't you going to say hello to your old Aunt Nadia?'

'Hi,' he said curtly and slouched out to the long hallway to the kitchen, followed by Gitte, who moved with affected youthfulness, as if she were twenty and not four years older than him.

Lise watched Nadia as she put on her coat in front of the mirror in the small, dark entryway. Maybe she could rely on her, maybe she really knew nothing about any of it.

'It's funny,' said Nadia, smiling to herself in the mirror, 'how he still has his father's face.'

'Funny?'

Lise stared at her suspiciously, and suddenly Nadia was too big for the room, like the china doll from her childhood that she had put into the little cardboard theater her father had pasted together from a pattern in *Family Journal*. But people just said things like that out of the blue, she thought with horror, without giving a thought to the incredible difficulties involved in sharing your face with someone else. They couldn't both use it at the same time, and Lise didn't know – since children kept those kinds of things to themselves – what kind of complicated agreement had been reached between father and son. A Section Chief has a great need for his face, and it must not bear visible traces of the nightly dreams and secret excesses of an adolescent boy. And when it was Mogens's turn to wear it, the face was ravaged with adult worries and lack of sleep, and he had to stretch it and smooth out wrinkles before he put it on in the morning, before he went to school.

'Goodbye, Lise,' said Nadia somberly. 'Take good care of yourself, OK? And keep away from those stupid pills. You can sleep just fine without them.'

Lise stood there for a minute looking at the closed door after Nadia had left. Her thoughts fumbled for Dr Jørgensen's face as if she were rummaging in a drawer for something she hadn't used in a long time. She found it underneath a lot of other faces and stared at it, terrified. It was long and flat and endless, like an illustration of the theorem that two parallel lines never intersect. It was overwhelming, and she let go of it again as she went into the dining room and turned off the record player.

4

'Once upon a time there was an old woman who was a very evil witch. She had two daughters; one was ugly and mean, but that's the one she loved, for she was her very own daughter. The other was beautiful and good, but that's the one she hated, for she was her stepdaughter . . .'

'The ugly one is Hanne, and the beautiful one is Gitte.'

'So I'm the evil witch?'

Lise pressed Søren closer to her and, smiling, gazed into his little face, which was suddenly much older than his seven years. He had used it up too quickly and had to put on a future face, because there was no one to parcel out the children's treasury of time for them – even though you would never think of giving them all the licorice at once that was meant to last their entire childhood. Gert always said with naive pride that the boy was advanced for his age, without thinking further about what terrible consequences that sentence contained.

'Yes, you're the witch.'

He laughed, teasing her, and looking at her with that guileless lack of empathy that only children can manage.

She continued reading from the rare edition of *Grimms' Fairy Tales*, which she had bought during her happy period, running from one antiquarian bookstore to another to find it. She read without comprehending the words. Søren lay back against the pillow. His mouth smelled faintly of supper, because Gitte said you got holes in your teeth by brushing them. There was a rushing sound in her ears again. It had been going on all afternoon, ever since Nadia had left. But when she stepped into Søren's messy room, it had stopped. It came back when he mentioned Gitte's name, which always lay on his lips like drops of saliva. It came back and reminded her of the bathroom with the long, twisting, mysterious pipes, whose function only plumbers knew anything about. On the other hand, she knew nothing about plumbers, and she thought about Rapunzel from her childhood, the girl downstairs with the golden braids, the girl whom a drunken old plumber had gotten pregnant when she was fifteen years old. She had hated him because he took away a beautiful dream from her. Now he was taking revenge with this rushing sound in her ears. A doctor could cure noises in the ears; he was a better plumber than that other one. But it made it difficult to distinguish their voices from each other, as if she had suddenly become slightly deaf.

She finished the fairy tale and discovered that Søren had fallen asleep. It always happened so abruptly, like the click of a shutter in a camera. He slept, and she suddenly felt superfluous. The noise from the TV had a threatening ring to it; a hostile world seemed to be calling to her with its urgent demand for involvement. A verse from a poem rose up in her mind:

> more than anyone else, you yearn for wings,
> the earth has burned your feet

and it comforted her so she had the courage to leave the room and join the others, the way you enter a recurrent dream in which you know that everything is predetermined and nothing can be changed.

The telephone rang as she walked past it out in the hallway.

She picked up the receiver and said her phone number. 'Excuse me for disturbing you,' said a girl's perky voice. 'I'm calling from the newspaper *Aktuelt*. We're doing a survey on the question: "Are mini-skirts destroying marriage?" The background for this is an article by . . .'

The door to the dining room was partly open, and she saw Gert and Hanne sitting next to each other. Their backs expressed that intimacy between people that makes words superfluous. She kicked the door shut with her foot.

'Excuse me,' she said, 'I didn't hear the last part.'

'Yes, well, the question is whether young girls in mini-skirts are such a temptation to men that they're endangering the institution of marriage. I'm talking especially about housewives 40 to 50 years old who stay home. We've asked a number of important women about this.'

'Not if the marriage is a good one.'

She heard an unnatural freshness in her voice and had a fleeting feeling that this conversation had taken place before, the way you recognize a landscape when you know you've never been there.

'If men in that age group fall for young girls it's because of an immaturity in themselves, it has nothing to do with fashion.'

'No, I don't think so either. Thank you and I'm sorry to have bothered you.'

She went in and sat down next to Hanne as she considered whether they had heard the conversation. Hanne's long, honey-colored hair hid her profile. In front of Gert there was a whiskey bottle, seltzer, and a glass, and he leaned forward politely to catch her eye.

'How about a little drink?' he asked. 'You look like you could use one.'

His eyes shone dully like raisins, and his ears, she noticed with relief, looked the same as they always did.

'No,' she said, 'I'm tired. I'm going to bed soon.'

She stared at the TV. The anchorman's gaunt, bespectacled face grew suddenly distant, as if she were looking through the wrong end of a telescope.

'There were violent disturbances in front of the American Embassy this afternoon,' he said. 'Police and demonstrators are still fighting . . .'

He vanished and they saw demonstrators marching toward the embassy.

'There's Gitte,' said Gert.

'And Mogens.'

Hanne leaned forward, and Gitte turned her head and seemed to look straight at them for a moment. Then she marched on triumphantly with the others.

'You shouldn't have let Mogens go,' said Gert and took a big gulp from his glass. 'He isn't interested in politics. If his real father knew about this, he would be furious. But of course it's none of my business.'

'Oh, he won't get mixed up in anything,' said Hanne with her little twelve-year-old voice that hadn't caught up with her real age. 'Unless Gitte makes him.'

'This is the first time since Gitte came here that she isn't home,' said Lise, 'and then we see her on TV.'

It was as if it couldn't be a coincidence, as if it were part of what was approaching, part of the lurking evil that surrounded her.

'The world has gone mad,' said Gert gloomily, staring into his glass. 'We can sense what Baudelaire calls "the terrible wings of time".'

She glanced quickly at him, through Hanne's childishly fragrant hair. She remembered their Baudelaire period from the time when the children were small. They lived with quotes from him on their lips, and Gert had bought a rare edition of his works, but didn't really know enough French to get anything out of them. What on earth had happened in the meantime? It was ages since he had been home in the evening. When her stepfather wasn't home, Hanne usually kept to her room. Was he still thinking about his dead mistress? She didn't think so because, all things considered, his strength lay in his lack of imagination. He couldn't see with other people's eyes and couldn't feel with their nerves.

The TV blared on with clips from the war in Vietnam. The picture grew blurry and she saw Gitte's face again, staring at her. In her frugality, it was as if she had bought her face second-hand, intending for it to last a long time. That's why the faces of poor people were often so incongruous; they bore traces of a childhood that was not their own, which always seemed to have been bitter and unhappy. She looked down at the table and took a deep breath – suddenly there wasn't enough air in the room.

'I think I'll have a drink after all,' she said and stood up.

Gert turned toward her.

'If you're going out in the kitchen,' he said, 'would you mind looking in Gitte's room to see if that English biography of Tolstoy is there? I lent it to her the other day, but I'm not through with it yet.'

'OK,' she said from the doorway, and it seemed to her that Gert and Hanne smiled faintly at each other, with relief, the way you do when a difficult math problem is finally solved. Out in the narrow hallway, which was so dark that they kept the light on all day long, she stood still for a moment, as though she had forgotten what she had come for. The noise in her ears had vanished and the silence filled her mind like a poem. Then she went on through the kitchen and into Gitte's room. She closed the door behind her, but still had a distressing feeling of not being alone. On the table was Mogens's tape recorder, whirring with one reel empty. He and Gitte recorded homemade radio plays on it. She shut it off and noticed the pills still on top of the dresser as they had been that morning. The image hadn't been out of her mind for a moment. Frightened and fascinated, she stared at the brown medicine bottle as reality disappeared behind her like someone on a railway platform as the train pulls away. She heard indistinguishable voices from the basement apartment; Gitte knew so many awful things about the people who lived there. The book about Tolstoy lay next to the tape recorder, and there was a bookmark in it. She opened the book and read what Gitte, in her impersonal grade-school handwriting, had written on the bookmark. 'Tolstoy never bathed,' it said, 'and his wife was frigid.' All the pages of the book hadn't been cut open. It was obvious what Gitte had gotten out of the book, as if she had forced from the author his most important secret. She read like a detective looking for clues in an apartment, without for a moment concerning herself with the whole picture. The voices from below grew louder, and as if driven by someone else's will, Lise went over and knelt down, placing her ear against the base of the hot-water pipe near the floor.

'She never shows herself outside the apartment. You don't have to believe me, but they're trying to drive her crazy. I've heard the husband and the girl talking about it.'

It was a man's voice, and terror shook her whole body like an attack of fever.

'If I were her I'd go to the police. It's criminal.' Now it was a woman talking.

'No, the methods are probably legal, all right. The husband is apparently an attorney.'

'What are you talking about?'

It was an old, squeaky voice, and Lise remembered that according to Gitte the mother was deaf, and that they always talked as if she weren't there.

'Shut up, old woman, it's none of your business.'

She stood up with difficulty and stared at the wall, which seemed stained with suffering and pain. Her heart was pounding in panic. She had to get away before the catastrophe struck her. Suddenly she was overwhelmed by a terrible weariness and she sat down on a chair. She longed for peace and tried to imagine what that word meant. She thought about those evenings during her childhood when her parents weren't home. She would write verses in her poetry album that they weren't supposed to see. She imagined how they were preoccupied with something other than her now. Peace meant not existing in other people's consciousness. Now they were sitting in there waiting for her to take the pills. As a child she had always done what the grownups wanted her to do, but now her anger and rebelliousness awoke like a proud pillar of fire within her. She wasn't ready to die. There was still something that she loved. She saw Søren's lost face before her. He was growing up to a world of violence, and she was the only fragile bulwark against it. The weariness and despair left her. She would fool them. She would take the pills and then call Dr Jørgensen so he could make sure she was taken to the hospital. They wouldn't be able to get her there. Friendly souls would surround her, and in the other beds would be women she could talk to about children and love, as she had done with Nadia when they lived together as young girls. In hospitals there was a white peace that smelled of ether – like the white peace after giving birth, when the pain had been endured. Gripped by a kind of gloomy agitation, she went over and picked up the bottle of pills. She had to move the telephone into her own room without their noticing. Her life depended on it. She tiptoed back down the hall and put the bottle on her nightstand. Then she went out in the kitchen again for a glass. She filled it with water at the sink in her room. Then she unplugged the phone in the hall, carried it over to the windowsill, and knelt down to plug it in under her bed. She turned on the overhead light and the sharp glare slipped in underneath her eyelids like a corrosive fluid. The door to the dining room opened and Gert called:

'Where did you go? Wasn't the book there?'

'Oh yes, I'll get it right away.'

She ran back to Gitte's room again, grabbed the book, and rushed in and placed it in front of him. They were still watching TV, and the whole thing had to be done before the program was over and before Gitte and Mogens came home.

'I think I'll go to bed now,' she said, 'I feel so tired.'

'You go ahead. Good night. Sleep well.'

He gave her a look full of ironic sadness. That's the way he would say goodbye to someone about to die, she thought. He had often said that there were enough people and books in the world. Any addition was merely a repetition. And love was a disease that you later looked back on with horror. Love for children was the only exception, because it was free of desire. But he also cultivated desire without love, which often led him to prefer prostitutes to mistresses. Her thoughts let go of him completely when she went into her own room after a fleeting glance at Hanne, who was sitting biting her thumbnail, intensely involved with a movie on TV.

She looked up Dr Jørgensen's number in the phone book. Hope moved like gentle, melodic sentences through her body where the terror had lain down to rest like a dog in its basket. She got undressed and put on her nightgown. She got into bed and poured the pills out in her hand. They were white and innocent and she didn't count them. She swallowed them without thinking and washed them down with water. She didn't know how fast they would work, but maybe there was no time to lose. She went over and lifted the receiver from the phone and asked for the doctor's number. A woman's voice answered.

'Is Dr Jørgensen home?' she asked politely. 'This is Lise Mundus.'

'Just a moment.'

There was a humming on the line and the sound of laughter, as if there were a lot of people. Maybe he was having a party.

'This is Dr Jørgensen.' His voice was cheerful and self-confident.

'This is Lise Mundus. I've taken a lot of sleeping pills and now I don't know what to do. I don't want to die.'

'Fine,' he said as if he had been expecting this for a long time. 'I'll send an ambulance right away.'

He laughed, as if she had told the joke of the century, and she held the receiver away from her ear and stared at it. It sounded the way glass objects do when they're smashed into a thousand pieces, and fear welled up in her again. She hung up the phone and Gert and Hanne's laughter pierced through the noise of the TV. Hell enveloped her and she hid her face in her hands. Tears slid down her cheeks and it felt like her face was melting and running through her fingers.

5

The little ballerinas danced across the grass with a sweetness and innocence in their movements, as if there were still mother's milk in all their limbs. They were dancing to music that only they could hear. Their radiant skirts were lifted by the wind and the delicate, completely identical faces wore enraptured, solemn expressions, which nothing from without seemed to disturb. The grass was greener than any other grass in the world, except for the grass on the lawns of Søndermarken during her childhood; on Sundays she would lie there on her stomach between her parents, whose youthful laughter filled the whole world. Suddenly a long shadow fell across the lawn, as if a storm cloud were passing in front of the bright sun. A gigantic policeman emerged from the trees in the background and approached the dancing children with steps as stiff as a wound-up robot. The children didn't seem to notice him at all. He went over to one of them, just as her curry-colored skirt flew up and revealed her golden legs – her calves had the mature curves of a grown girl. Something flashed bright and clear through the air, and the girl fell to the ground like a doll. The knife was sticking out through her back, and the blood spread over the grass like a red, flaming flower. The policeman fumbled with his fly and threw himself on top of the murdered child, whose face turned slowly, like a sleeper whom no dream can disturb. She saw that it was Hanne's face, and she wanted to scream but could only manage a faint whisper. The other children kept on dancing as if they hadn't seen a thing. She wanted to stand up but something was holding her tight around the waist, and she heard a clear, authoritative voice very close by.

'Are you awake?' it said. 'Do you know where you are?'

Something blue and white fluttered past her, and she looked into a face as smooth and fresh as a newly laid egg.

'Yes,' she said, and her vocal cords felt as dry as hay. The horrible sight had vanished, and she had probably just been dreaming. They always said that she had been dreaming whenever they didn't want to have witnesses to something she had seen or heard.

'Yes,' she repeated with difficulty, holding her hand in front of her eyes to shut out the bright light, 'but I don't know where I am.'

'You're in the toxic trauma center. You've been unconscious for 48 hours.'

Suddenly she remembered everything and smiled with relief. She had escaped them, she had fallen out of their memory like a fish through a gap in the net. She had never existed before for this girl with the egg-like face.

'What's your name?' she asked gratefully and repeated the question a little louder when she saw that the young nurse had turned away from her and was now busy staring at a bubbling lavender liquid in a tall glass tube hanging attached to another bed. In the bed lay a naked woman whose skin was as dark and weatherbeaten as an old man from India. She was sleeping with her mouth open, and a whistling sound forced its way through her teeth, just like when the boys in her old neighborhood whistled by sticking their fingers in their mouths. A hypodermic needle was fastened to the back of her hand with adhesive tape, and connected by a rubber tube to an apparatus in which the liquid rose and fell with a rhythm that was demanding the full attention of the girl.

'My name is Miss Jensen.'

She wanted to roll over to face her but something hard and stiff cut into her waist, and she saw that she was tied to the bed with a wide leather belt covered with bolts and screws. They looked like all the merit badges on Mogens's old boy scout sash.

'Why am I tied down?'

'So you won't fall out of bed. People are always restless before they wake up completely. They want to get free right away.'

You could hear that she had said these same sentences hundreds of times before, and Lise felt guilty because she wasn't a real suicide. She had fooled the people here too and sneaked into the system like a grain of sand in a perfectly functioning clockwork. She looked at the unconscious woman and felt the shadow of a strange sorrow at the edge of her mind. At least they could have covered her breasts. They were limp and emptied, as if many children had nursed at them. Her body was covered with purple spots as if she had been beaten, and Lise suddenly noticed a terrible ache in her earlobes. She touched them, and they were so tender that she let go of them at once. At the same moment she saw Miss Jensen twist the woman's earlobe between her fingers as she watched her face intently. She winced in pain, and the nurse looked satisfied.

'Now she'll wake up soon.'

'What time is it?'

They had taken her watch, and the gold chains around her neck and wrist were gone too.

'Eleven in the morning. After the hospital rounds you'll be moved to the state hospital. That's what Dr Jørgensen has requested.'

His name aroused all of her fear like a sharp needle against a newly healed wound. She remembered his hearty laughter on the phone, which had sounded as if she had just walked into a trap set long before.

'I don't want to go there,' she said, afraid. 'Why can't I stay here?'

'You're one of his patients, and he's the chief of staff at the state hospital.'

She closed her eyes, and the ballerinas were there again, as if they were painted on the inside of her eyelids. They were dancing, absorbed in ethereal delight, and in a little while the terrible thing was going to happen. Quickly she opened her eyes. If this keeps up, she thought, I won't be able to sleep at all. Now there was a rushing in her ears again. She discovered that the woman in the next bed had no chin. Her lower lip went right into her neck like on an animal. What a crime to bring such a deformed human being back to a life she wanted to leave.

A doctor stepped in through the door and came over to her bed. His face looked as if he had just reached some major decision.

'So you're awake,' he said and sat down on the chair next to her. 'Is your mind perfectly clear?'

'Yes,' she said.

'Can you tell me why you did it?'

She looked him straight in the eye – his pupils were totally surrounded by white, just like fried eggs.

'I had such a terrible need to see some new faces,' she said candidly.

He jumped up as suddenly as though he had been stung by a bee.

'This is no time for jokes,' he said, ice-cold. 'It costs the government 110 kroner a day to have you lying here.'

He gave her a look that said she had just lost a friend for life, and went over to the unconscious woman and began slapping her cheeks as methodically and dispassionately as a piece of meat that needs to be tenderized. Then he left the room after exchanging a few words with Miss Jensen. She couldn't catch what they said.

'As a child,' she said mournfully, 'people always laughed at me whenever I was the most serious, and when I said something funny, they would get mad. But the doctor was mistaken, I didn't mean to be funny.'

'That's what it sounded like,' said Miss Jensen coolly. 'But let's not talk about that anymore; the ambulance will be here soon.'

She was totally superfluous here, she had poisoned the atmosphere for them. At the state hospital she would have to be very careful with her words, the way you had to be with children who said what they thought, without inhibition. Something had forced its way in here too, the noise in her ears, the suspicious voices, and the images behind her eyelids. She longed for an untouched place, a virgin territory that her feet had not yet walked on, a path without memory where young lovers strolled, for whom she meant no more than the nail on their big toe.

'I have to pee,' she said, childishly. 'Won't you get me loose from this belt?'

Miss Jensen went over to her and selected a key from a big key ring she wore on the belt of her apron.

'Lean on me,' she said. 'You're probably a little dizzy.'

It was a long way to the floor, and her legs ached as they had when she was a child and they had been growing all night. Miss Jensen stood leaning against the open door of the toilet stall while she finished. An incredibly fat woman came into the white-tiled room. She wore a red-checked hospital dress, and Lise practically fell into her arms when she stood up and pulled down her short white gown.

'Lise,' exclaimed the woman, 'don't you recognize me? It's Minna. We went to school together. And to think that you're famous now. We all thought you were awfully stupid. Just shows how wrong you can be.'

She looked surprised, as if her obesity had ambushed her overnight. Deep in her face Lise found the features of a little girl with pretty brown eyes and two dark, skinny braids.

'Have you got a cigarette?' she asked, overcome with nicotine craving.

The woman laughed so her double chin jiggled.

'It's not allowed here,' she said. 'No smoking. That's one of the worst things. But it's even worse to have no lipstick. I wasn't a human being until I got one in here.'

Lise felt her lips – they were dry and covered with little blisters that hurt.

'Come on,' said Miss Jensen impatiently. 'You're finished.'

When she was lying in her bed again, her past rose up like a wall whose supporting building next door has been torn down. It stared at her with the vulnerability of her entire childhood. Moisture dripped down it like tears or rain. She suddenly longed to be somewhere else, away from her school classmate, away from the animal-like, unconscious woman, and away from the happy ballerinas beneath her eyelids.

'Well,' said Miss Jensen, 'the ambulance is here now. Don't worry, you'll probably be in an open ward.'

Two men in uniform came in and carried her down on a stretcher. With experienced hands they wrapped her in a red blanket and carefully carried the stretcher down the stairs. Inside the ambulance one of them sat and held her hand. His mouth was crooked, as if he had facial paralysis. It was as quiet as a cathedral. Hope burned gently in the young man's eyes, which were clear and bright like Søren's. He gave her hand a friendly squeeze, and she thought that she would soon be lying in a white bed, surrounded by gentle, kind women with whom she could talk quietly about men and love. In that new place the terrors would be gone. The man's gaze seemed to caress her, and she closed her eyes without seeing the ballerinas anymore. Sleep cradled her in its arms like warm water, and she didn't notice when the man let go of her hand.

6

The silence from the ambulance persisted, but she felt that there was only a fixed amount of it, and that she might use it up too quickly with any rash movement, the way men confined in a submerged submarine had to save on oxygen. She was lying in bed and staring out into the dimness, trying to orient herself. The room was large, with a high ceiling, and the beds resembled boats with white sails, rocking gently in a sea that was peaceful for the moment. The nurse had said that she should be quiet, because the patients were taking an afternoon nap. The room was divided by chin-high wooden panels into small, open compartments with four beds in each. In the middle there was a wide passageway where two nurses were sitting at a table across from each other, whispering. The headboard of her bed was up against one of the wooden panels. It was raining outside, and a poem fluttered through her mind on its gentle way through the world:

> It's raining in all the streets
> and in my heart as well.
> I traveled so far through the world
> and yet I found no peace.

Poetry was the only thing she had had to herself at home, since it was unknown territory for Gitte, just like classical music, which sounded like noise to her ears. She closed her eyes but quickly opened them again because the children were dancing behind her eyelids and they had to be protected from the terror of the world. Why had she made a policeman a sex murderer in her book? You shouldn't pick a fight with the enforcers of the law because you never knew when you might need them. The nurses were whispering much too loudly. It sounded like a kettle of water about to boil. One sentence tore itself loose and entered her ear as if it came from her pillow.

'Is she ever ugly in person! You wouldn't think so if you'd only seen her picture.

She felt the blood shoot up to her cheeks. She no longer belonged to herself. No matter where she sought refuge, people had unashamedly formed an image of her over which she had no control. If you find your name on others' lips, Rilke wrote someplace, then take another. She moved her fingers over her face, as if to assure herself that they hadn't taken it away from her when she was unconscious and unable to watch out for it. Her skin was cold and dry, and the blisters on her lips were starting to burst, secreting a clear fluid that slowly ran down her chin. She was dreadfully thirsty, but even more she craved a cigarette. She realized how bereft of possessions she was. No cigarettes, no money, no clothes, no lipstick, comb, or toothbrush. Gert wouldn't bring her any of those things, because he got sick whenever he set foot in a hospital. Once he was supposed to visit his mother when she was in the hospital, but he fainted on his way up the stairs. The smell of a hospital made him nauseated and unable to breathe. She carefully turned over on her other side, and the clear laughter of a young girl resounded in her other ear.

'We've asked a number of important women,' said an ironic voice, which had discovered that she had sneaked into those ranks the way you sneak over a national border with a passport expired long ago. She wasn't important and it wasn't her fault that grown people read her book. She cautiously lifted her head and moved her hand over the pillow; the voice had come from inside it, and there must be a reasonable explanation for this. Through the pillowcase she got hold of a hard round object as big as a five-kroner coin. That must be a loudspeaker; more angry than scared, she sat up in bed.

'Nurse,' she said sharply, not caring if she woke up the others. 'Come and take away this loudspeaker – I've found it.'

One of the nurses rushed over to her.

'Shh,' she whispered, 'what are you talking about?'

She held up the pillow in front of her.

'The loudspeaker,' she repeated, 'take it out.'

'There isn't any loudspeaker,' said the girl calmly. 'You still have the poison in your body, that's all.'

'Take a look at this.'

She examined the pillow, her frantic hands trying to find the round object again, but now it had vanished. She felt uncertain.

'The poison,' she said, 'when will it be gone?'

'In a couple of days,' said the girl very kindly. 'And in the meantime you should just stay calm, or else they'll put you in the locked ward.'

The nurse went over and pulled the curtains open. A gray light poured into the room, and there was movement in the other beds around her. Something furry poked out over the comforter next to her, and a woman with a donkey head sat up and stared at her with moist animal eyes that were completely bloodshot.

'Hello,' she said. 'My name is Mrs Hansen. What's your name?'

Frightened, she turned away without answering. Another donkey head was lying on that side, staring at her. She turned onto her back and looked up at the ceiling while her mind was convulsed with terror. She knew that there were institutions filled with deformed and monstrous human creatures who were kept hidden from the world, and who lived and died without anyone other than the hospital personnel ever seeing them. Had they brought her to that kind of place? She thought about the expression 'the locked ward' and longed to go there without having any idea what the term meant: a different place, another reality, where it might be possible to exist. For the time being she would have to pretend nothing was wrong, the way you did when confronting people with a harelip or bad breath. That was the most tactful.

'It's time for some hot chocolate.'

It was the nurse. Her face was like a childish sketch absent-mindedly scribbled in the margin of a composition book. The girl tried to fill it out from within, the way you stick your fingers into a glove to see whether it might fit. She was trying to live up to the world's expectations of how young girls ought to look, and her round eyes were full of good will and the fear of doing something wrong.

'Come on,' she said, holding up a white bathrobe. 'You look like you could use something to drink.'

She allowed herself to be led to a table on the other side of the room. The animal-like women were sitting around it, but one of them had a human face, and it was just as cheap and ready-made as Gitte's. She was wearing a hospital gown like the others, and she was about to light a cigarette. Lise felt it would help her to smoke. It would clear her thoughts, and that's what she needed, above all else.

'Could I possibly borrow a cigarette?' she asked, pointing at the pack on the table.

The woman shoved the pack over to her without answering. Turning to the others, she said:

'It's the same old story with the new ones. They borrow a bunch of cigarettes and you never see them again. They don't have any money either, and before you know it, they're written out of here.'

Written out! she thought unhappily. That was what they said about her because she hadn't published anything in two years.

'I'll pay you back,' she promised meekly. 'I have plenty of money at home.'

She lit the cigarette with a lighter on the table and inhaled deeply. A pleasant dizziness came over her, and she smiled cautiously at the human face.

'Where's your bed?' she asked, making conversation.

'Right behind yours. We can whisper to each other through the partition. That's what I did with the woman before you.'

A smile crept like a worm across her mouth, then afterwards it looked as if she had never smiled.

'What are you going to do this afternoon?' asked one of the donkeys.

'Lie on my bed and read. What else is there to do in this boring dump?'

She would have to get used to this jargon, the way a child has to when she joins a new class. She would have to get used to the donkeys with the female bodies and the woman who wasn't a donkey, but whom she feared more than the others for some reason.

A new nurse with a tired, worn-out face came over and took her by the arm.

'Time for you to go back to bed,' she said. 'And you aren't allowed to smoke yet, I forgot to tell you that.'

Obediently she let herself be led over to the bed and turned over the pillow before she lay down. A little while later she saw the other woman go over to her bed behind the partition with a magazine in her hand. A sharp whisper sounded in her ear:

'We've found out what kind of person you are. When you're going to write a book, you go around looking at all kinds of other books written by people who know their stuff. You steal a sentence from every book and put them together like a puzzle, and then you make people think that you've written every sentence yourself.'

'That's a lie!'

Wild with rage she jumped out of bed, ran behind the partition and over to the vicious woman, who was lying in a relaxed position on her bed, pretending to read.

'That's a lie,' she repeated, stamping the floor with her bare foot. 'I've never plagiarized anything. That's a rumor started by jealous people.'

The woman put down her magazine and stared at her with eyes as astonished and inhuman as the eyes of a teddy bear.

'What are you talking about?' she exclaimed. 'I haven't said a word to you since you borrowed that cigarette.'

Lise was on her in one bound, just like when the children used to tease her on the playground. She dug her nails into the woman's face and watched with furious satisfaction as the blood trickled out of two long gouges.

The woman screamed and tried to cover her face with her hands. The nurse came running and pulled Lise away by force.

'What in the world is going on?' she said heatedly. 'Why are you attacking Mrs Halvorsen this way? Get back to your bed and I'll see that you're taken to the locked ward right away. This ward is only for peaceful patients.'

She was breathing hard and she let herself be led back to her bed without resistance. That witch had just gotten what she deserved. Whatever was in store for her in the locked ward, it couldn't be worse than this.

'Are there donkeys in there too?' she said caustically.

The nurse left her without replying. She lay there with her heart pounding hard and stared up at the ceiling. Once she had actually stolen a sentence from one of *Grimms' Fairy Tales* and used it in a different context in one of her children's books. The thought of it had always filled her with shame and the fear of discovery. Now, while her thoughts fled in all directions, she felt that everybody knew about it, and the little feathers had turned into five chickens, as in Hans Christian Andersen's tale. She had been mercilessly unmasked, and there was no more peace in the world.

'Come on, it's time for you to see the doctor.'

She stuck her feet into the clumsy slippers that the girl put down for her, let herself be wrapped up in the bathrobe and led down the long corridor and into a room with a door that said: Examination Room. A woman in a white smock was sitting at a desk and leafing through some papers.

'Sit down,' she said curtly and pointed at a chair.

The doctor regarded her for a moment in silence. Her face was fragile and glass-like, as if a sneeze from six feet away might make it break into a thousand pieces that could never be put back together again. It must have taken all of the doctor's concentration to make sure that wouldn't happen.

'Don't you think it's wrong to scratch another patient in the face?' she said slowly.

'Wrong?' exclaimed Lise, startled. 'If you only knew what she said to me!'

'What did she say?'

'Something about a cigarette,' Lise lied. 'She loaned me one and said that she'd never get it back again.'

'I see.' The woman played with a penknife absentmindedly. 'The only thing you're going to get out of this is that now you'll be taken to the locked ward. You're too undisciplined to stay here.'

'I won't mind at all,' she said defiantly. 'At least *she* won't be there.'

The doctor stood up and went over to the door.

'Stay here,' she said imperiously, 'while I call the nurse.'

In a little while the young girl with the unfinished face came in and said with hypocritical cheerfulness: 'Come along, Mrs Mundus, you're going to be moved now.'

She took her big jangling key ring and opened the door at the end of the corridor. Lise looked down another hallway where the beds were so close together that it would be difficult to walk past them.

'Anyone here?' called the girl. 'Here I come with a new patient.'

From the distance a shape came toward them with light steps, as if she were walking on rubber soles. Before she had reached her, Lise heard the door behind her lock. Then she screamed and held her hands to her mouth while her eyes stung as if from the heat of a burning spotlight.

She was standing face to face with Gitte.

7

'Stop screaming like that!'

Gitte tried to take her by the arm, but she pressed herself against the locked door with her arms spread wide, as if she were pinned to it.

'Gitte,' she said, 'why are you here? I didn't know you were a nurse.'

'My name's not Gitte. I'm Miss Poulsen.'

Lise stared at the close-set eyes beneath the eyebrows that had grown together, at the stubby nose and the wide mouth with its hungry expression. She felt as if her blood were turning to ice in her veins and her heart tumbled around inside her like a bird that wants out of its cage.

'Come on now.'

Another nurse had appeared and they grabbed her by the arms and tried to haul her away from the door.

'No!' she yelled and tore herself loose. 'I'll walk myself.'

She had never been able to stand having Gitte touch her.

She walked between them as if under arrest, and her legs were shaking. Formless shapes wandered around in the hallway, and one of them, an old woman, stood in their way and cautiously touched her bathrobe.

'Manfred,' she whimpered, 'have you come to take me away?'

'Get out of the way,' said Gitte. 'This isn't Manfred.'

I'm with the insane, she thought, and her will to survive

shot up inside her like a clear flame. It was a matter of preserving her sanity, then they couldn't seriously harm her in any way. She lay down on the bed they showed her and let them fasten the belt around her waist. It cut into her flesh and was so tight that she could only turn over with difficulty. They walked away from her bed, and she heard them laughing.

'That's that,' said Gitte. 'Now it's the next one's turn.'

She saw them disappear around the corner at the end of the hallway, and a few minutes later they came back, dragging a very old, totally naked woman between them. The woman was screaming.

'Not yet,' she shouted. 'It's not my turn yet. I don't want to be drowned.'

They laughed and continued dragging her through a door. The patients who were wandering back and forth through the room didn't seem to notice the incident, as if it were a perfectly ordinary event.

'What are you doing to her?' yelled Lise. 'What's going on here?'

'It's our way of solving the problem of the old people,' said Gitte's voice close to her ear. 'Didn't you recognize her? It's the deaf woman from the basement apartment. There aren't enough nursing homes, and somebody has to take care of the social problems.'

The voice was coming from her pillow, and she proceeded to examine it and wasn't surprised when she found a speaker there too, inside the pillowcase. She held onto it tightly and tried to pull off the pillowcase. She had to have proof. She wanted to show it to Dr Jørgensen, because he didn't know what kinds of crimes were being committed here.

'We always take the oldest one,' said the voice cheerfully. 'Someday it will be your turn.'

A short fat woman with madness shining in her watery eyes

came over and let her fingers glide over Lise's face, and she let go of the pillow and screamed in terror. She screamed as though she'd never stop, and the two executioners rushed over to her.

'Let's get her out to the bathroom,' said the one she didn't know. 'There's obviously nothing else to do.'

The words increased her terror, but she stopped screaming as they pushed her bed out through the same door where the old woman had vanished. She closed her eyes and heard them laugh as if they were enjoying themselves immensely.

'So,' said Gitte, 'now she's finally here.'

She heard the door close and slowly she opened her eyes. She was alone in a huge bathroom, only dimly lit by a narrow window high up on the wall. In the middle stood a deep, old-fashioned bathtub with rust in the bottom and lion's-claw feet. There was a multitude of pipes running along the walls at various heights, and there were two gratings as well – one high up and the other close to the floor. The screens on the gratings were covered with a thick layer of dust. She felt relieved to be alone and tried with all her might to think about the world outside. It was run by a well-organized system, and there were numerous offices filled with people who saw to it that the laws were administered. She would see that the world found out what monstrous crimes were taking place here. She would write to the Minister of Justice and tell him they ought to investigate the situation immediately. She put her thumb between the belt and her gown and carefully turned over. Then she heard the rumbling in the pipes just like at home and a voice said:

'Put your hand over your mouth, you've got bad breath.'

She put her hand to her mouth and the sweat poured out over her whole body.

It was Gert's voice; he must be somewhere behind the pipes.

She remembered what the man in the basement had said: 'They're out to drive her crazy.' But why? she thought. What was the plan?

'She does what they tell her to do.' That was Gert again. 'I think she's learning.'

'Not yet,' said Gitte disconsolately. 'Then she would have learned it at home. I did what I could. Look over here, Lise.'

She turned her head and stared at the floor grating. Behind it she saw Gitte's face pressed against the screen.

'If you had understood the new times,' she said gently, 'you would have liked me. That was all I wanted. Then you never would have come here.'

She propped herself up on her elbow, and hope made a bright border around her thoughts.

'I really was fond of you,' she said softly. 'You've just misunderstood me. When I come home, I'll prove it.'

The face vanished and there was a sound from the pipes as if someone were running through them and beating on a drum.

'Just listen to how meek she is,' said Gitte triumphantly. 'She thinks she's going to go home again. As if anyone has ever gotten out of here alive.'

'It'll be fun when Jørgensen arrives,' said Gert.

'I'll tell him everything,' Lise threatened. 'He'll get me out of here. He'll see that you're punished.'

'He was the one who put you in here,' said Gert sarcastically. 'Don't you realize that he's behind the whole thing?'

She was silent with horror, remembering his hearty laughter on the telephone. Who could she trust anymore?

'Nadia,' she said, 'I'll call and ask her to come.'

Gitte laughed maliciously.

'Call?' she said. 'How are you going to do that? And who was the one who got you to call the doctor? Nadia said he was your friend, I heard her quite clearly.'

She thought about her conversation with Nadia and suddenly saw her as part of an enormous plot, whose purpose she had to figure out. She closed her eyes and there was blessed darkness. The little girls were gone. She was mercifully alone and helpless in a world of evil. But if she preserved her sanity, there was still hope. Someone would sooner or later come through the door and discover the crime. A person from outside, someone who would take her at her word and help her find justice. People would start to ask about her out in the world. How long had she been here? Her sense of time had dissolved, the way it does when you're sitting in the dentist's chair. She had to get away before it was too late. They couldn't hold healthy people against their will.

The door opened and Gitte came in wearing her neat uniform. The stiff white cap on her head looked like a halo. She had a glass of red liquid in her hand, and she put it on the stool beside the bed.

'Drink this,' she said in a friendly tone of voice. 'You need a lot of fluids. It's juice.'

Lise stared at the glass and felt her thirst slide through her guts. The liquid had dark particles on the bottom, and all at once she knew there was poison in it. They wanted to murder her, just as they had done with the old woman.

'I'm not thirsty,' she said, and she could barely separate her dry lips. 'You won't get me that easily, Gitte.'

She stared angrily at the smug, self-satisfied face, which looked as though it were fastened to the cap with invisible pins.

'My name isn't Gitte. How many times do I have to tell you that?'

She went out and closed the door behind her, and a little while later her breathless voice sounded in the pipes.

'She won't drink the damn juice, it would have been so easy. Maybe Jørgensen can make her drink it.'

The voice hadn't been there when Gitte was standing next to her, because she couldn't be in two places at once. When she was behind the floor grating, the voice had come out of her there. So she wasn't crazy, thought Lise. On the contrary, she had never felt her brain work so clearly and logically before. There must be long corridors behind the pipes, which you entered from behind. And there must be peepholes so they could look at her. Now they were talking and laughing with each other, and she tried hard not to hear what they were saying. She had to be patient and make the best of things. But she was about to die of thirst. She looked at the poisonous filth in the glass and licked her lips.

'Look at the blisters on her lips,' said Gitte in disgust. 'They look like maggots.'

She tried to remember a poem, but they had all vanished, and she searched for them the way a child searches for her pacifier.

'There burns a candle in the night,' sneered Gert hatefully, and Gitte continued: 'It burns for you alone.'

She flushed with shame and anger. It was one of her own poems.

'They're awful,' said Gitte. 'Enough to make you throw up. She's never caught on to modernism. The young people laugh at her.'

The door opened and Dr Jørgensen stepped in, dressed in a white coat. He had shoulders like a clothes hanger and his tired face had slipped so far down that it was almost covering his neck. He sat down on the stool and moved the glass over a bit. His brown eyes were full of empathy.

'Well,' he said kindly, 'I hear you've been a little restless.'

'That's not so strange,' she said indignantly. 'The most horrible things are going on here. They kill the oldest patients. I've seen it myself.'

'You're mistaken,' he said calmly. 'You're just hallucinating a little.'

'You hear that?' said Gert. 'You're crazy as a loon.'

She stared stiffly at the doctor's face, but his expression didn't change, even though he couldn't avoid hearing it. Maybe he was the most dangerous of them all, and she should watch what she said to him.

'I want to get out of here,' she said. 'You have to get me discharged.'

'No. Not as long as you are ill.'

Something dawned on her. He knew that she wanted to complain to the Minister of Justice, but if he could make her believe she was ill, there would be no reason for it. With terror she realized that she had seen and heard too much for them ever to let her go.

He patted her hand but she pulled it away.

'What happened at home before you took the sleeping pills?' he asked. 'Were you afraid of something? Something to do with your husband, perhaps?'

'Yes, something to do with me,' Gert howled with laughter behind the pipes. 'Why don't you tell him? Don't you trust him?'

'No,' she said firmly. 'I was just nervous and overwrought, that's all.'

'Yes, I see,' he said. 'We can talk about that when you're feeling a little better. You should drink something, your mucous membranes are all dried out. Take this.'

He held the glass up to her lips, and she pulled her head back with a jerk and pressed her lips together tight.

'You know very well that there's poison in it,' she said.

'No,' he said gravely, 'there isn't.'

He put the glass down and looked at her thoughtfully. She remembered how he had helped her many times in a pinch.

Had he really allied himself with all the others against her? And why?

'He needed money,' said Gert. Now they were answering her thoughts too. It must be telepathy. 'He's been living beyond his means and gotten into debt. It was stupid of you not to take your checkbook along.'

The doctor's expression didn't change. He was putting on a great act.

'I've spoken with your husband,' he said and stood up. 'He said that you haven't been well for some time. You didn't dare go outside, for example. But things will get better. We'll give you something to make you sleep.'

He left, and the two in the pipes laughed exultantly.

A new nurse came in and turned on the light. They shook hands.

'Hello,' she said. 'My name is Mrs Nordentoft. You just have to call loudly if you need a bedpan.'

'Can't I go to the toilet by myself?' she asked dejectedly.

'No. The head doctor said that the belt has to stay on for the time being.'

The nurse disappeared, and the light reassured her somewhat. Everything was better in the evening; they had to go home to sleep, at any rate. She searched for a face that would give her some rest and remembered Søren's face in the morning with a milk mustache on his mouth. Suddenly she heard him crying in despair: 'Mommy, Mommy,' he called, 'come and help me!'

She looked around in panic. Behind the grating up near the ceiling she saw his face against the screen. Tears were streaming down his face and his little fingers were clutching at the screen as if trying to tear it loose.

'Søren,' she shouted in horror, 'what's wrong? Why are you crying?'

'It's Gitte,' he whimpered. 'She's putting out her cigarettes on my back.'

Gitte's face popped up behind Søren's and stared down at her.

'Don't let it bother you,' she said. 'Don't feel anything. You don't worry about the bombed children in Vietnam because you only love your own. It's people like you who create all the unhappiness in the world. If you can be indifferent about Søren, you can come home. Then you will be cured.'

She screamed wildly and held her hands to her face. Red flames leaped up behind her eyelids, and her tears could not put them out.

8

It was still raining outside. It was raining from a sky that she would never see again. It was the sky of her childhood, and the evening star pricked a hole in it with a bright, delicate light that flooded the windowsill in her bedroom where she sat with legs drawn up and lost herself in gentle dreams. Behind her was the darkness and the fear and the smell of sweat, sleep, and dust. Behind her was the bed with its heavy, clammy quilt that was like the lid on a coffin. Behind her were her father's and mother's woolen nighttime voices from the world of sex, which she didn't understand. Behind her was the imprisoned night, fermenting like a sealed jar of jam that no air could reach.

It was quiet in the pipes, but Gitte's face appeared behind the grating near the floor, the one she negotiated from, which was the one Lise feared the least. As long as Gitte was there, Søren was safe.

'In the kibbutz,' said Gitte longingly, 'all the children belong to everyone. The mothers don't love their own children any more than the others. It's the same way with deer in a flock. Lion cubs nurse from the closest female, and she doesn't care if she's their mother or not.'

'People always overrate the importance of what they don't have,' said Lise. 'I haven't always been equally fond of my mother.'

'I haven't either.' Hanne's childish voice, full of annoyance, rang from the speaker in the pillow at her ear.

'If you knew how much I envied my girlfriends because their mothers talk to them when they come home from school. I was just supposed to read your disgusting book chapters; they made me sick. You thought they were about me, but you were always writing about yourself. You've never seen anything but yourself in the whole world.'

'And so you took your revenge,' said Lise softly, as a stab of guilt pierced her heart.

'Yes, then she took her revenge.' That was Gitte's voice from the pipe.

Mrs Nordentoft came in. She looked suspiciously at the untouched glass.

'You have to drink something,' she said sternly. 'What do you want? Water, milk, tea? It doesn't matter so much if you don't eat, but we can't have you lying here dying of thirst. That won't do at all.'

'No,' said Gert, 'you have to drink something. Then your suffering will be over.'

He laughed, and the nurse played her role just as well as Dr Jørgensen had. Lise's tongue was swollen and tender, and she could only speak with difficulty.

'I'm not thirsty,' she said, 'but can't you loosen the belt a little? It's cutting into me like knives.'

Mrs Nordentoft felt the belt and took out her keys.

'All right,' she said, 'it doesn't have to be so tight.'

Lise looked up into her gray eyes, which were not the same size.

'Couldn't I have a cigarette?' she asked.

'No, then the bed will just catch on fire.'

She left, and Lise noticed a burning smell in her nostrils. She sat up and to her horror saw frantic little flames darting up from the comforter.

'It's on fire,' she yelled, 'the bed is burning! Help me!'

The fire spread quickly and was nearing her face. She screamed wildly and yanked at the belt to get loose.

Mrs Nordentoft came back in.

'What is it now? Why are you screaming like that?'

'The bed,' she said, her body shaking all over. 'It's on fire.'

'Nonsense,' said the other woman, passing her hand lightly over the bedclothes. The flames sank down and disappeared, and the quilt bore no trace of them.

'Now I'm going to bring you your injection. Then you'll fall asleep right away.'

She came back accompanied by Gitte, who was holding a full hypodermic in her hand.

'Should this be the final one?' she said as if to herself. 'Then we'd get it over with.'

'No,' Lise pleaded, terrified. 'Don't kill me now. I'll do anything you say, but just let me live tonight.'

'No. When I think of all the bread you made me bake for your beastly children because you didn't feel like doing it yourself . . .'

'I didn't know it was a nuisance for you,' she said in despair, but they had already pulled back the comforter. She thrashed around in the belt and screamed, the way you scream to wake up from a gruesome nightmare.

'Come on, stop making such a fuss. We're only doing it for your own good.'

She noticed a momentary pain in her thigh and, exhausted, rolled onto her side, whimpering like a sick dog.

'Stop crying,' said Gitte. 'This time we were only teasing you. You won't die yet. It's all much too amusing for that.'

They were pounding away on the drums, and Dr Jørgensen said with eerie gentleness:

'Close your eyes now and sleep. Then we won't bother you anymore.'

She closed her eyes and there stood Gitte with a sign from a demonstration held up in front of her. She was standing as motionless as a photograph, and on the sign it said in childish printing: SLEEPING FORBIDDEN! Quickly she opened her eyes again, and at the same moment Mrs Nordentoft came in and turned off the light.

'Good night,' she said. 'Sleep well.'

The darkness was so dense you could cut it with a knife. It covered her face like a sweaty hand. She felt a deathlike weariness, and her thoughts rose up in the air like balloons whose strings have been let go.

'I've never been able to understand,' chatted Gert, 'why she didn't take a lover.'

'She's a lesbian,' replied Gitte. 'She's in love with Hanne.'

Suddenly she heard a whirring sound close to her bed.

'Now you're going to hear the tape, Mother,' said Mogens. 'I put it under Hanne's bed. Gitte and I played it after you fell asleep.'

'No,' she cried. 'Mogens, how did you get in here? Why are you doing this to me?'

She put out her hands to take hold of him but he was out of her reach. The whirring sound stopped, and Gert and Hanne's laughter filled the whole world.

'I've studied the marriage statutes,' said Gert. 'We can only be married if she dies or goes insane.'

'Gitte can help us with that,' said Hanne's little voice. 'It worked with Grete. Why shouldn't she fall for the same trick?'

'Wait a minute! Stop it, Mogens. I don't want to hear any more.'

She held her hands over her ears and sobbed in despair into her pillow.

'Help!' she shouted. 'Take him away. Turn on the light. I can't stand it!'

Mrs Nordentoft came in and turned on the light. There was no sign of Mogens or his tape recorder.

'What's the matter now?' she asked patiently. 'You must try to sleep while the injection is working.'

She bent down over Lise and wiped away the tears with her handkerchief. Her face was made of thin paper that had torn in several places. Underneath, the flesh was a suppurating wound. The smaller eye was rigid and expressionless like a glass eye.

'Don't turn off the light,' Lise begged. 'I'm afraid of the dark.'

'You can't sleep with the light on. And it's also against the rules.' She frowned and bit her lip thoughtfully. 'Do you hear voices?' she asked.

'Of course,' said Lise. 'You hear them too.'

'No,' the woman said adamantly, shaking her head. 'All the voices you hear come from inside yourself.'

It dawned on Lise that the whole staff must be in on the plot.

'If I believed that,' she said, 'I would be insane.'

'You aren't well, you know.'

'Close your mouth,' said Gitte, 'she's looking at your ugly teeth.'

'False teeth are cold,' Gert said with loathing.

Mrs Nordentoft turned off the light and left. The darkness was hot like a steam bath, and the voices in the pipes grew distant and indistinct. She closed her eyes, and Gitte's form with the sign slowly became blurred and hazy. In her dreams, Dr Jørgensen's face appeared before her like a close-up on TV. It was gentle and kind, and the brown eyes were moist as if with tears.

'Reality,' he whispered, 'only exists in your mind. Things would be much better for you if you understood that. It has no objective existence.'

'Then where do I exist myself?' she asked.

'In the consciousness of others,' he said patiently, as if speaking to an obstinate but talented pupil.

'I don't want that,' she said, afraid. 'I just want to be myself.'

'Yes, but don't you know that everyone exists in numerous editions, just like books? Copies are made of them in the office for the secret files.'

'Oh,' she said, astonished, 'that explains a lot of things. So are you still my friend?'

'Yes, of course I'm your friend,' he said and laughed suddenly with Gitte's mouth. She saw that he had a hypodermic in his hand.

'Here's some LSD for you,' he said and stuck the needle into her leg. 'It will teach you to love your neighbor.'

She screamed and opened her eyes. The morning light that filled the hideous room had a gray, hopeless sheen to it, like on school days when you hadn't done your homework. It smelled of sweat and she noticed that the bed was wet and her gown was clinging to her body. Her thirst was so intense that it seemed to weaken her hearing. From the pipes came an indistinct murmur of voices, and there were no faces behind the two gratings.

The door opened and a man in a white jacket with brass buttons came in. He was carrying a basin and pushed down the door handle with his elbow. When he turned around, she saw it was Gert, but that didn't particularly surprise her. She had gotten used to her world of terrors the way you get used to a physical pain. Maybe there really were several versions of the same person, and this was just a copy.

'Gert,' she said, 'why do you hate me? Have you forgotten how happy we once were?'

'My name isn't Gert,' he said stubbornly. 'My name is Petersen, and I'm a nurse here. It's time for you to be washed.'

He placed the basin on the stool, and she saw that the water was thick and murky.

He dipped a washcloth into it and opened her gown at the neck. Then he rubbed the washcloth over her face, and she felt her skin tighten and stiffen like under a mask of egg whites. She ran her fingers across her face.

'If you try to remove it,' said Gitte's voice in the speaker, 'the skin will come off too.'

'Stop that, Gert,' she said, full of fear, 'or I'll report you to the police.'

'You wouldn't look for help from a band of child murderers,' scoffed Gitte.

Gert didn't answer, but, unconcerned, went out again with the basin. He had barely closed the door behind him before a woman in a hospital gown came in. She had some knitting in her hand, and her face was disheveled and cheerful, like the face of someone who lives for others to such a degree that she has never placed any importance on what kind of face she wore. One face was just as good as the next. She sat down on the bed, and at the same moment the room was filled with silence. All the voices were quiet and there wasn't the slightest rushing in the pipes. The woman looked at her with a kind, friendly gaze.

'I've come to help you,' she said. 'I was in here before you, and I know what it's all about. First of all you have to have something to drink. Now I'm going to get some water from the tap for you, some without poison in it.'

She left her knitting on the bed while she went out, and Lise thought with indescribable relief that finally someone had come to her who was totally well and normal just like herself.

9

While she greedily drank the water, her childhood seemed to be staring at her through the dull, calm eyes of the woman. She saw her mother before her, when she would sit under the lamp in the evening and sing for her while her father slept on the sofa. The living room was an island of light and security in the wild sea of the world. Now the memory of it glided through her mind like a warmth that had always been there and was just waiting for someone to call it forth. The woman patted her on the cheek.

'If anyone asks you if you hear voices,' she said in a broad, muted voice, 'just say no. It's very important.'

'But that's no use,' said Lise, surprised, 'everyone can hear them.'

'Oh, no.' She was knitting cheerfully away and there wasn't a sound in the room except for the clicking knitting needles. 'You can only hear your own voices.'

She said this in such a matter-of-fact way, as if she were explaining that everybody has their own toothbrush.

'Then Dr Jørgensen can't hear them either?' she asked, full of hope.

'Of course not. Tell him that you don't hear any voices except his.'

'Why?'

Tove Ditlevsen

'Otherwise you'll never go home. If you talk about the voices, they'll think you're insane.'

'That's what they want me to believe.'

'That's obvious. This is an insane asylum, after all, and it can't exist without patients.'

'How do I get out of here?'

'You have to write to the ombudsman. That's what I've done and I'm expecting an answer any day now. And above all, you should humor the voices. It's stupid to fight with them the whole time you're here.'

Gert came in carrying a tray with a cup of coffee and a plate of sandwiches on it.

'Why are *you* here?' he said, frowning. 'You shouldn't be bothering Mrs Mundus, she needs rest.'

The woman calmly collected her knitting and left the room as if she were walking out of a painting in which she had been the central figure.

'It's time to eat your breakfast,' said Gert with a borrowed voice that must have belonged to the nurse whose role he was playing.

'Yes,' she said obediently and looked at the open-faced sandwiches, which had a faintly greenish surface and smelled sharply of ammonia. I wonder how long you can live without food? Her hunger wasn't as bad as her thirst had been. Maybe the woman would bring her some uncontaminated food. She thought of her as her only friend, someone she could count on in the midst of this hell, someone who wouldn't betray her.

Gert disappeared again, and at the same moment Gitte appeared behind the negotiation grating.

'You never understood young people,' she said. 'The writers who don't understand can't survive the new times. Do you remember when you were interviewed by two high-school boys for their school paper? They asked you why you never participated in the current debates. Do you remember what you answered? You quoted Hemingway. Repeat what you said.'

As she tried to remember the words she had used, she looked at Gitte's hands, which were holding on to the grating. It struck her as somehow deeply disturbing that there were twice as many hands in the world as faces. Then the words came to her, strong, clear, and bold.

'Let those who want to save the world do so,' she said slowly, 'if only I can be left in peace to comprehend it clearly and distinctly and in its entirety.'

'Yes,' said Gitte, satisfied, 'that's what you said. And thus your fate was sealed. Hemingway shot himself in the head. He was too old, like you. He belonged to the dead world. It's a shame there aren't any mirrors here. You should see your own face now. It looks like the face of a corpse.'

Fury made Lise abandon all caution.

'I hate you,' she cried. 'I should have thrown you out a long time ago.'

'That was a dumb thing to say,' said Gitte mildly. 'You should realize that I'm just trying to save you. But you're not being cooperative.'

Her face vanished and a little while later she heard Søren scream, hoarsely and abruptly from the torture grating. Filled with horror, she stared up at it. His face was shrunken and ancient-looking, like those of the Indian children you saw on the TV programs about underdeveloped countries. His hunted gaze met hers, full of hopelessness, as if he expected no help from her.

'Søren,' she yelled, 'run out to the ward and find your father. He's here, and he'll make sure that you get home.'

She tugged at the belt, trying to pull it down over her hips, but it was impossible.

'Gitte,' she screamed, 'what are you doing to him?'

'I'm pulling out his fingernails,' said Gitte gleefully. 'Since you won't bear your share of the world's suffering, *he* has to do it.'

'But I will,' she cried in despair. 'I'll agree to all your conditions, if you'll just leave him alone.'

'Be indifferent,' Gitte admonished sternly. 'There are billions of children in the world, and two thirds of them are suffering. Not until you direct your coldness at your own children will you begin to feel something for all of them.'

'Yes,' she said with the feeling that her mind was suddenly emptied of its contents. 'I understand what you mean.'

Søren's sobs grew fainter, and her despair was blunted in an eerie way, as if her center of feeling was momentarily numbed.

'I'm starting to understand what you mean,' she repeated, suddenly recalling what a relief it had been when her love for Gert had been replaced by a clear, pleasant indifference. She had a sweet, nauseating taste in her mouth, while the echo of an old sorrow brushed her heart. She discovered that her memory of Søren as a baby had vanished. She saw the face of a baby before her, but it might just as well have been a strange child she had seen in a buggy on the street. Was there some form of love that she didn't share? She thought about Fröding's poem:

> I bought myself love for money.
> For me nothing else could be had.
> Sing prettily, vibrating strings,
> Sing prettily still about love.

Her eyes filled with tears. All the voices had vanished, just as when the woman had been sitting with her, knitting.

The sweet poison of a kind of comfortable weariness glided through her body. The light in the room had grown soft and cloudy like the water in an aquarium you've forgotten to clean. She felt as if she had been here for years and was now a very old woman. Then she remembered that they always murdered the oldest patient, and the fear came back like a faithful friend who doesn't care whether you return his feelings or not. Her life depended on getting away from here. Like the woman had said, it was important to humor them. But she hadn't been humoring Gitte. For a moment she had actually felt a false, eerie comprehension of what it was all about, and she had betrayed Søren. The memory of his childhood painfully returned to her, and she knew that she had been insane a moment, when his sobs became like a distant noise in her ears, like the noise of the trolley cars down in the street. They drove screeching and rattling through her head, and inside them sat the people whose faces were as empty as houses no one lives in anymore. They were poor people who sold their time for money. They made a certain amount for each hour, and the ones who bought all this time added it to their own, the way rich people hoard food during the build-up to a world war. In the evening the trolley-car people participated in the government-approved entertainments, and they felt guilty when these entertainments gave them no joy. Their death was humble and remote, and they crept hastily into it as if it were some random garment that might fit them if they were lucky. She had to bear their destiny like a habit abandoned long ago, which could be resumed with a little effort. For she had no home any longer, no money, no influential friends. She had only her sanity, which they were trying with all their might to steal from her. She remembered her dream and again heard Dr Jørgensen's voice: 'Reality exists only in your mind.'

Quiet and slender as a thought, he stepped into the room and sat down on her bed. His brown eyes had a sly, untrustworthy expression, which she had never noticed before. Her mother always said that people with brown eyes were treacherous. That was one of the false truths that she had never been able to tear herself away from.

'When you're calmer,' he said, 'you'll be moved out to the ward. We've only put you in here so you won't disturb the other patients.'

She didn't answer, just looked at his hands, which were lying on his knees like two dead objects he had put down for a moment.

'You're hallucinating,' he said. 'Do you know what that means?'

'Yes,' she said guardedly, 'it means you see and hear things that don't exist. But I don't. I don't hear any voices except yours.'

'That's a lie,' said Gitte in the pipe. 'He knows it's a lie. He doesn't dare let you out, because then you'll report him to the police. He's been given 50,000 kroner either to keep you here for the rest of your life or to liquidate you.'

The woman had said that he couldn't hear the voices. She tried to look as though she hadn't heard it either. Suddenly his face was very big, and she saw that tufts of black hair were growing out of his nostrils.

'You're ugly,' flew out of her mouth.

'Yes,' he said softly, 'that's probably true.'

'Mogens was here last night with his tape recorder,' she said, because it wasn't certain that he knew about it. 'He played a tape that he had made underneath Hanne's bed.'

'You're mistaken,' he said with urgency. 'This is a locked ward, and no outsiders can come in here after visiting hours. You are ill, Mrs Mundus, and I'm here to help you.'

'That's the one thing you can't fool me about.'

She looked him straight in the eyes, which were full of multicolored specks just like her father's, ruined by the fire in the furnace he had shoveled coal into for a lifetime.

'I have always despised patients who wouldn't face the truth.'

The words came, but he wasn't moving his lips. His adam's apple didn't move either, and that was an art he must have practiced for a long time. Gitte had learned the same trick; she had noticed it that last day at home.

'I can only help you,' he said in an offended tone of voice, 'if you will tell me what the voices are saying to you. You have to be a little cooperative.'

That was the same word Gitte had used.

'Tell him what we're saying,' sneered Gitte from the speaker in her pillow. 'But turn your face to the wall. Your breath is poisoning the air for him.'

Terrified, she turned her head away from him and burst into tears.

'Leave me alone,' she sobbed. 'I've never wanted anything else. I don't care about the world. I just want to write and read; I just want to be myself. If you let me go I won't give anything away. I'll rent a room. I can work in an office again. I'll send Søren to a day care center after school. I just wish that all of you would forget about me. Even though Hemingway committed suicide, he was right.'

'You'll go home as soon as you're well. Your husband and children miss you. Grete's suicide shook Gert up so badly that the only thing he wants is to come back to you. You have so much to live for, but I can only help you if you tell me the contents of the tape Mogens played for you last night.'

'But you know what was on it,' she said. 'Why should I tell you something you already know? Hanne and Gert –'

She stopped talking, because a brilliantly colored kaleidoscope was swirling around in front of her right eye. It spun faster and faster, and the doctor's face spun with it, as if he had lost control over it.

'Miss Poulsen,' he shouted in a voice that echoed down through all of her ages, 'hurry, bring a spoon, she's having convulsions.'

A sensual ecstasy overwhelmed her and eradicated everything. Her body tensed upward in an arch and she lost consciousness.

IO

Time raised its terrible wings and flew away toward a reality that was not her own. All weight was lifted from her, and she stared up into a blue sky that was studded with memories. Her hand was hidden in Gert's, and from his lips, which were pressed against her neck, came a strong, sweet smell of childhood and fear endured. The sun glowed on her upturned face, as if it came from within her, torn away from the season of the year.

'I love you,' she said, turning her head and looking at his delicate face with its fragile, melancholy mouth.

'Love,' he said, 'makes you selfish. You don't care about anyone else in the world.'

'I feel sorry for them,' she said, letting her fingers run through his smooth blond hair. 'I feel sorry for all the women who don't know you.'

Suddenly his eyes left her face, and she followed the direction of his gaze. She caught sight of Hanne, who was sitting on the grass with her knees pulled up and her honey-colored hair almost covering her adult, secretive face. There was loneliness about her, like a child who has broken the rules of the game and is excluded from the dancing and singing circle of friends. In a distant, sad voice and without taking his eyes from the motionless figure, Gert said:

Oh, these honorable bourgeois youths,
they must restrain their hearts.
Gracefully the strong reseda grows
in father's little garden.

'Sophus Claussen,' she said with a smile, while a chill, as if from her childhood bedroom, ran through her body so that she involuntarily reached for the quilt to pull it closer around her. Gert's face grew bigger, his lower lip fell, revealing a row of dull gray teeth that didn't belong to him. Afraid, she wanted to let go of his hand, but his grip on her tightened, and a dusty gray light pricked at her eyeballs like a scratching insect.

'You've had convulsions,' he said. 'Take these two pills.'

He let go of her hand and she saw a bottle of medicine standing on the stool. She saw the deep bathtub and heard the rhythmic dripping sound from the faucet, which looked like a twisted mouth. Her thoughts fumbled for support like loose pieces of algae in a stagnant pond.

'Gert,' she said softly, 'we were so happy.'

'My name is Petersen,' he said patiently, 'and please take these pills or the convulsions will start up again. You don't have enough barbituric acid.'

'Then I'll take them without water,' she vowed. 'I can swallow them plain.'

She recognized the pills; they were the same ones Gitte had given her.

She sat up in bed and swallowed the little white pills without difficulty. They had unfastened the belt, but it was still attached to the bed.

'That's right,' said Gert, satisfied. 'You're starting to behave quite sensibly.' His face was suddenly blurred, the way it looks when you've forgotten to wind the film and you've taken two pictures on top of each other.

'You have two faces,' she said, astonished. 'That's not allowed. You can only wear one face at a time.'

He patted her on the hand without replying. Then he went out through the closed door, the way people move in a dream. She shut her eyes, and a sunset was there, painted behind her eyelids, as banal as a bad painting.

'Even then,' said Gitte through the speaker in the pillow, 'he realized that love between two people is selfish. He always wanted to free himself from it. Now we all love each other at home, just like at the junior college. And we have enough money for LSD, enough to make the whole world happy. When you get out, you'll be the housekeeper for us and live in the maid's room. Then you'll have some LSD too, and Gert will sleep with you again the way he does with the rest of us. The sexual urge must be satisfied just like hunger. It's all on the same level.'

'And romance?' she said, depressed.

'That was invented by the troubadours. It's completely out-of-date nowadays.'

The door opened and the knitting woman came back with her round, dissipated face folded up sloppily and absentmind-edly, like a dress thrown in the bottom of a closet by someone who has always had plenty of clothes.

'I saw that the chief of staff was in here,' she said. 'You have to watch out for him. He's the one who decides when we can go home. You didn't tell him anything, did you?'

'No, nothing special. I just told him about the tape recorder, because I don't think he knows about everything that's going on.'

'That was stupid. You should never talk to them about tape recorders or speakers or hot-water pipes or radiators or anything like that. You should just say that you know where you are and what year it is and which king is on the throne.'

She kept knitting cheerfully, and Lise's heart practically overflowed with gratitude.

'When you're here,' she said, 'all the voices are quiet. Isn't that strange?'

'No,' said the woman, whom nothing seemed to surprise. 'My voices are only in the TV room now, and I don't go in there anymore.'

She sounded as if she were talking about some unruly children she had finally put away so they could no longer bother anyone.

'What's your name?' asked Lise.

'Mrs Kristensen, and I was a social worker before I came here. I'm used to giving people advice.'

'My name is Lise Mundus,' she said, and the feared glimmer of recognition did not appear in the woman's eyes.

'Where do the voices come from?' Lise asked. 'There must be a natural explanation for them.'

'Oh, yes.' Mrs Kristensen laughed so heartily that she dropped a stitch. 'There's probably an explanation for the telephone and the radio and TV too, but ordinary people wouldn't be able to understand it, even if some technician tried to explain it to them. One thing isn't any stranger than the rest.'

'What do the voices say to you?' asked Lise, feeling her mind react like an old relative you can always count on when it comes to being tactless.

Mrs Kristensen gave her a wounded look.

'That's not something you really ask about,' she said reproachfully. 'You ought to know that. Shall I get you some water?'

'Yes, please,' said Lise guiltily, 'but how do I get any food? I don't dare eat what they give me.'

'My husband brings me food every day. I'll give you some of it when I get a chance.'

When Lise had satisfied her thirst, she said contritely: 'Don't be angry about the question I asked you just now. You're the only one I can trust, and I don't know what I'd do if you left me.'

'I won't. But it'll be easier when you join the rest of us. We have a great time, as long as we watch out for the nurses. When they hear what we're saying, they write it down in the report.'

'If you get a letter from the ombudsman,' said Lise, 'are you sure they'll give it to you?'

'Oh,' laughed the woman, 'it'll be sent to my home address. If it was sent here, they'd never give it to me. If you aren't married, just list your parents' address.'

Miss Poulsen came in and her smile was like an optimistic crescent moon between two ears sticking out, just like in a little child's drawing.

'There's a visitor to see you,' she said. 'You'd better go, Mrs Kristensen.'

'A visitor?'

The word was mundane and ordinary and produced a long echo of memories down through the years. Who would visit her here? Did they really have visiting hours in hell, too?

Her mother came in through the door just as the nurse and Mrs Kristensen went out. She was wearing a silly, modern hat that didn't suit her age. She had stubbornly put on her youth; from behind it her age laughed between the false teeth like the troll in old fairy tales.

'Lise,' she cried in a whimpering tone of voice, 'how could you do this to us?'

She sat down heavily on the stool and gasped for breath.

'You're getting more and more like her,' jeered Gitte from her pipe. 'You're just as scared of old age as she is. And you understand your own children as poorly as she does.'

'It's not something I did to you,' she said. 'I just felt so unhappy.'

'Well, how about that,' said her mother indignantly. 'You, who have everything! And you're famous, besides. Just yesterday, the women in the dairy store showed me an article about you in the paper. They asked you whether you didn't think fame had its obligations, and do you remember what you said?'

'No,' said Lise, filled with vague anxiety.

'That you hadn't won it in a national election. That was clever; just give them what they ask for.'

'That was the answer that brought you here,' said Gitte.

'My God,' said her mother, looking around with distaste. 'Why on earth are you lying in a bathroom? Now that you could afford to go to the rest home in Skodsborg if you felt like it.'

'Mother,' said Lise, trying to conjure up the solid, secure foothold from her childhood before her inner eye. 'You've got to help me. I'm here against my will, and they're trying to make me think I'm crazy. They're trying to murder me, and they're all in it together.'

'Have you gone mad? Who would try to murder you here?'

'There's poison in everything they give me,' she said wearily and with no hope of being believed.

The silly hat was almost falling down over her mother's eyes; she pushed it back with annoyance, the way she always did when something didn't suit her. 'You're really sick in some way,' she said, 'but that's just a sensible punishment for all your snobbishness. You always thought you were better and smarter than your father and me, and you were ashamed to invite your fancy friends home because your father was only a stoker.'

'No,' she yelled and burst into tears. 'That's not true, Mother. I've always loved you.'

'What are you talking about?' said her mother anxiously, slipping out of her egotism like a nut out of its shell. She stood up and leaned her made-up face over Lise's as she held her head in both hands.

'Don't cry like that,' she said. 'Look, I brought you some apples. Do you miss the children? I was over there yesterday, having coffee with them and Gitte. She's like a mother to them, she really is.'

Lise turned her face to the wall and kept on crying.

'You hear that?' said Gitte from the pillow. 'I've told her all about it. She's totally on our side.'

'Be quiet,' shouted Lise and began desperately to turn the pillow over and over to find the little, hard object. Her mother watched her with fear in her eyes.

'I'm not saying anything,' she said, confused. 'What are you doing with that pillow?'

She let go of it and looked at her mother from the depths of her childhood, which suddenly rose up out of her memory through thousands of irrelevant adult days. The sharp face became young and round, and she felt a peace as if an ether mask had been placed over her nose and mouth.

'Mother,' she said quietly, 'sing one of the old songs for me, the ones you always sang when I was little.'

'All right,' she said, 'I'll see if I can remember one of them.'

Then she started singing with a sweet, metallic voice that sounded as crisp as the hourly chimes from the Church of the Holy Spirit:

> Down in Saxony there lived long ago
> a girl so young and so fair.
> She was a gypsy. With her band she rode
> round about in the Saxon land.

There were many verses, and while she was singing, all the voices were silent, the way they were when Mrs Kristensen sat with her. She closed her eyes, and behind her eyelids was the picture of the sailor's wife on the wall in her childhood home. She was holding her hand above her eyes, gazing out to sea for her husband. Lise stared at her happily, as if reunited with a beloved childhood friend. Her mother's voice grew fainter, and a large, friendly hand was placed over her eyelids and erased the sailor's wife as if from a magic slate.

Slowly the terrors were stretched out between the small nails of routine, and sometimes it was possible to regard them as something outside of herself. Then a faint, tolerable sense of relief would appear, which she had to hide as if it were a stolen object that she didn't dare keep for very long. It seemed to her that she had been here forever and that she would never get out. They had tied her firmly to the bed again because once, when the torture in the upper grating had been especially vicious, she had run screaming out into the ward. She could understand that it must have scared the other patients, who didn't know the reason behind it. And the belt only bothered her whenever the bed caught on fire. Then she would scream and someone would come in and put out the fire, just before it reached her face. If only she had had a mirror. The scabs on her lips had fallen off, and her skin was smooth and leathery to the touch, like Mogens's soccer shoes. In the evening Gitte and Mrs Nordentoft would pull her gown up over her head and wash her all over her body with the sticky, corrosive fluid that couldn't be removed without taking the skin with it. She looked down at herself in disgust. It was an unused body with a flabby, caved-in stomach and empty breasts with dark, hard nipples. A body that no one desired anymore. Gert, watching from his pipe, catalogued its anatomy in such obscene terms that nothing within the old realm of her imagination could match such pure, undisguised malice. When Gitte came in with the hypodermic, she never stopped fighting for her life. And Gitte would always throw the home-made French bread into her deliberations about whether to give her a lethal dose, the way mad Mr Dick in *David Copperfield* always mixed the head of Charles I into all his impossible petitions. There was order and routine to everything now, and she was afraid of any changes, to such a degree that she felt her whole world shudder and collapse whenever they promised her that she could come out into the ward as soon as she stopped being so restless. She thought of the donkey-women behind the locked door and realized that she had been seeing things. Doubt seized her too, when she remembered the old woman they had drowned. They had only done it to scare her. It was the same thing when the ward nurse had painted her face so it looked like Mrs Kristoffersen's, her housekeeper before Gitte. She did it to confuse her and break down her resistance, but Lise saw right through such childish tricks with her healthy, clear sense of judgment.

'Wash your face,' she said coldly, 'it's good enough the way it is.'

'You're learning to tell the difference,' said Gitte approvingly from the negotiation grating. 'You're learning to use your mind in the right way.'

This praise made her feel as proud as a child, but she couldn't hold on to that feeling, or any other feeling. The safest thing was not to feel anything at all. All her memories had become distant and vague for her, and important things had dropped out of them, replaced by sharp glimpses of completely irrelevant events. Her skin was rubbed raw where the belt cut into her waist, and the physical pain softened the dread in her heart. Time did not move, and you couldn't let it out because the window wasn't a real window. It was painted on the wall, which was made of damp, filthy-yellow cardboard, whose outer side you couldn't even imagine. There were days and there were nights, and she didn't know when she was sleeping or when she was awake. She never thought 'yesterday' or 'tonight', but always 'once', the same way she thought that in her childhood she had once been to Søndermarken with her parents, without knowing whether this simple memory had grown out of one or a hundred Sundays.

Once Gitte said: 'Are you sure that I exist? Think about it. Did I ever get a letter or a phone call? Did I ever go out?'

'I have proof that you exist,' she replied. 'How could I have talked to Nadia about you otherwise?'

'Ask her,' said Gitte. 'If she's never seen me, then will you believe that you're insane?'

'Yes,' she said, 'then I'll believe it.'

She had gotten a letter from Nadia, who wrote that she was in Finland for a psychologists' conference that would last two weeks. When she came home, she would visit her. But Lise didn't like having visitors. Her mother had left her voice behind when she went home, and inside the pipes it had lost its metallic sweetness and had become flat and toneless and worn-out, like when she haggled with sales clerks over prices. Her mother's vocabulary was ridiculously limited, and she wasn't intelligent enough to really get to Lise. After her attack of weakness, the fragile memory of the old songs had grown as boring and irrelevant as when other people talked about their dreams. Instead she remembered a rip in a red dress that her mother had stretched across the palm of her hand. 'If you keep on like this,' her mother had said, 'we'll end up in the poorhouse.' That prospect hadn't frightened her at all. She could be anywhere, if only she was allowed to keep her poetry book with her. The only thing in the world that she wanted was to write poems in it, and anything that prevented her from doing this aroused her hostility.

She almost always lay on her side with her legs pulled up and her hands folded under her cheek. It was easier to placate the voices by keeping totally still, and the whole time she felt as if she were being observed like a beetle under a magnifying glass. Mrs Kristensen brought her some of her food and watched her contentedly while she ate it from the waxed paper. The voices never spoke of her, and Lise had formed the impression that they didn't know anything about her existence. The staff left them alone too and stopped chasing Mrs Kristensen away whenever they found her there. Lise could tell her everything without fear, and she answered all questions practically and sensibly.

'If I get out of here,' said Lise, 'where should I go? I don't have any home anymore, and they've divided up my money.'

'I'll tell you what to do,' said Mrs Kristensen. 'Go out to the women's home on Jagtvej where you can take your little boy with you. From there you can get in touch with the organization for household help; I'll give you the name and address of the director. Then you'll be placed in a good home where you can learn to clean and cook under the guidance of the housewife, and you'll have some spending money too. It'll all work out. If you feel lonely, you can visit me. My children are all married and I'm alone all day long. I put adhesive tape over the mail slot so my neighbor can't peek in.'

'Thank you,' said Lise, totally satisfied with this solution. 'But if you hear from the ombudsman, you'll be home before I am. And then who'll give me anything to eat and drink?'

'Then I'll come and visit you,' she promised, 'because it's essential that I go home soon. The chief of staff wants to transplant a new brain into my head.'

'A new brain?' asked Lise, astonished.

'That's right.' Mrs Kristensen looked up from her knitting with a patient expression. 'They transplant hearts, don't they?'

Everything she said was as convincing and matter-of-fact

as two and two makes four. Everything became simple and straightforward and was smoothed out like threads in a fine embroidery. Lise felt as though she had known her forever and would never lose her. But little by little a longing began to gnaw at her like a mouse in a crumbling skirting board. She was hungry and thirsty, and once when Mrs Nordentoft was carrying out her untouched food, she said:

'Would you ask Mrs Kristensen to come in here? I haven't seen her in a long time.'

'That's not so strange,' said the nurse in an indifferent tone. 'She's been moved to St Hans Asylum.'

'St Hans?' she repeated, horrified. 'But there was nothing wrong with her.'

'I don't think you're the right person to judge that,' said Mrs Nordentoft with a friendly smile. 'But hopefully she'll get well there.'

The feeling of being utterly alone and helpless returned to her mind like a violent shudder that made the sweat break out all over her body. A young girl she hadn't seen before came in and put her hand on Lise's forehead.

'Are you feeling bad, Mrs Mundus?' she asked gently. 'Do you want something to drink?'

Lise looked up into a face that for some reason inspired her trust. The young girl's features seemed to be sunk in the memory of an old sorrow, and the pupils of her eyes were unnaturally large, like Hanne's pupils the time she had iritis and every morning had to have drops of atropine in her eyes. It gave them an expression of continual worry.

'Yes,' she said, 'but please give me something that doesn't have poison in it. Take the water from the faucet and don't let anyone touch it.'

'All right,' said the girl, 'and I can drink a little of it first, so you'll know that it's pure.'

After that she gave Lise both water and food, and she always ate a little herself before she fed her, the way you feed a little baby. Lise always warned her to be cautious, because she knew what a risk she was taking. It was the same as being a prisoner in a concentration camp, fearing for the life and safety of the guard who secretly eases her suffering. Her name was Miss Anesen and she was a trainee. If they discovered that she was helping her, she would certainly lose her job.

'Won't you lend me a cigarette,' asked Lise one day, embarrassed at her poverty.

'Sure,' said Miss Anesen, 'but I have to sit with you while you smoke it.'

She lit it for her, and Lise happily smoked herself dizzy. The voices left her alone when the young girl was with her, just like when Mrs Kristensen was there. She felt the need to warn her new friend.

'The nurse who calls herself Miss Poulsen is really named Gitte,' she said. 'She's my housekeeper.'

'I think it's just a coincidence that she looks like her,' said Miss Anesen, holding the ashtray out to her. 'They say everybody has a double.'

'That's true,' said Lise thoughtfully. 'There are also some people who have two faces. Gert does, and in reality one of them belongs to the male nurse named Petersen.'

'He's so nice,' said the girl, changing the subject. 'You can tell him anything. Who's Gert?'

'That's my husband,' she said, and the word sounded idiotic. 'I was in love with him once, but now he loves only youth. He said before that everyone between 35 and 45 ought to be frozen until they're so old that nature will do the rest.'

'When did he say that?'

'Right before you came in,' she said, 'but he's quiet whenever you're here.'

'You must be mistaken,' said the girl calmly. 'Mr Petersen has gone home, and your husband is probably at work, isn't he?'

'Yes, that's true.' Lise remembered that she was never supposed to talk about the voices.

Miss Anesen stroked the damp hair from Lise's face.

'As soon as you stop screaming and crying so much,' she said, 'you can come out into the ward. It'll be much better there.'

The minute she was gone, Gitte appeared behind the negotiation grating.

'Do you remember,' she said coldly, 'the time Nadia asked you to send 100 kroner a month to the striking mine workers in Spain?'

'And I did, too,' she said, afraid. 'I did it for at least a year.'

'Yes, but it annoyed you to do it. You only did it so that Nadia would think you were a good person. You didn't feel anything at all for the people you were helping. You couldn't picture them, because you lack imagination. You only know mine workers from D. H. Lawrence's novels. And besides that, you've had plans to move to Spain to avoid taxes.'

'That was Gert's plan,' she defended herself. 'He wanted to see the old Europe.'

'Spain is a sore on the face of the world,' said Gert. 'I've changed. I've learned to see things through the eyes of the young people. When I take an LSD trip, I'm filled with love for all the creatures of the earth. All of them except you. You write in a language only spoken by five million people. It's so important for you to create sentences in that language that everything else takes second place to your perverse obsession. Haven't you noticed that people flee out of your life like they would from a burning house?'

'Why don't you flee too?' she asked defiantly. 'What's really binding you to me?'

'Hanne,' he said brutally. 'I love her, and we're just waiting for you to disappear from the picture. Then we can get married, since you and I haven't had any children that it would harm.'

'There's Søren,' she said in despair. 'He can't have his sister as a stepmother.'

'I'll take care of him,' said Gitte with cruel mirth from the torture grating. 'We've thought of everything, dear Lise. Now I'm going to throw sulfuric acid in his face.'

'No,' she screamed in the utmost pain, 'spare him, let him go. I'll take him with me to the women's house on Jagtvej; we'll both disappear out of your lives. I'll do anything you ask me to. I won't go to the police, I won't write to the ombudsman, I'm willing to go to St Hans Asylum for life, if you just spare his face. I'm willing to love you, I'll be your mother, I'll support you for the rest of your life.'

She thrashed around wildly, and the belt bit into her flesh but didn't cause her enough pain.

'Look,' said Gitte calmly, 'here's the bottle. If you really love that insignificant boy so much, then let me take you instead. Then you'll never be able to show yourself to anyone again. You'll be so disfigured that not even your mother will recognize you anymore. That's the price if I spare him.'

Lise's hands fumbled over her face, and Søren's desperate screams cut through her head like the rattling, screeching trolley cars. Suddenly she was filled with the same numbing sense of well-being she had felt before she had the convulsions. Her damp legs separated, and the scene behind the torture grating grew distant and irrelevant, like a boring movie.

'No,' she said absently. 'I need my face more than he needs his. If Mrs Kristensen can get a new brain, then he can get a new face.'

'Fine,' said Gitte in a sated tone of voice. 'Now that you're indifferent to him, I'll leave him alone for the time being.'

Lise slipped away on a wave of joy and fear and pain, and

Gitte's face grew large and distinct, as if a warm rain were streaming down it. She felt love for Gitte flowing through her body, and she surrendered to it, the way you cross a border from which there is no return. And in one clear, observant spot in her mind, she knew that now they had won. She had gone insane.

12

She was sitting up in bed, knitting. Knit five, purl five. It was supposed to be a pot holder, and the yarn cut into her forefinger the way it did in Home Ec classes in school. Knit five, purl five. She was proud that she could figure it out. With every fifth stitch a drop fell from the faucet into the bathtub, and it never failed. There was order and a system to everything. They had removed the belt from her bed. She had been given a bath in clean hot water, because they no longer had any reason to try to kill her. She ate and drank what they gave her, because now that she was insane, they didn't put poison in it anymore. All the faces were clear and alert, like after a long night's sleep, and Gitte had stopped using Miss Poulsen's face, which had found its way back to her like an exhausted child who finally comes home after wandering around on strange, unfamiliar pathways. She was only in doubt about Mr Petersen, for he still had Gert's ironic, melancholy eyes, while his own were probably out at the cleaners. But she coped with this by avoiding his glance. Miss Anesen had cut and cleaned Lise's fingernails, and one day she lent her a mirror, and in it she saw a totally new, very young face, whose past wrinkles seemed to have been smoothed out with a hot iron. Even the triple necklace of wrinkles around her neck was only faintly visible, as if time had run backwards like the reel of a tape recorder. Mogens didn't bring it with him at night anymore; he needed his sleep, after all, before putting on his father's face in the morning. The voices came less often now, and their words were tired and gentle, like after a job well done. She was allowed to go alone to the toilet that didn't lock. The other patients would open the door and mutter apologetically when they caught sight of her. Their faces were white full moons, and she couldn't tell them apart. Whenever Dr Jørgensen said that she could move out of the bathroom now, she would beg as if for her life to stay where she was. She didn't want to leave Gitte, whom she could still entice down to the negotiation grating once in a while. She never appeared in the torture grating anymore. Ever since the day when Lise had sacrificed Søren's face for her own, Gitte had stopped torturing him. She wasn't a sadist and had only used cruelty in the service of a greater cause.

One evening Mrs Nordentoft came in and asked her if she wanted to come and watch TV with the other patients. She remembered that Mrs Kristensen's voices were in there and she had no right to hear them, but Gitte said through the pillow speaker that she should go because there was an important message for her. So she let herself be wrapped up in her bathrobe, shoved her feet into her slippers, and went into the unfamiliar room, leaning on Mrs Nordentoft's arm. She stared at the anchorman's face, which resembled Dr Jørgensen's. He was talking about the disturbances in Paris, where students and workers were demonstrating against the president. They showed clips of the street battles. The demonstrators threw down their signs and with their bare fists attacked the police, who flailed their clubs at their heads and shoulders. Bonfires flared up, and tear gas flowed through the streets like sulfuric acid, blinding the young faces covered by frail, transparent hands that offered no real protection. She was gripped with excitement and felt a wild triumph at seeing a picture of the president being slashed with knives. Suddenly she saw Gitte step out from the crowd and pick up a poster at the foot of the Arc de Triomphe. Her face filled the whole TV screen, and she lifted the sign up to it with outstretched arms. Lise stared at the words, written in a childish, grade-school script. It said: *Love everyone or no one!* At once her excitement sank like the flames of a bonfire that receives no fuel. The verse of an old poem passed soothingly through her mind:

> – and if you will be free of loss and sorrow,
> then you must love nothing here on earth.

She lost interest in what was gliding across the TV screen. She tried to picture her children, but she had forgotten their faces. Instead she saw a boy's face from her childhood street. He was much older than she was, but he was saying a formal goodbye to his childhood in the presence of the children in the trash-can corner. 'I'm going to Spain,' he said, 'to sacrifice my life for freedom.' She loved him because he was going to die soon. One time he had jumped out of the stairwell window from the third floor in the front building. The fall had compelled everyone's respect and admiration for him, but when he came home from the hospital, his hip was twisted, and that had sealed his fate. One of his feet was always dangling half an inch above the other, and his eyes saw something no one else could see. Soon an enemy bullet would strike him in the heart, and sorrow and poverty and boredom would never again rise up in his throat like nausea.

'I'm tired,' she said to the nurse sitting next to her. 'I'd like to go to bed.'

Now she pulled up her gown herself whenever they gave her the injection, and a little while later her brain would be listless and empty – a mirror that doesn't reflect anything or anyone. Her sleep was deep and dreamless, and the frightening images behind her eyelids never appeared anymore. Hanne's face and voice had disappeared too, and of the three faces left, her mother's was the most annoying.

'Do you remember,' her mother said reproachfully from her pipe, 'that time you were home alone and out of pure and simple meanness you smashed that vase I liked so much?'

'Yes,' she replied, 'but I've regretted it ever since.'

'That won't make the vase whole again,' said her mother drily. 'We had it in my childhood home, and it was the only memento of my mother that I had. You've always been cold-hearted.'

'I didn't want to repeat your lives,' she defended herself. 'I wanted to have my own.'

'When there wasn't any food in the house, you would go and eat dinner with the whore next door. You didn't care if we got any.'

'I know,' she admitted, 'but I've been punished for that. Today I'm just as poor as you were then.'

Dr Jørgensen came in without his white coat on; he was dressed in a neat custom-tailored suit and a shirt so white that it made his face look as if he had just been sitting in bright sunlight.

'You look good,' he said, satisfied. 'Don't you feel much better?'

'I'm insane,' she told him happily.

'You're not as ill as you were. In what way do you feel insane?'

'I don't care about my children,' she explained. 'I've almost completely forgotten about them.'

'It'll come back,' he promised. 'You'll love them again as soon as you see them.'

'Yes,' she said, 'but only when I feel something for the Spanish mine workers and the arrested Russian writers and the political prisoners in Greece.'

'But that's not up your alley,' he said with surprise. 'You can't feel anything for people you've never seen.'

'He's an individualist,' said Gitte with contempt. 'He doesn't understand a thing about it.'

She grew confused and studied his dark, affluent face, which smelled faintly of aftershave.

'Have you paid off your debt?' she asked.

'What do you mean by that? I don't have any debt.'

Smiling, he let his finger glide along her nose.

'Keep quiet,' said Gitte. 'We've paid him off. We have no use for him anymore.'

'Nothing,' she said. 'It's just something I was thinking.'

'Hasn't your husband visited you?' he asked. 'He would be pleased that you're getting well.'

'No,' she said in a fit of candor. 'He's going to marry Hanne while I'm insane, and then it won't matter much afterwards.'

He scrutinized her for a moment, and the shadow of her old trust in him passed through her mind.

'So you believe,' he said slowly, 'that there exists an intimate relationship between the two of them?'

'Yes, of course,' she said calmly, 'it's been going on for a long time.'

'Who told you that?'

'They told me themselves. And you know all about it too. You got the 50,000 kroner to get me out of the way.'

'Did they tell you this while you were still at home, or after you came here?'

She thought about it for a moment. 'They didn't tell me until I was here,' she admitted.

'I don't think it's true,' he said earnestly. 'You must not believe everything the voices tell you. They can easily be lying.'

'That old hypocrite,' said Gert contemptuously. 'I never could stand him. He was the one who made you indifferent to my unfaithfulness, and that wasn't what I intended. He took you away from me, and that's where it all started.'

Terrified, she retreated.

'I don't know what voices you're talking about,' she said. 'I don't hear any voices.'

'All right, all right, never mind.'

He pushed back her newly washed hair behind her ear and patted her lightly on the cheek.

'Do you have anything against Gitte visiting you?' he asked. 'She's asked me for permission.'

'Say no,' said Gitte. 'She's just a carbon copy.'

'No,' she said obediently, 'I don't have anything against it.'

'You'll have to resign yourself to coming out in the ward tomorrow,' he said. 'The bathroom is badly needed, and it's not very comfortable in here, after all.'

'Oh no,' she begged in terror, 'I don't want to leave the voices.'

She regretted it at once.

'I mean you and the nurses,' she said unconvincingly.

'The voices will go with you,' he promised gravely. 'They'll be out there too.'

'Am I going home soon?' she asked. 'I won't report you, and you can keep the money. And besides, the police wouldn't believe me anyway, now that I'm insane.'

She stretched her arms up over her head, as if to show him how harmless she was. Harmless, not worth worrying about. That was her attitude at school. She remembered the encounter with Minna at the trauma center. 'We always thought you were awfully stupid.' The world shouldn't be afraid of her, because then she would be afraid of the world. It hit her hard whenever she forgot about this and revealed something of herself which she now fiercely denied, the way she had done in that damned interview Gitte and her mother had mentioned.

'You'll go home as soon as you're well,' he said.

'Then I'll have to learn how to bake bread.'

'It's probably not that hard,' he said with a smile.

When he had left, Gitte appeared in the negotiation grating. She pressed her face so hard against the screen that her nose was completely flattened.

'You didn't handle that very well,' she scolded. 'You've got to learn to behave as if you are well. It's just a question of practice. And you also have to do it when my copy gets here. Talk to her the way you did at home, like you would to someone of a lower caste than you.'

'I didn't expect that of you,' Lise said, alarmed. 'I come from poor circumstances myself. All people are created equal, that's what it says in the American Declaration of Independence.'

'Don't love America,' warned Gitte. 'Not until they've pulled out of Vietnam.'

'I've always detested the world beyond Valby Hill,' she said, so softly that she didn't think Gitte could hear.

'That's why you clung to your children so they were almost smothered. Do you remember the little poem by Henry Parland that you liked so much? Recite it for me.'

She obeyed, and as the words slid across her lips, she realized she really hadn't understood them until now:

A mother came to me:
tell me
what is missing
in my love.
My children don't love me
as much as I love them.

I said:
indifference,

a little soothing indifference
is missing from your love
– then she went away
looking at the ground.

'Yes,' said Gitte, 'and you didn't learn that until you were indifferent about Søren's face. But it won't last forever. When you start to feel something for the whole suffering human race, then you will love Søren again.'

But she thought that the question then would be whether Søren would love her. Would he ever forgive her for sacrificing him to save her own skin?

Gitte disappeared, and all the voices were silent. A thin ray of sunshine fell through the high window, and it surprised her. Could it be springtime outside? She had no idea how long she had been here.

13

The patients were wandering up and down the long corridors wearing dresses that were either too small or too big. Their random faces were gray and flaccid and fit them as poorly as the dresses did. But they seemed content as long as they could reach their eyes and look out through them, as if through dusty windows no one had thought of cleaning. They fumbled with one hand along the wall, which tilted into the room slightly, and they knew that one day, in its yellow, neglected weariness, the wall would fall on top of them and crush them. They kept their voices inside themselves as much as possible, because they couldn't be sure that a voice like that would find its way back once they let it out. It was best if they only let it form easy, ordinary words that didn't express any personal thought but might have been spoken by anyone at all. Now and then they stopped, as if someone from outside had called them – a husband, a child, a memory. They shook their heads and for a moment lost control over the tilting wall. Then they would forget about it and resume their strenuous work of keeping the hours apart from each other, so the evening wouldn't trickle down over them in the middle of the afternoon, and so the nights wouldn't flow together in long chains without their knowing what the days were doing in the meantime. Every time they reached the end of the corridor, they would stare up at the big, creaking clock whose hands so often forgot to move.

Among the patients moved the quick, slender nurses, wrapped in their confident sexuality and disinfected against contamination, like the staff of a leper colony.

Certain things happened that slid under Lise's skin with the quiet regularity of routine. One patient seemed to leave herself and came over and touched her arm as if to convince herself that Lise was real and that you couldn't walk through her like a rainbow. 'You look so kind,' she said dully and absentmindedly. 'Won't you please tell me where the exit is? I need to go home and send my grandchild to school.' Lise showed her the door to a stairway she had never seen and whose steps she couldn't visualize. The woman grabbed the door handle and discovered that the door was locked. Then, with no sign of disappointment, she went over to a nurse and very politely asked her for the key.

'But you can't go home before you've had lunch,' said the girl. 'After you've eaten, we'll let you out.'

The patient seemed completely reassured with that reply, even though she had heard it a hundred times before, and it was all like a ritual whose original meaning no one remembers any longer.

Lise had accepted her new, fragile reality the way a box accepts a lid that only fits if it expands and makes a great effort. That's the way things went, and she could only hope that nothing else would change. Dr Jørgensen hadn't lied to her. The voices were here too. They had settled into the radiators beneath the barred windows, in her pillow, and in the pipes in the toilets, which she visited more often than necessary. Now there were only Gitte's and Gert's voices, and they guided her thoughts in the right direction the way you guide the steps of small children who wouldn't be able to find their way on the steep, tilting floor themselves. They spoke to her so tenderly that the sweetness of surrender filled her like a drug. But she still had much to learn. There were things she hid from them; for instance, that her lack of love was not absolute, and that on the edge of her insanity there was a frayed, trembling border of something normal and familiar that would put her in danger again if anyone caught sight of it. She was only allowed to love Gitte, and slowly that love would expand to include every creature who suffered from poverty, injustice, disability, dictatorship, and persecution by those who thought differently. Gitte never reminded her of the last, crucial scene behind the torture grating, but she knew that it would be repeated if she revealed her weakness and doubt even for a moment. Most of all she had to guard herself against Dr Jørgensen and the treacherous attacks of old trust in him, which seized her all too often. She didn't always succeed in making him believe in her harmlessness. She felt transparent under his searching eyes, and fear took hold of her whenever he said that she was getting well. 'But I hear voices,' she would defend herself. 'That only happens when you're insane.' She no longer heeded Mrs Kristensen's warning, for it was no longer her goal to go home. The faces were waiting for her there, and her eyes would strike them like sulfuric acid. And besides, Gert and Hanne would have to get married first, because that's what was demanded by the uncomprehending, difficult world in which Gert had placed himself, as in an old painting whose frame he didn't dare step out of. He wanted to be up in the 28th salary bracket, and he couldn't get there if he didn't fit into the middle-class system. It was all right to have an insane wife, but then he had to legalize his and Hanne's relationship in some other way. Only in marriage could the love of youth be validated; on this wave he would be carried out over the old world and into his only chance of survival. Then Gitte could retire and live on Lise's abandoned youth, and every morning Lise would bring her coffee in bed and they would talk quietly together about men and children and love, just like in the conversation you could never hold with a dead person except in pleasant dreams.

Once Gitte said through the toilet's cisterns:

'If the situation came up, would you marry a Black man?'

'Yes,' she lied, shocked.

'You don't mean that,' said Gert sternly.

'I never had time,' she defended herself, 'to form my own opinion about that. It was my resolve to describe the world I saw, not to participate in it.'

Then Miss Anesen was suddenly standing in the doorway, regarding her with a gentle smile.

'Who are you talking to?' she asked.

'Nobody,' she said, startled, and flushed the toilet unnecessarily.

'We know very well that you hear voices,' said the other woman. 'Don't be so afraid of losing face.'

Terrified, she touched her face, which was creased and wrinkled like her mother's, because she had forgotten to hold it back when it ran through the future as if through a sewer where the light falls seductively through a fake window at the end onto the old garbage and scurrying rats.

She went in and lay down on her bed next to the woman whose head was always raised several inches off her pillow. In her gray, timeless face only the eyes were alive, attentive, and observant. Whenever they tried to feed her, she would press her lips tight together and only open them in response to the most gently caressing words, taken from old lullabies. She never answered when you spoke to her. Next to Lise's bed there was a table with a soap dish, a comb, and a toothbrush on the shelf underneath; all of it belonged to the state and had no connection with the similar articles in the home she had abandoned like a dream that leaves no lasting traces. Mr Petersen came over to her with his borrowed eyes fastened to his face like some foreign burden that made him embarrassed, so she constantly had to help him get over it and pretend nothing was wrong, the way children remove the paper from a present whose contents gives them no joy, because the adults have always forgotten the most important thing: the key to the wind-up mouse or the battery for the lamp in the dollhouse.

'There's a visitor for you,' he said. 'It's a girl – she's sitting in the waiting room.'

Gripped by a vague uneasiness, she stepped into that room which held no memories; the patients sat across from the visitors with featureless faces from the past, selected from the cloakroom where they hung on hangers like the dresses that never fit. Gitte was sitting in a corner, carrying on a lively conversation with a patient whose face was torn out of its context, like the sentences Gitte pulled out of books at home and wore like a suit that no one would ever dream had not been made especially for her.

'Hello, Gitte,' she said, and noticed with alarm how the old loathing passed through her consciousness like a clear, erect thought from that disturbing world she had once abandoned, the way you give up on an insoluble, insurmountable question. Gitte's face stood out from her dress like a flower in a vase when the water hasn't been changed. It was wilted and forsaken, and the dreamy expression in her eyes resulted from an error in construction and not from a noble character.

'Lise,' she cried. 'It's so nice to see you again. We weren't allowed to visit you before, because you were so sick. Sit down and let's have a good talk.'

Lise sat down, pulling the stiff dress over her knees. Her stockings were sagging and the loose slippers suddenly reminded her of all the small, elegant shoes Gert had bought for Hanne. She missed her voices, which had never penetrated into the waiting room. Doubt settled into her heart, which was suddenly pounding like the drums in the bathroom pipes. Maybe this was the real Gitte, and the face behind the negotiation grating was just a copy.

'How are things at home?' she asked without interest.

'Fine,' said Gitte, 'but we all miss you. Especially Søren. He was wounded on the cheek by an explosion in physics class, but now it's starting to heal.'

'It's the sulfuric acid,' she said, appalled. 'You promised to spare him.'

'What do you mean?'

Her cold, inquisitive eyes rested on Lise like a painful, inescapable memory.

'Nothing,' said Lise. 'I'm just crazy.'

'Yes,' said Gitte contentedly. 'And you should stay here until you get well. Look, I've brought you some cigarettes, and I remembered your lipstick.'

She took a pack of Prince cigarettes out of her purse, and Lise grabbed the lipstick and held the shiny tube in her hand as if it were a precious gift, a tender greeting from a world to which she would never return.

'Do you have a mirror?' she asked.

Gitte held up her little pocket mirror for Lise as she let the red lipstick glide over her pale, dry lips.

'Thank you,' she said, 'that was nice of you.'

The words were flat and dry in her mouth, just like the other patients whose voices sounded as if they were wound-up dolls whose batteries were almost dead. All of the visitors talked very loudly, as if to deaf people, and they rustled the bags of fruit and the sandwich paper and brushed their fluttering hands across the faces and hands of the patients, as if to reassure themselves that they were still alive.

'Why did you do it?' asked Gitte. 'Gert was terribly upset. He was already very depressed over Grete's suicide. I don't know how he would have managed without Hanne. She's so unselfish, and she does everything she can to console him.'

'What does she do?' asked Lise absently.

'Oh, lots of things. Tonight they're going to a performance: "The novel in space". Modern authors don't have their books published, you know. They hang them up in a room and the spectators go in and participate, like one of the characters. It's very interesting. If you want to keep up with things, you'll be writing like that too.'

Silence suddenly slid inside her like a new kind of reality she had to assume. The humming sound in her ears disappeared, as did the quivering, temporary character of the walls and furniture. Gitte's face was solid and physical, and her skin was only slightly stretched across her cheekbones. Poor people got used to these things, just like wearing second-hand clothes. She was wearing Hanne's hand-me-down dress, which had molded itself to her thin figure and was only too tight across the breasts. She had left one of the buttons open, and you could see her pulse beating below her collarbone. Nervously, Lise dangled one foot and saw that the other patients were doing the same thing. They were longing for their visitors to leave so they could wander up and down the corridor again with listening, inward-looking faces and a hand moving along the tilting wall. They were as flat as paper dolls, while Gitte and the other strangers had a reverse side that they weren't afraid to show. They had skin, bones, blood, and nerves underneath, and they gave off an odor of memories and seasons of the year that struck the nostrils of the insane with a fear that they wouldn't be able to tolerate for very long.

'I've learned to like you,' said Lise cunningly, 'as much as my own children.'

'That's a lie. You can't stand me, but you don't dare throw me out because I know too much.'

Gitte's throat was completely relaxed and her narrow lips were pressed together over her small milky teeth. She revealed them with a smile.

'I like you too,' she said. 'In my opinion, the generation gap doesn't exist. Mogens is chairman of the student council. They've been holding meetings every evening. There's a teacher they want to get rid of at the school. He doesn't understand anything about the new times.'

'But I do,' Lise said, afraid. 'You go to bed with each other for the sake of friendship, and sex and kinship play no role. I understood it all when I went insane. Do you mind if I go to the toilet?'

She had to go out to Gitte's voice in the cistern, because she couldn't do without it anymore. Gitte herself didn't know that her voice had been robbed of its echo. She didn't know anything about Lise's frayed doubt or her dangerous, dawning normality which felt like a deep ache far inside her bones.

'Gitte,' she called, 'say something to me.'

But there was only a distant rushing from the cistern, and she knew that the voices had betrayed her because she didn't feel any love for the girl in the waiting room, even though she had brought her cigarettes and lipstick. She had taken her own voice back, and it lay shiny and fat on her tongue like a coiled snake ready to strike. Lise felt helpless and forsaken and she realized, filled with horror, that the sickness was on its way out of her mind, the way a snail abandons its house – naked, trembling, and unprotected. She longed for the bathroom as if it were her lost childhood home.

'*Lolita*,' said Gitte as she put on her coat. 'It was an experience to read it again. I see myself in it. I was only twelve when the principal's husband seduced me. He would come when I licked his eyeballs. They were rough and salty like mussels. The witch hated me, the way Lolita's mother hates her. Hanne says hello, I forgot to tell you.'

With cruel cheerfulness, she stared at Lise's suddenly aged form, which was bending forward as if to accept the coming years quickly.

Gitte put out her hand and for a moment it lay on Lise's, as cold and dry as a stone.

'I'm looking forward to you coming home,' she said.

'It won't be long,' said Lise, 'but as long as I still hear voices, I can't.'

But she didn't hear voices anymore. And she had to hide this fact from everyone until Hanne and Gert were married. Silence rose up in her mouth like gall as she took her place in the line of wandering patients. Mr Petersen put his hand on her arm, and she saw that he had gotten his own eyes back. They had shriveled up a little, like two pieces of dried fruit, and didn't quite fit in their sockets, but she knew that they would soon adjust.

'You're supposed to go to the Examination Room,' he said. 'Dr Jørgensen wants to talk to you.'

14

She saw at once that he had taken special care with his face that morning, the way you send out a suit you seldom wear to be dry-cleaned and pressed for an important occasion. But now when the late afternoon was already leaning toward dusk, fatigue was breaking through his skin like stubble on dark-haired men who have to shave twice a day. His gaze resembled the dying embers behind the mica-glass panes on a country stove. Tenderness rose up in her like a fever, and it was colored by the same fear for his safety that she had felt for Miss Anesen when she had risked her life to help her.

'Was it nice to see Gitte?' he asked.

'Yes,' she said. 'I'm not afraid of her anymore, now that I've learned to love her.'

She noticed that the words fell as slowly as if they were falling from an eyedropper, and they were somehow all wrong. They were supposed to fit his image of her, because only in that way could she appease the evil forces in the world.

'That's not required of you,' he said, astonished. 'There must be other people who are closer to you than your housekeeper. Is that something the voices have demanded of you?'

'Yes,' she admitted. 'There's so little love in the world that the person we have to love the most is the one everyone else has overlooked. The person it takes the most work to love, the one we deep inside find repulsive because she prevents us from getting by easily. The one who is suffering, the one who has been wronged, the spiritually destitute, and the anonymous child who every morning must sit down at his school desk with the nauseating stink of fear handed down for generations.'

As she was saying all this, something melted in her throat and heart, and she saw his face through a veil of tears.

'Don't be afraid of me,' she said softly. 'I'll never expose you. Money means so little to me, and I'll reconcile the others to you. I see everything as if it were happening on another planet. Gert is welcome to marry his depraved little nymph, who has taught him everything right from the start. Through her he'll experience the new world with all its demands to love your neighbor; and this even applies to the man on the trolley with his insufferable bad breath and his sweaty, crumpled transfer.'

'I think you're getting well,' he said gently.

'No,' she said, terrified, staring at the radiator under the window; no voices were there to help and support her.

'No,' she repeated, 'I still hear voices, and that doesn't happen if you're well. And I'm no good at housework.'

'You don't have to be,' he said earnestly. 'It's enough that you're good at poetry. In my opinion, you've written some quite brilliant poems.

'They're hopelessly banal,' he added, 'full of confessions of what you feel that you feel when you feel.' This last part he said with closed lips, and his adam's apple didn't move.

'Sometimes,' she said slowly and with difficulty, 'I hear things that you don't really say.'

'It's good that you're aware of that,' he said, holding his face up at the temples with his forefingers because it was too tired now to hold itself up.

'Do you know Nordahl Grieg's poem about the blitz in London?' she asked.

'I don't think so,' he said wearily, 'but I'd like to hear it.'

She recited two verses, stumbling over the words because she had to hurry now. Somewhere dinner was waiting for him, prepared with that personal love, like a slow-acting poison, which condemned him to destruction in that old, discarded world he belonged to. At the table sat little Hassan with the crooked legs, who one day would grow into his heart the way beans run up a pole, only to break suddenly and unexpectedly under their weight.

> Churches and pillars and salt-gray Elizabethan buildings –
> how calmly the people take leave of all that was turned
>   to rubble.
> The bombs have to strike *something*. Blessed is every
>   bomb that arced down
> into a Gothic structure, if only one child was spared.
> Art must not be purchased with slavery, evil, and
>   infamy.
> What good is it to lose your freedom and save your
>   Notre Dame?
> Art too has the right to bloody wounds that throb.
> And the world will love London for its lack of
>   monuments!

'That's very beautiful,' he said, 'but that way of thinking is foreign to you. It's your destiny to express yourself, just as it's the gazelle's destiny to be devoured by the lion.'

The comparison seemed to offer him quiet amusement, and the untrustworthy expression again passed over his face like a cold shadow.

'Write to me,' he said. 'Write what the voices say to you. I'll see that you have something to write with. And trust me. I'm your friend.'

He held the door open for her, and she lost one of her state-owned slippers as she went out. Embarrassed, she stuck her foot into it again and joined the ranks of wandering patients with one hand against the tilting wall, which she now knew quite well was solid, shored up by white, plaster-spotted masons, whose lives ran along unnoticed like bursting raindrops down a drainpipe.

15

She wrote: 'When I was eight years old, they gave me a doll that could open and close its eyes. They stood at the foot of my cot, and my father's pajama pants were not quite closed. I could see some damp black hair sticking out. In the night the bed had rocked under them, and I had heard my mother say in a strange, laughing voice: "Don't do it so hard, you'll wake up Lise." With fear and disgust, I thought that what my girlfriend had said was true: "Your father and mother do it too." A few days before, a child had been murdered on our street. A lame bachelor shoe-maker had strangled a little girl and stuffed the body into a cupboard in his mother's apartment, where it was discovered when she came home from the hospital. My mother told me that I should never go anywhere with any strange men on the street. I should find a policeman if any man ever offered me candy or ice cream. It was my birthday and my happiness was supposed to be like a shiny round ball that they could hold in their hands so everybody could see it. When the doll's naked, cold body with the bent arms and legs lay in my arms where they had clumsily placed it, I knew that something had become a part of my world that I would have to keep to myself forever. I smiled in the electric light that slipped in between my teeth like bits of meat, and I pushed the doll's arms up and down so much that they were completely loose in the shoulders. It was supposed to look as though l was playing with the doll. My parents seemed satisfied, and it struck me like a new kind of loneliness, that they were so easily deceived. The hideous pink doll stared at me with its dead glass eyes, and I put it down quickly so that the eyelids would hide them. Later I discovered that its papier maché body would dissolve when I washed it, so in that way I soon got rid of it. Someday, I decided, I would have a real, living child, and it would not have any father. I didn't want to ever get married. Then I was lying in the grass next to Gert, whose hair smelled of melted candle wax like the memory of a Christmas Eve. Hanne had thrown her thin, golden legs across his. She was eating a striped lollipop with an innocent, absentminded expression. Mogens was sitting a little apart from them, picking flowers. Gert let his hand slide over the little hairs on Hanne's naked calves, and I thought suddenly that the girl resembled that revolting doll of my childhood. Hanne had never owned a doll. She was given little cars and picture books for her birthday, and I assumed that her joy at these gifts was genuine. It wasn't until today that I realized that I have never really known her.'

She looked up with a start and stopped writing. A sound like a tin box rolling across the floor filled the quiet room, and over by one of the tables stood a tall, heavy-set woman who was spreading something out to show Mr Petersen, who seemed to be making a great effort to admire it. Then she folded it up and stuck it under her arm as she looked around with a self-satisfied expression. She caught sight of Lise, who was sitting on the edge of her bed with her feet resting on the shelf under the table.

'Why, that's Lise Mundus,' she cried, rushing over to her with one of her fat, soft hands thrust out.

'Imagine meeting you here,' she said. 'I saw what you said about girls in mini-skirts; oh, it was so true. But I can see that the picture must have been several years old. You're thinner now and you have more wrinkles in your face, but I recognized you at once. I've read *The Deviant*, and the ending sure was a surprise. I have a bone to pick with the police, myself. They're the ones who committed me. That's how it always is. And what had I done? Handed out raisins on Nørrebrogade to all the poor kids. As if that would bother anybody.'

Laughter spread across her baggy cheeks as if it had spilled out of them.

'I've wanted to meet you for years,' she said. 'I'm an artist myself. I paint pictures of flowers, and I'm in here for the sixth time. They feed you well here.'

She spoke as if it were a spa that she honored with her presence every year. She had sat down at the table, moving the paper and ballpoint pen onto the bed. Lise's heart was pounding just like in a nightmare.

'You're mistaken,' she said. 'My name is Mrs Albrechtsen and I'm just an ordinary housewife.'

'Really?' shouted the other woman. 'You look exactly like her. Do you want to see my painting?'

She unrolled it on the bed, and it was atrocious.

'That's pretty,' said Lise dully, 'but I need to be alone for a little while. I'm writing a letter.'

'You'll have to learn to love her too, someday,' said Gitte through the pillow, and Lise forgot her fright in the joy of hearing her voice again.

'Where have you been all this time?' she asked. 'I was afraid that you'd abandoned me.'

'I'm the remnants of your illness,' she explained, 'and it's not certain that you'll hear from me again. You know that you're well. You have to go home soon and bake French bread. Gert and Hanne have gotten married and they love to have coffee in bed.'

'But I want to write books again,' she said softly, 'under a completely different name. Dr Jørgensen says that I don't have to be a good housewife.'

But no one answered her, and she searched feverishly for the speaker inside the pillowcase, but someone had removed it.

Then the procession making the hospital rounds came over to her bed. A young doctor with a conceited expression stopped in front of her and paged through her case record. At his side stood Miss Brandt, the ward's head nurse, who no longer pretended to be anyone but herself. Somewhere in the room the tin-box voice of the new patient rolled around, imprisoned between the walls, which would not be able to withstand the pressure for very long.

'How's it going?' asked the doctor without looking at her. 'Are you still hallucinating?'

'Yes,' she said and added truthfully: 'But it's not as bad as before.'

His face was like the consummation of a lengthy, harmonious pregnancy. She saw with relief that it was not one of those that she would have to take upon herself.

'I see that you've started to write again,' he said kindly. 'I think you'll be able to go home soon. You can move into the open ward, at any rate.'

'No,' she said, terrified. 'I don't want to.'

In there was that woman who knew all about the sentence she had plagiarized.

'You don't?' he said, astonished. 'You'll be able to talk more with the other patients. In here they're quite sick, you know. But I'll discuss it with the chief of staff.'

He went over to the next bed, where the woman with the raised head regarded him with no interest whatsoever.

'Well,' said the doctor to Miss Brandt, 'there's no change here. But we'll be hearing from St Hans Asylum soon; then she can be moved over there.'

He spoke as if she weren't present, the way the people in the basement apartment at home discussed without embarrassment when their mother was going to do them the favor of dying so they could get the insurance money.

She started writing again, holding her arm protectively over the paper, afraid that the horrible artist would see it. All of the silently wandering patients were separated from each other like a flock of birds cut straight through by an airplane. Their faces were about to fall right off, and their frightened hands fumbled over them so that the unknown that was beneath the skin wouldn't reveal itself to be a secret illness hiding behind what was visible to everyone. She wrote:

'There is no pathway to love. Love places itself across the path, and when it disappears, the path is destroyed.'

The sentence wasn't her own. It was Colette's, and she hadn't thought about it for years. A poem by Yeats rose up to the surface of her mind like a fish in a quiet forest lake. As she wrote down the poem, her heart was once again moved, the way it had brought her solace after her divorce from Asger.

> Down by the salley gardens
> > my love and I did meet;
> She passed the salley gardens
> > with little snow-white feet.
> She bid me take love easy,
> > as the leaves grow on the tree;
> But I, being young and foolish,
> > with her would not agree.
> In a field by the river
> > my love and I did stand,
> and on my leaning shoulder
> > she laid her snow-white hand.

She bid me take life easy,
          as the grass grows on the weirs;
But I was young and foolish,
          and now am full of tears.

She stared at the words as if they were a secret message, written on the wall of her heart. For a long time she had spent days in the Royal Library because there was no peace at home. She had tried to translate the poem, but discovered quickly that she could spend a whole lifetime on it and it still wouldn't be good enough.

Miss Brandt came over to her.

'Your husband is on the telephone,' she said. 'Patients aren't really supposed to use it, but he said it was important.'

She followed the nurse in her flopping slippers, still filled with the sweet pain of the poem, like a strong, bitter wine.

'Hello, Lise,' said Gert, 'listen to this. I've talked to Dr Jørgensen, and he says that you can come home.' He added shyly and subdued: 'I miss you so much; we all do.'

'Gitte too?' she asked.

'I've thrown her out,' he said. 'She gave Mogens LSD and he smashed all the windows in his room. So I figured that was enough.'

'But she'll take revenge,' she said, horrified. 'She can go to the police and tell them everything. Have you thought about that?'

She saw the sly, nutcracker face before her, and love and fear made their way out of her through a thick crowd of faces, above which the dwarf from her childhood rose up like a balloon, growing smaller and smaller under the infinite vault of the sky.

'What in heaven's name would she go to the police for?' he asked. 'Nothing criminal has been going on in our house.'

'But I'll miss her,' she cried without knowing if she meant it or not. 'She introduced me to a whole new world.'

He laughed his old, crisp laugh.

'The old world is good enough,' he said. 'I'll come and pick you up tomorrow.'

'When I come home,' she said slowly, 'there's something I want to ask you, something I want to know the truth about. Dr Jørgensen said the other day' (or maybe it was ten years ago, she couldn't remember) 'that he despised patients who wouldn't look the truth in the eye.'

'I don't agree with him,' he said, 'but I'll answer your question completely honestly, no matter what it's about.'

'Thank you,' she said. 'How is Søren?'

She saw his little old-man's face before her, the way it had looked that last time behind the torture grating, the face of a starving child from India.

'Fine,' said Gert, 'but he misses you too. Gitte filled his mind with confusing sexual information instead of fairy tales. He misses the life we used to have before all the craziness started. But we can talk about all that when you get home. I'll buy a bottle of whiskey to celebrate.'

'Thank you,' she said. 'I'm looking forward to having you pick me up.'

And as she walked back to her bed, she pulled the belt tighter around her red plaid dress, which was much too big. She felt as though she had received a blood transfusion from an unknown donor. Normal life, with all its burdens and joys, ran gently through her veins, and when the artist stopped her out in the hallway, she said loud and clear:

'You were right. My name is Lise Mundus. And I'm going home tomorrow to start writing a new book.'

16

The artificial light had preceded the stars. Warm and golden, it flowed under her eyelids, through the pores of her skin, and into her blood, where it dragged a net through her memory and touched gently on half-forgotten remembrances. They were walking across Town Hall Square, and Gert's face was alternately lit and shadowed by the glow from the blinking neon signs, which had always been the same.

'When I was seventeen,' she said, putting her arm through his, 'I stood in front of the B.T. building and waited for a young man who never came. When I went home, I thought my future was just as cold and gray as the buildings on Vesterbrogade.'

'That's a sensitive age,' he said gently. 'Hanne is cooking dinner – something special, I think. She wants to celebrate your homecoming. I guess she's relieved that Gitte's gone. She didn't like her, and for some reason she was a little afraid of her.'

Lise stepped aside for a blind man who was fumbling with his cane along the curb. His alert, listening face was remote and turned inward, and it wasn't necessary to take it upon herself. All of the faces in that fleeting blue hour passed effortlessly through her as if through a ray of sunshine, and some of them took others along with them, as if in distraction, so her mind felt transparent and light, like all the quick steps that the street pulled down.

'Don't you miss her?' she asked and suddenly saw before her that small, vengeful, lonely face behind the negotiation grating.

'For years,' he said sadly, pressing her arm tighter against him, 'I've only missed you. I've behaved like an idiot.'

'Why don't we go somewhere and have a drink before we go home?' she said suddenly. She felt strangely afraid of entering those rooms again, just as if she were entering a childhood that had never belonged to her.

'All right,' he said amiably. 'Let's go to "The Pearl".'

It was a dirty little pub where they had often gone before, after the children were in bed and the day was over. There were rings left by beer glasses on the bare table, and in the background some bricklayers in work clothes were playing pool.

'Two double whiskeys,' he said to the listless waitress who reluctantly tore herself away from the group of workers. She didn't seem to remember them. She had a broken blood vessel in one eye, and her skin was gray and porous like an eraser. The blinds were pulled down and the lamp on the table was lit. There was a rip in the parchment lampshade, as if it had been sliced with a knife by a drunken guest. Lise felt the radiator under the window – there was a faint rustling in the pipes, like a bird chirping on a branch.

'What month is this?' she asked.

'The middle of March,' Gert informed her. 'You've been in the hospital for three weeks. Why did you really take those pills?'

'Because Gitte left them out,' she said, 'even though you had asked her to hide them away.'

'I never told her that!' he cried. 'We never talked about them at all.'

'Then she lied to me,' she said. 'She told me you were afraid I would do the same thing Grete did.'

'With her,' he said, holding his glass absentmindedly up to

the light, 'I made the mistake of arousing feelings that I could never return. But what was it, by the way, that you wanted to hear the truth about?'

'Not now,' she said. 'Not here. Later.'

The faint intoxication veiled his face from her, and she saw that his pupils had grown bigger than before, as in children who blink at the light when you wake them up from a bad dream.

'Sometimes,' she said slowly, 'you do something to another person, and afterwards you're not the same. You do it in order to save yourself. And what you previously thought was the most important thing in the world isn't very meaningful anymore.'

'That's true,' he said, downing his whiskey. 'But that doesn't apply to you. You've never been any great sinner.'

For a moment she felt angry at the harmless image of herself that he had, although it corresponded to the image she wanted the world to have. But if she revealed her coldness and egotism and told him what had happened behind the torture grating in the bathroom, it wouldn't have any reality for him – not the way it would for her for all eternity.

Someone dropped a coin in the jukebox, and a nasal female voice sang:

> He came in the summer
> and the sun was shining.
> He made me promises
> and said sweet words . . .

The rest was drowned in the noise from the bricklayers playing pool, but the sentimental, banal melody touched a memory. It was one of the records that Mogens and Gitte always played. It was the one she had stopped the afternoon Nadia had been there.

'How is Mogens taking it now that Gitte's gone?'

'He's a little sad. I think he was dumb enough to fall for her. It's easy to turn the head of a boy like that. And then her whole crazy evangelism about loving your neighbor. He swallowed it whole, even though the truth was that she wasn't even capable of loving a cat.'

He placed his hand awkwardly over hers, and the warmth from it streamed in over her whole body.

'I love you,' he said frankly. 'Can you forgive me for betraying you?'

'I betrayed you too,' she said. 'I only cared about my stupid books.'

'They're not stupid,' he said warmly. 'One of your stories is in Hanne's schoolbook, and a poem too.'

'I've never written anything that's good enough,' she said, 'I only dared write for children.'

'Maybe that's a greater art than writing for grownups.'

She stared at his face with the vertical furrows in his cheeks and the taut, transparent skin. His melancholy mouth touched her like a fingertip against her heart.

Love stretched between them, as delicate as a piece of gauze. She knew that it wouldn't last. Hatred and resentment and indifference and selfishness would come back again like old, faithful friends, and nothing could persuade them that they weren't welcome. As soon as she was wrapped up in her writing again, the demon of jealousy would possess him and he would feel excluded from the circle of her little world, which was like the childish chalk markings she had once drawn on the playground around her own feet: 'Whoever steps on the line can't play anymore.' And if she now yielded and began to love him again, his vengeance would strike her unprotected heart. Yet she still thrilled to that old feeling of happiness under his dark, caressing eyes.

'Let's go home,' she said. 'It's a shame to make them wait with dinner.'

'Yes, it is,' he said and called the waitress, and as he paid, she seemed to hear a distant, gloating laughter in the radiator pipes. But that might just be her imagination; after all, she was well now.

The evening was cold and windy, and Gert put his arm around her shoulders as they walked the few steps home.

'By the way, Hanne has a boyfriend,' he said, 'from high school. I've said hello to him a few times; he's a very nice boy.'

She thought he spoke with studied indifference, and she heard Hanne's cold voice, the way it had sounded through the speaker in the pillow.

'It's about time,' she said, 'that she's allowed to live her own life.'

She was lying with her face against his bony shoulder, which smelled sharply of new-mown grass. His finger slid along the curve of her lip, tenderly.

'Let's start all over,' he said. 'Let's forget about all the bad feelings there have been between us.'

They had spent a pleasant evening with the children, whose faces were again hanging in place like the pictures on the walls. On one of Søren's cheeks there was a scar from the explosion in physics class. It would always be there, and she would have to keep the memory of the bottle of sulfuric acid to herself, along with the faces and the voices from the bathroom.

'I've been through a crisis,' she said. 'I've realized that you can't turn away from the suffering people in the world.'

'Oh,' he said with a smile, 'Gitte managed to brainwash you with that too. But you know what – it takes more bravery to worry about your neighbor's calluses than about the Blacks in the Congo. I'm thinking about Albert Schweitzer. There must have been many suffering people in the streets of Strasbourg, but he wouldn't have become world-famous by helping them.'

'The Vietnam War,' she said uncertainly. 'All those bombed children?'

'Take care of your own children first,' he said somberly. 'Not to reproach you – but you've neglected them a great deal lately.'

'I want so much to write a book for grownups,' she said seriously.

'Do it,' he said. 'I'm sure you can.'

Suddenly the wall leaned very slightly inward, and she put out her hand to support it. She seemed to hear Hanne's childish voice again, full of resentment:

'I despised your disgusting chapters.'

'Will you answer one question?' she said.

'Yes.'

His fingers ran through her long hair, and underneath she had a fleeting impression that her face was swiftly aging and becoming old and shrunken like Søren's, behind the torture grating.

Full of dread, she said, 'Has there ever been anything between you and Hanne? I just want to know the truth.'

Without taking his fingers away, he said calmly, almost with indifference: 'The truth, Lise, is just as irritating as a hangnail. Have you ever known anyone who has derived the least benefit from the truth?'

'No.'

Suddenly the truth was completely irrelevant and unimportant. Long sentences glided through her open mind. Tomorrow she would start to write and to take care of her children. And this meant it was tremendously important to learn to bake bread. Then the people who wanted to would continue taking care of the rest of the world.

Gert turned off the light, and with a contented sigh she snuggled up to him.

'I wonder where Gitte has gone?' she asked sleepily.

'To a kibbutz, I think,' he said. 'She was always talking about it.'

'Yes,' said Lise, and thought she had only heard that from the negotiation grating. As far as she could recall, Gitte had never talked about it before she was in the hospital. But what was real in this world, and what was not real? Wasn't it a kind of sickness that people could walk around holding onto their own ego? – that whole chaos of voices, faces, and memories that they only dared to let slip from themselves drop by drop, and never could be certain of retrieving again.

'Tomorrow,' she said, 'I'm going to start writing.'

But he had already fallen asleep.

F

EAT, DRINK,
and Be KINKY

A Feast of Wit and Fabulous Recipes
for Fans of KINKY FRIEDMAN

★

MIKE McGOVERN

A FIRESIDE BOOK
Published by Simon & Schuster

FIRESIDE
Rockefeller Center
1230 Avenue of the Americas
New York, NY 10020

FIRESIDE and colophon are registered trademarks
of Simon & Schuster, Inc.

Designed by Gretchen Achilles

Manufactured in the United States of America

10 9 8 7 6 5 4 3 2 1

Library of Congress Cataloging-in Publication Data
McGovern, Mike.
     Eat, drink, and be kinky : a feast of wit and fabulous recipes
for fans of Kinky Friedman / Mike McGovern.
     p.   cm.
  Includes index.
  1. Cookery. 2. Cookery—Anecdotes. I. Title.
TX714.M3837 1999   99-39144
                                                       CIP

ISBN 0-684-85674-3

ACKNOWLEDGMENTS

★

A lot of slurping and burping went into *Eat, Drink, and Be Kinky*.

Many people offered up their choppers in pursuit of fine taste. Many thanks. Especially to a couple of Sheilas from Down Under, Kate Paul and Suzie Smith. They helped develop recipes, too. Other Aussies contributed excellent tucker, including the Akermans, Tessa, Pia, Suzanne, and Piers.

Kinky inspired both me and this book. The entire Friedman tribe got in on the deal—Kinky's father, Tom, his bride, Edythe, his siblings Marcie and Roger. They all put a lip-lock on a Chicken McGovern feast. Three generations of hungry Friedmans got down that lemonade summer's day under the black walnut trees of the sprawling family ranch outside Kerrville. Kinky forked over the name Chicken McGovern and used the recipe as a prop in one of his funny stories, *The Love Song of J. Edgar Hoover*.

With deepest love to Beverly Morris, for her invaluable help and the warm country kitchen she provided through the long New York winter. And gracias to Rosie Mendoza and Elese Deptwa, Lottie Cotton, Joanna Pettet, Carol Becker, Ethan and Jennifer Morris, Evie Righter, Sandy Wolfmueller, Lee M. Fuller Jr., Pete and Ellie Donaldson, Chick Slepian, Big Bill Thompson, Mica Minden, Roberta Katz, Maria F. Krieger, Don Hancey, Laurie and Danny Hutton, Stevie Hays, Joe Heller, Speed Vogel, Dwight Yoakam, Mike and Lilly Brennan, John Bal, Kent Carroll, Frank McCourt, Downtown Judy, James Charlton, Akila and Audrey Couloumbis, Jim Fitzgerald, Leonora and Tony Burton, Anne Gerasimos, Will Hoover, Cleve and Mary Hattersley, Doug Holloway, Willie Nelson, Lucianne Goldberg, Terri and Chinga Chavin, John McCall, Larry ("Ratso") Slavin, Steve Rambam, Peter Winterble, Nick Tosches, F. Murray Abraham, Stephanie DuPont, Dorothy Nicholson, Becky Priour, Martin Persson and Jennifer, Irene, and Peter Myers.

FOR BRIAN

CONTENTS

EAT, DRINK,
and Be KINKY

INTRODUCTION

As a famous homosexual once said, "Every time my friends succeed I die a little." Happily, this is not the case with my friend Mike McGovern's new killer bee cookbook, *Eat, Drink, and Be Kinky,* upon the puissant pages of which millions of Americans will soon be spilling extremely tasty pasta sauce. McGovern's not only my favorite Irish poet, he's also one hell of a chef. This is especially true when he's not cookin' on another planet.

I also believe this book may provide some long overdue remedies to the spiritual malaise that has overcome America since chain restaurants have turned us all into chain people. The work you are about to read is far more than a cookbook. *Eat, Drink, and Be Kinky* will have a broad, engaging appeal not only to serious gourmands but also to alcoholics and sex perverts as well. In fact, I think of this book as sort of a culinary version of James Joyce's *Ulysses.* McGovern's masterwork, to my mind, compares quite favorably with Tolstoy's *Anna Karenina.* For one thing, it's shorter. For another, it's funnier. If, indeed, a recipe book can ever be said to be funny. I certainly hope it's funnier than this introduction.

The problem that seems to have arisen with McGovern's mighty effort is that he appears to be taking his handiwork even more seriously than I do. He sees himself as a modern-day Ernest Hemingway; our mutual editor, Chuck Adams, as a vaunted Maxwell Perkins; and myself as a pesky F. Scott Fitzgerald, consumed with envy at the possibility of being eclipsed upon the timeless literary horizon. Nothing, believe me, could be more ridiculous. I want McGovern's book to do well. I just don't want it to do so well that he moves up from a friend to a contact. That could get pretty tedious. Of course, now that I think about it, our relationship has always been pretty tedious.

But Mike McGovern is certainly not without charm. He pedals his large white luminous buttocks around New York on a bicycle. His somewhat decrepit, lox-colored couch has been across the Atlantic twice. He's the only tenant in his building who steadfastly refuses to let the entire complex go condo. His taxes are prepared by the old man who runs the neighborhood pizza shop. He was friends, in younger days, with Martin Luther King Jr. He was also quite friendly with Al Capone's chef, a worthy mentor for the young McGovern, though he bore the rather unusual name of Leaning Jesus. McGovern also got the first jailhouse interview with Charles Manson while working for the *New York Daily News.* It should also be noted that he once combed his hair before meeting a racehorse. And, not to bury the lead, he's also the best cook I've ever met in my life.

Though the wit and wisdom of the Kinkster is liberally sprinkled throughout this book, along with various sordid anecdotes and recipes from the Village Irregulars, the true centerpiece on the table is McGovern's cherished collection of divinely wrought, hellishly sought, and sublimely thought-out recipes. From time to time McGovern himself will wax lyrical about Italian heroes and American whores and how you shouldn't eat anything bigger than your head. McGovern himself, of course, has an enormous head. I myself have a much smaller head (uncharitable people have, on occasion, called me a pinhead) and over the years I've developed a rather severe case of head envy. But I suppose this is hardly the place to be parading my personal problems.

If you try these recipes I know you're going to love them. But they're not for everybody. It's possible a few people might experience a mild form of projectile vomiting. A rare individual here and there might try one of McGovern's more exotic concoctions and find himself squirting out of both ends. In the unlikely event this should happen to you, you could try fasting until there's peace and freedom in the world. If this doesn't work (and it usually doesn't) you could try pouring Vodka McGoverns down your neck until you find yourself out where the buses don't run. If you see a large man with a large head pedaling his large, white, luminous buttocks by on a bicycle, you'll know you're there. I'll be the guy puking in the alley who comes up to you and says, "Are you new in town, sailor?"

In closing, I'd like to thank my parents, teachers, and rabbis, and Mike McGovern for being Mike McGovern. He's possessed of great intelligence, kindness, and honesty, not to mention an incessant, rather annoying Peter

Pan–like innocence that never fails to get up my sleeve somewhat severely. I hope you eat, drink, and be kinky. I hope you never wear a white shirt when you're eating pasta. I hope you never have McGovern for a housepest.

Yours in Christ,

Kinky Friedman
December 7, 1941
Buttflaps, Montana

STARTERS AND SNACKS

Kinky Friedman got his "start" on a ranch in Texas, and ever since then his life has been one big banquet. Here are a few recipes to get you started on your way to culinary ecstasy, with a few passes for some Kinksterisms on life and food and the state of the onion.

In six days the Lord created the heavens and the earth and all the wonders therein. There are some of us who feel that He might have taken just a little more time.

—*A CASE OF LONE STAR*

CAJUN NUTS

MAKES 2 CUPS

EQUIPMENT NEEDED: PARCHMENT PAPER

1 pound shelled raw peanuts (available at health food stores and some supermarkets)
1 extra-large egg white
2 tablespoons packed light or dark brown sugar
½ teaspoon salt
¼ teaspoon paprika

1. Preheat the oven to 375 degrees F. Line a baking sheet with the parchment paper.

2. In a medium bowl, mix the peanuts with the egg white, brown sugar, salt, and paprika until coated. Spread the nuts in a single layer on the prepared baking sheet and bake for 15 minutes, turning halfway. Let cool before serving. Store any leftovers in an airtight container in the refrigerator.

Morning, like anything else in this world, is relative. Some people had probably been up since six A.M. doing squat thrusts in the parking lot, eating fibered cereal, and disturbing other Americans with early morning phone calls. If you want to get up at six A.M. and pretend you're Tevye the Milkman, that's your problem. For me, morning begins when I realize that the soft warm body curled up next to me is a cat.

—FREQUENT FLYER

NUTS ABOUND

MAKES 2 CUPS

3 tablespoons canola oil
1 pound pecan halves or blanched whole almonds
1 tablespoon sugar or 2 packets aspartame
1 teaspoon cumin seeds, toasted and ground
1 teaspoon dried thyme
1 teaspoon garlic powder
1 teaspoon onion powder
½ teaspoon salt
Pinch of cayenne pepper (optional)

1. Preheat the oven to 300 degrees F.

2. Heat the oil in a medium skillet until hot. Add the pecans and toss to coat. Remove the skillet from the heat.

3. In a small bowl, stir together the sugar, cumin, thyme, garlic and onion powders, salt, and cayenne, if using. Add to the skillet and toss to combine.

4. Spread the seasoned nuts in a single layer on a shallow baking pan and bake for 15 minutes. Remove from the oven, turn the pecans over, and bake for 15 more minutes. Let cool before serving. Store leftovers in an airtight container in the refrigerator.

The shuttle from La Guardia flew low over the Potomac in preparation for landing in Washington, the city where William Henry Harrison steadfastly refused to wear his overcoat for his inaugural parade. He died about two weeks later of pneumonia. I wasn't about to make the same mistake. I wore a heavy blue peacoat that looked like it'd been handed down to me by Oliver Twist along with a bright red Sydney Swans Australian football scarf and a black cowboy hat. I might not blend in too well at some of the more upscale restaurants, but it's always better to look like a squirrel, I figured, than it is to freeze your nuts off.

—*THE LOVE SONG OF J. EDGAR HOOVER*

Mexican Guacamole

3 ripe large Mexican avocados, if available, or your choice avocado

3 tomatoes, peeled, seeded, and diced

1 large onion, diced

Juice of 1 lemon

⅓ cup finely chopped fresh cilantro, or to taste

2 hot green chili peppers (such as jalapeño peppers), seeds and ribs removed, minced

½ teaspoon salt

Peel and pit 2 of the avocados, mash them in a medium bowl. Peel and pit the third avocado, dice it into ½-inch pieces, and add it to the bowl. Add the tomatoes, onion, lemon juice, cilantro, chilies, and salt, and stir gently, just to combine. Serve with toasted tortilla chips or toasted pita wedges.

It's almost as hard to get good Mexican food in New York as it is in Mexico. You've got to know what you're doing in this world or life passes you by.

—*A CASE OF LONE STAR*

Sesame Dipping Sauce (for Veggies)

This is a crowd pleaser, and easy to do. Just steam up a head of
broccoli or cauliflower, or zucchini spears, and serve with this.
You won't believe how fast it all disappears.

MAKES 1 CUP, ENOUGH FOR 6 SERVINGS OF VEGETABLES

EQUIPMENT NEEDED: BLENDER

6 tablespoons smooth or chunky peanut butter
3 tablespoons low-sodium soy sauce
3 tablespoons rice vinegar
1 tablespoon sesame oil
1 tablespoon honey (Tupelo, if available)
1 tablespoon chopped fresh ginger, or to taste
1 scallion, chopped
2 garlic cloves, chopped
½ teaspoon crushed red pepper flakes
Tabasco sauce, to taste
3 tablespoons chicken or vegetable stock, heated

1. Put in blender the peanut butter, soy sauce, vinegar, oil, honey,
ginger, scallion, garlic, red pepper flakes, Tabasco, and stock, and
puree. Transfer to a bowl and serve at room temperature.

2. The sauce will keep in the refrigerator, covered, for three days.

. . . I realized . . . that women and cats had a lot in common. For one thing,
neither of them had a particularly well-developed sense of humor. For another, they both went through life governed only by things that either comforted them or intrigued them. They both liked to be stroked and cuddled
and they both could pounce when you least expected it. On the whole, I
preferred cats to women because cats seldom if ever used the word "relationship."

—*GREENWICH KILLING TIME*

EAT, DRINK, AND BE KINKY

What makes a Kinky woman? Here are a few examples.

A sweetheart of a blonde who teaches dance to Playboy Bunnies strutting their stuff on stages around the world.

A lean, not mean, highly successful suit among the predominantly male hierarchy running New York's Madison Square Garden.

And one who sounds like a kookaburra made the deepest—for a time—impact on Kinky. This former Miss Texas teaches line dancing on TV.

In any case, Kinky, like his pal, radio personality Don Imus (and most garage mechanics and millions of other men and boys), likes his women without whiskers or similar adornments. That doesn't apply to his cats, Dr. Scat and Lady Argyle.

Kinky's current standout is not too popular down at the local synagogue, either. She's yet another drop-dead blonde, the kind Raymond Chandler liked to dwell on when he pulled out his typewriter.

She's funny and young and smart and an incorrigible flirt (to Kinky), with dancer's legs and a love of learning. In fact, she's still in school, studying law.

An heiress to one of America's grandest fortunes, she was raised in the ways of the very rich. Like Kinky, she enjoys foods that enchant the soul and inflame the senses. When asked to contribute a Kinky recipe, she came up with a succulent oyster dish.

Kinky has an advantage over most competitors. If he likes a woman, she is elevated into his oeuvre. In the Kinky literature, she goes by the name of Stephanie DuPont.

STEPHANIE DUPONT'S OYSTER-MUSHROOM PÂTÉ

First rate not only as an appetizer, but also as
a stuffing for roast chicken.

SERVES 6 AS AN APPETIZER

EQUIPMENT NEEDED: FOOD PROCESSOR OR BLENDER

8 ounces white mushrooms, wiped clean and coarsely chopped
1 bunch scallions, both green and white parts, roughly chopped
2 garlic cloves, roughly chopped
1 pint fresh oysters, liquor reserved
2 tablespoons unsalted butter or canola oil
1 to 2 cups bread crumbs (Panko, if available)
1 tablespoon dried basil
Cayenne pepper and freshly ground black pepper

1. In the food processor, finely chop the mushrooms, scallions, garlic, and oysters.

2. Melt the butter in a skillet over moderate heat. Add the mushroom mixture and sauté it, stirring, for 2 to 3 minutes, or until the oysters are lightly cooked. Remove the pan from the heat and stir in enough of the bread crumbs until the mixture holds together and is only slightly moist. If the mixture becomes too dry, stir in some of the reserved oyster liquor. Stir in the basil and cayenne and black pepper to taste. Let cool, then transfer the mixture to a bowl, pressing it in slightly.

3. Serve the "pâté" as a dip with toasted tortilla crisps or as a spread on toasted French bread rounds.

"Hi, darling," I said, moments later when I got Stephanie on the phone.

"Hello, dickhead," she said.

. . . Stephanie DuPont, for one so young, was well on her merry way to becoming the biggest ball-buster of all time. But she was funny. She was brilliant. And she was beautiful beyond a shipwrecked sailor's dream. Beneath her icy exterior, where few if any prospectors had survived the caustic blizzard of her nature, there beat a heart of gold. I was crazy, perverse, misguided, romantic, egocentric, stupid, and smart enough to believe that if I followed my map I could reach the motherlode.

"Eight o'clock?" I said. "The Derby?"

"I'll see you there, dickhead."

—*SPANKING WATSON*

SOUPS AND SALADS

Salad days is a term generally used to refer to youth and the joys thereof. In Kinky's case, that salad got tossed a little early on, and the result has been a lifetime of peeling and shredding—with the occasional julienne thrown in, lest things get a little too dicey—in an effort to keep the great slicer in the sky at bay.

As far as soups are concerned, Kinky isn't.

I didn't like maître d's much, I reflected, and to be fair I must report that most maître d's I'd encountered didn't like me much either. I did not have what you might call a Judy Garland–like rapport with that distinctly Cerberean species. Nobody really liked maître d's at these coochi-poochi-boomalini frog places anyway, I figured. They were effete, power-hungry, phony, officious little boogers for the most part. Not even the most misunderstood child in Belgium wanted to grow up to be a maître d'. About the only charitable thing you could say about them was they were good diversionary subject matter to think about when you were freezing your Swedish meatballs off.

—*GOD BLESS JOHN WAYNE*

TOMATO SOUP

SERVES 6

EQUIPMENT NEEDED: LARGE HEAVY-BOTTOMED SAUCEPAN;
  BLENDER OR FOOD PROCESSOR

½ cup extra-virgin olive oil

3 medium onions, sliced

7 medium ripe tomatoes, peeled, seeded, and quartered

Salt and freshly ground black pepper to taste

4 cups chicken stock

2 tablespoons flour

3 garlic cloves, or to taste

3 tablespoons chopped fresh basil

6 tablespoons nonfat plain yogurt

1. Heat the olive oil in the saucepan until hot. Add the onions and cook over moderate heat, stirring, about 5 minutes, until softened. Add the tomatoes and salt and pepper to taste, and simmer, stirring occasionally, for 15 minutes.

2. While the tomatoes are cooking, stir together the stock and flour in a bowl. Pour into the blender, add the garlic, and puree. Add the stock mixture to the saucepan, stir to combine, and simmer for 5 minutes. Remove the pan from the heat and let cool.

3. When the tomato mixture is cool, puree it in the blender. The soup can be served sprinkled with basil, hot or cold. If serving hot, reheat over medium heat. If serving chilled, refrigerate, covered, until cold. Serve in bowls, each garnished with a dollop of yogurt.

Children, it has always seemed to me, have a greater inherent understanding of many things than adults. As they grow up, this native sensitiv-
ity is smothered, buried, and destroyed, like someone pouring concrete
over cobblestones, and finally replaced by what we call knowledge. Knowledge, according to Albert Einstein, who spent a lot of time, incidentally,
living with the Indians when he wasn't busy forgetting his bicycle in
Princeton, New Jersey, is a vastly inferior commodity when compared
with imagination.

—*ROADKILL*

EAT, DRINK, AND BE KINKY

BUTTERNUT SQUASH SOUP

SERVES 6

EQUIPMENT NEEDED: LARGE HEAVY-BOTTOMED SAUCEPAN;
BLENDER

2 tablespoons extra-virgin olive oil or butter
1 large onion, diced
1 medium butternut squash (about 2½ to 3 pounds), seeded, peeled, and cut
    into 1-inch pieces
6 cups chicken stock
Salt and freshly ground black pepper to taste
1 cup light or nonfat sour cream

1. Heat the olive oil in the saucepan over medium heat until hot. Add the onion and cook it, stirring, about 5 minutes, until softened. Add the squash and stock, and bring to a boil. Lower the heat and simmer for 20 minutes. Let cool.

2. When cool, puree the mixture in the blender. Pour the puree into the saucepan, season to taste with salt and pepper, and stir in the sour cream. Heat the soup slowly, over low heat, before serving. Do not let it boil.

When I thought about it, there'd been an absence of music lately in both my life and the cat's. I killed the shot and thought about it, took a reflective puff or two on the cigar, and thought about it some more. Because of my years on the road as a country singer I had come to hate the sound of the human voice singing. That was understandable, I figured. Sonny Bono never lets his young wife play rock-'n'-roll music. Elton John never goes to concerts unless they are his own. Of course, his closest friends call him Sharon, but the point is that too much of a good thing can get pretty tedious.

—MUSICAL CHAIRS

DOWNTOWN JUDY'S TORTILLA SOUP WITH CHILI PUREE

SERVES 5

EQUIPMENT NEEDED: BLENDER

THE TORTILLAS
1 tablespoon corn oil
8 corn tortillas (about 7 inches in diameter), cut into strips

THE CHILI PUREE
4 ounces dried pasilla chilies (also called *chile negro*), seeded and deveined
Chicken broth, as needed

THE SOUP BASE
2 tablespoons corn oil
1 large red or yellow onion, thinly sliced
7 large garlic cloves, minced (or fewer if you wish)
1½ cups canned tomato puree
4 cups chicken broth
Salt and freshly ground black pepper

THE ACCOMPANIMENTS
1 pound fresh Mexican cheese (such as *queso ranchero* or *queso fresco*), diced
2 ripe avocados, Hass, if available, peeled, pitted, and diced
1 cup nonfat sour cream
2 pasilla chilies, cut into strips
2 medium limes, cut into wedges

1. Prepare the tortillas: Heat the corn oil in a large skillet until hot. Add the tortilla strips and, turning them, fry until crispy. Remove and reserve on paper towels.

2. Prepare the chili puree: Preheat the broiler. Roast the chilies on a baking sheet for 15 seconds; turn; and broil for 15 seconds more. Remove. Bring 2 cups water to a boil in a saucepan; add the chilies and soak them for 30 minutes. Drain. Put the soaked chilies and enough chicken broth in the blender to be able to puree the chilies. Remove. You should have ¼ cup chili puree.

3. Prepare the soup base: Heat the corn oil in a saucepan until hot. Add the onion and sauté, stirring, until golden. Add the garlic and cook, stirring, for 1 minute. Add the reserved chili puree and bring to a boil. Lower the heat and simmer until the mixture is reduced to a paste. **Be careful: Do not let the mixture burn.** Add the tomato puree and chicken broth, bring to a boil, then simmer, covered, for 30 minutes. Add salt and pepper to taste.

4. Serve immediately in wide bowls, topped with the reserved tortilla strips, cheese, avocado, sour cream, and chili strips. Squeeze fresh lime juice over all.

leve Hattersley: To get to Kinky's place, you tool along Route 16 through a half-dozen German towns, cross a small range of mountains, and leap over several streams that are either at flood stage or as dry as Kinky's humor.

You eat dust for three miles of dirt roads and cattle guards and be on the lookout for razor-sharp rocks. You'll know the El Rancho Friedman Deluxe by the patriotic decor—red, white, and blue buildings.

Kinky may even welcome you. Maybe you'll get the rain dance ceremony if Kinky's Apache chums, led by the Hollywood handsome Robbie Romero, are in from La-La Land.

Kinky never considers himself lonely. Not with God's creatures his constant companions. Hummingbirds, armadillos, cats, dogs, scores of horses and braceros, all live in harmony with the blessed Kinkster.

And that's a good thing, since very few civilians venture that deep into the Hill Country. John Wayne once did. And he didn't stop until he got to Bandera, with its old-movie-set Texan saloon. But if you're only for the lonely, you'll be fine at Echo Hill. And if Kinky is reflecting somewhere, the only voice you're likely to hear will be your own, bouncing off thousand-foot Echo Hill itself.

So if you go, it's BYOK (Bring Your Own Kitchen). Literally. Pots. Pans. Cooking equipment. Eating utensils. Food, too. How old are Kinky's pots? Carbon dating might unravel the answer to that one.

"Anybody can cook, if you can read," says Kinky, who employs three basics in cooking: boiling, searing, and smoking. He boils pasta, sears bloody big, hairy steaks, and smokes fat Havana cigars.

All that aside, I like cooking for Kinky. Why? I know the menu by now.

By the time I'm prepared to simmer, parboil, or flambé, I'm in my foxhole mentality. You need your cool as the emotions of battle flare around you. Still, I ease through the firefights with the animals pacing or snoozing on key pieces of equipment. Kinky? He blows smoke. I never waiver from my assignment. Never let a green pepper die a miserable, shrunken death.

In the end I always win. The triumph at battle's end comes when Kinky sits back in his chair, places his napkin on his lap, and pats his tummy, lights a half-chewed stogie, and belches one for the gods. That Kinky enjoys these meals is sometimes left unspoken. But he invites me back—always.

CHILLED AVOCADO AND MANGO SOUP

SERVES 4

EQUIPMENT NEEDED: BLENDER

1 large ripe avocado, Hass, if available, peeled, pitted, and cut into chunks
1 large ripe mango, peeled, pitted, and cut into pieces
1 cup apple juice
1 cup nonfat plain yogurt
¼ cup chopped chives or scallion greens, for garnish

Put the avocado, mango, apple juice, yogurt, and ½ cup water in the blender, and blend until slightly chunky. Cover and chill for 1 hour. Garnish with the chives.

This is not to take anything away from the great Gabby Hayes, who was overworked, underfucked, and underappreciated in his time, and went on to be overshadowed by his younger brothers, Ira, Isaac, and Woody, and, of course, his sister, Helen. Even his illegitimate stepchild, Purple Haze, conceived on a curious one-night stand with Josephine Baker in Waco, Texas, went on to eclipse his father.

—*SPANKING WATSON*

Raking the dead leaves of the past is evil yard work. Whether you do it for two hours or twenty years, it leaves you feeling deader than the leaves you rake.

—*SPANKING WATSON*

WATERMELON SALAD

SERVES 6

EQUIPMENT NEEDED: JAR WITH LID

¼ cup extra-virgin olive oil

2 tablespoons cider vinegar

1 tablespoon vodka

Sea salt and freshly ground black pepper

4-pound chunk of watermelon, seeded, rind removed, and cut into bite-size
  wedges

1 large red onion, thinly sliced

¼ cup chopped cilantro (optional)

1. In the jar, combine the olive oil, vinegar, vodka, and salt and pepper; cover, and shake vigorously to combine.

2. Arrange the watermelon and onion in a large shallow bowl, sprinkle with cilantro, if using, and drizzle the dressing over all.

Funny the things you think about when your life hangs like a stray gray thread on Ratso's Hadassah Thrift Shop coat. Maybe it continues to cling there and you continue to live. Or maybe some well-meaning, neurotic broad puts down her plastic cup of white wine at a SoHo gallery opening and says, "Just a minute, Ratso, honey, you've got a thread hanging on your coat." She picks off the thread and you die. The landlord finds a new tenant and raises the rent. The cat goes to the city pound. The girl in the peach-colored dress calls, hears your voice still on the machine, leaves a message, and wonders why you never got back to her. Serves her right for waiting so damn long to call.

Answering machines tend to take on a life of their own. I remember the time the pope called Mother Teresa and told her she was needed in Los Angeles. . . . there were many poor people in the *barrios* there who needed her help. So, about three months later, the pope called Mother Teresa in L.A. She wasn't home but he got her answering machine. The message said, "Hi. This is Terri. I'm away from the phone right now . . ."

—*WHEN THE CAT'S AWAY*

POPEYE SALAD

SERVES 4

THE DRESSING

2 tablespoons honey

2 scallions, minced

2 large white mushrooms, minced

2 garlic cloves, minced

½ teaspoon crushed red pepper flakes, or to taste

1 tablespoon Dijon mustard

1 tablespoon rice vinegar, or to taste

Freshly ground black pepper

THE SALAD

2 plum tomatoes, seeded and diced

1 cup julienned red and yellow bell peppers

½ cup diced carrot

½ cup stemmed spinach leaves, washed, patted dry, and torn into bite-size
pieces

½ cup thinly sliced peeled jicama

1. Prepare the dressing: Heat the honey in a saucepan until warm. Add the scallions, mushrooms, garlic, and pepper flakes, and simmer for 5 minutes. Remove the pan from the heat and stir in the mustard, vinegar, and black pepper to taste. Let cool.

2. Prepare the salad: In a medium salad bowl, toss together the tomatoes, peppers, carrot, spinach, and jicama. Add the dressing and toss gently to combine.

If you play enough one-night stands, sooner or later you'll find that everywhere you go and everyone you know has become just another station on the way. On the way to where is, by this time, something you know even less about than you did when your journey started. But you feel like you have to keep going even if it kills you and, of course, in one way or another, it always does.

—*ROADKILL*

SON OF CAESAR SALAD

SERVES 4

EQUIPMENT NEEDED: BLENDER

THE CROUTONS
¼ cup extra-virgin olive oil
4 large garlic cloves, halved
3 cups cubes of French bread or another crusty bread (about ½ large loaf)
1 teaspoon freshly ground black pepper

THE DRESSING
½ cup extra-virgin olive oil
3 tablespoons fresh lemon juice
2 tablespoons half-and-half or whipping cream
1 tablespoon balsamic vinegar
1 teaspoon Dijon mustard
4 anchovy fillets, rinsed, patted dry, and chopped coarse
Freshly ground black pepper

THE SALAD
2 medium heads romaine lettuce, torn into bite-size pieces (8 cups of pieces)
¼ cup julienned fresh basil leaves
⅓ cup freshly grated or shredded Parmesan cheese

1. Prepare the croutons: Heat the olive oil and garlic in a large skillet over medium heat until the garlic turns light golden, about 2 minutes; remove and discard the garlic. Add the bread cubes to the skillet and brown them in the oil, turning, until lightly golden on all sides. Remove the croutons to paper towels to drain, and season with pepper; set aside.

2. Prepare the dressing: Put the olive oil, lemon juice, half-and-half, vinegar, mustard, anchovies, and pepper in the blender, and blend until smooth.

3. Assemble the salad: Toss the romaine and basil together in a large salad bowl; add the dressing and toss to coat. Add the croutons and Parmesan and toss again.

. . . [L]ife sometimes is like a kitten with a ball of yarn. It starts out going harmlessly along in one direction and before you know it, it rolls under the couch and you reach under there to get it and before you know it, you're staring into the limpid blue eyes of a twelve-year-old member of Future Hatchet Murderers of America who's hiding from imaginary Iroquois and he kills you and before you know it, the kitten is using your scrotum for a bean bag.

—*MUSICAL CHAIRS*

EAT, DRINK, AND BE **KINKY**

ROBBIE KATZ'S MAPLE SYRUP AND BALSAMIC SALAD DRESSING

MAKES A SCANT 1 CUP

EQUIPMENT NEEDED: BLENDER; CRUET WITH TOP

½ cup extra-virgin olive oil
¼ cup balsamic vinegar
2 tablespoons good-quality pure maple syrup
1 tablespoon red wine vinegar
2 garlic cloves, minced
1 tablespoon coarse-grained mustard
1 teaspoon dried mustard
1 teaspoon chopped fresh oregano
Freshly ground black pepper
1 tablespoon sesame seeds, toasted
1 tablespoon chopped capers

Put the olive oil, balsamic vinegar, maple syrup, red wine vinegar, garlic, both mustards, oregano, and pepper to taste in the blender and blend until emulsified. Pour the dressing into a small bowl and stir in the sesame seeds and capers. Transfer the dressing to the cruet and use immediately or store, covered, in the refrigerator.

Everybody dies an early death sooner or later. I'd always hoped mine could've been a little later. Dying's not what it's cracked up to be. But in all fairness, very few things are. Body surfing, for one.

—WHEN THE CAT'S AWAY

VEGETABLES

Being that vegetable gardens are somewhat alien to New York City, one should expect to find them there by the boatload, since in New York City just about everything is at least a little alien. Certainly Kinky found it a chore trying to make his garden grow on those mean streets (they're the ones that run parallel to Vandam), and has since retreated to a little green trailer in the little green hills of Texas, venturing forward only when responding to the siren call of food, women, or a big fat cigar, not necessarily in that order.

I smoke as many as ten cigars a day and I expect to live forever. Of course I don't inhale. I just blow the smoke at small children, green plants, vegetarians, and anybody who happens to be jogging by at the same time I'm exhaling.

—*A CASE OF LONE STAR*

ROASTED MUSTARD SPUDS

SERVES 4

EQUIPMENT NEEDED: NONSTICK BAKING PAN (13 X 9 X 2
   INCHES); MEDIUM HEAVY-BOTTOMED SAUCEPAN

6 medium red-skinned potatoes, cut into chunks
⅓ cup Dijon mustard
2 tablespoons extra-virgin olive oil
3 garlic cloves, minced
½ teaspoon caraway seeds, toasted

1. Preheat the oven to 375 degrees F. Lightly oil the baking pan.

2. Put the potatoes in the saucepan and cover with cold water. Bring the water to a boil and boil for 3 minutes. Drain and cool.

3. In a medium bowl, whisk together the mustard, oil, garlic, and caraway seeds; add the potatoes and toss to coat. Arrange the potatoes in the baking pan and roast 35 to 40 minutes, until crunchy on the outside but soft within.

It is a rather tedious fact of life that most of us who are confined to the human condition spend a great deal of time wishing to be something we're not. Or someone we're not. The proctologist, scrupulously washing his hands before and after each patient, dreams of being Dr. Albert Schweitzer. The rock star, as he worries whether to leave the Porsche with valet parking, dreams of saving the rain forest. The bank teller dreams of embezzling a million dollars and moving to Costa Rica. The average Costa Rican dreams of moving to Akron, Ohio, and becoming a bank teller. The many people who lead anonymous little lives long for fame. The handful of people who've become truly trapped in the thing that fame is, invariably long for anonymity. As far as the rest of us go, we have to deal with so many assholes every day we figure we probably should've been proctologists and at least get paid for it.

—THE LOVE SONG OF J. EDGAR HOOVER

BAKED POTATO DIFFERENT STYLE

SERVES 1

EQUIPMENT NEEDED: LONG-HANDLED WOODEN SPOON

1 large russet potato, well scrubbed
2 tablespoons extra-virgin olive oil
1 tablespoon white wine vinegar
Herbes de Provence, as needed
1 small onion, thinly sliced

1. Preheat the oven to 350 degrees F.

2. Bake the potato about 50 minutes, or until easily pierced with a fork. Let cool. Do not turn off the oven.

3. In a small cup, stir together the olive oil and vinegar.

4. On a work surface, place the handle of the wooden spoon along the length of the potato, actually touching it. Brace the spoon handle and the potato with one hand, and with the other hand, cut the potato, about three-quarters of the way through, just until the knife blade hits the spoon handle, into slices ⅛ to ¼ inch thick. Fan the potato slices slightly and brush with the vinaigrette. Sprinkle with the herbs, then insert the onion slices between the potato slices. Pour any remaining vinaigrette over the potato, and wrap it, still slightly fanned, in foil. Bake for 20 minutes. Remove the foil and serve at once.

Like Willie Nelson before him, Kinky was also being shunned by disc jockeys who would not play his music on the radio.

And, like Willie, Kinky wasn't about to settle for being a legend in his own lunchtime.

So when Willie and Kinky couldn't get airtime, each decided to go on the road with his band and bring his music to his fellow Americans.

Kinky and the Texas Jewboys worked behind chicken wire cages where they dodged insults and beer bottles in the hundreds of roadhouses splashed out over the American countryside. Bloodshed and flying glass aside, these venues happened to offer some of America's best home-style cooking.

In his travels Kinky began to compare himself not to Willie but to Jesus: "I noticed that Jesus and I have a lot in common. We're both Jewish, never married, and wandered the country annoying people."

The country western world didn't want him. The National Organization for Women nominated him Male Chauvinist of the Year, thanks to such memorable songs as "Get Your Biscuits in the Oven and Your Buns in the Bed" and "Waitreth, Oh Waitreth, Come Sit On My Fate."

But Kinky stayed tough. "God put her hand on my shoulder and said, 'Keep going.'" Now Kinky is inescapable. With a dozen novels to his name, he's best known worldwide for afflicting the comfortable and comforting the afflicted as the best-selling author of his own hilarious brand of rib-tickling, bar-thumping, foot-stomping whodunits. With titles like *Spanking Watson, Blast from the Past, The Love Song of J. Edgar Hoover,* and *Elvis, Jesus & Coca-Cola,* Kinky's books have been translated into eighteen languages. And wherever he wanders in this great big world, Kinky is as welcome as Magic Fingers in a no-tell motel. As a world traveler with an appetite to match, Kinky would go anywhere for a fine meal. And has.

FReNCH FRieS

SERVES 1 (KINKY, OF COURSE; IF YOU NEED MORE SERVINGS, IN-
  CREASE ACCORDINGLY)
EQUIPMENT NEEDED: CHIP OR MANDOLINE SLICER (OPTIONAL,
  BUT VERY HELPFUL); DEEP-FAT THERMOMETER; LARGE METAL
  SLOTTED SPOON

1 large russet potato, well-scrubbed but unpeeled
2 cups peanut oil, for deep-frying
1 tablespoon cornstarch
Salt

1. Using the chip slicer, if available, cut the potato into fry-size pieces, little-finger size, or thinner. Place in a bowl and cover with 1 quart cold water; add salt, if desired. Let soak for 20 minutes. Or, cover the bowl and refrigerate overnight.

2. In a deep, heavy saucepan, heat the oil to 375 degrees F on the thermometer. While the oil heats, drain the potato slices, then pat them completely dry with paper towels. Put the dried slices in a bowl, sift the cornstarch over them, and toss to coat.

3. Wearing oven mitts and using either a large metal slotted spoon or a Chinese skimmer, carefully add the potato slices to the hot oil. Deep-fry for 10 to 12 minutes, until golden brown, or longer if you like them extra-crisp. Remove with the slotted spoon or skimmer and drain on paper towels or brown paper bags. Salt and serve.

Sooner or later I was going to have to decide whether Texas or New York was truly my home. Then, in that quiet moment of reflection, I'd hopefully find the answer to the grand and troubling question that has haunted mankind through the ages: What is it that I really want out of life—horse-manure or pigeon shit?

—*ARMADILLOS & OLD LACE*

WRAPPED ASPARAGUS

SERVES 4

1 bunch green or white asparagus (at least 8 fat stalks)
Juice of 1 lemon
8 thin slices prosciutto
¼ cup balsamic vinegar
2 tablespoons extra-virgin olive oil
Salt and freshly ground black pepper
8 generous shavings Parmigiano-Reggiano cheese
4 julienned fresh basil leaves

1. Bring water to a boil in a 2-quart saucepan. Have ready a large bowl of ice.

2. Trim woody ends off the asparagus stalks. If the stalks are large, peel them with a vegetable peeler, starting just below the tip. Put the asparagus in the bowl of ice water. When the stove water boils, remove the asparagus from ice water and add to the saucepan. Reserve ice water. Boil for 1 minute, until stalks are slightly tender when tested with a fork.

3. Add half of the lemon juice to the bowl of ice water. Remove the asparagus stalks from the pan with a slotted spatula and transfer them immediately to the bowl of ice water. Let cool. Pat dry with paper towels.

4. Preheat the broiler.

5. Wrap a slice of prosciutto loosely around each asparagus. Arrange on a shallow baking pan. Drizzle with the vinegar and oil, and season to taste with salt and pepper. Broil about 3 inches from the heat for 2 minutes, turn, and broil 2 more minutes. Transfer the stalks to a serving platter and top with the Parmesan shavings, basil leaves, additional fresh pepper to taste, if desired, and the remaining lemon juice. Serve.

"[E]ven the spiritual surveillance of all our lives doesn't infallibly turn up every mundane detail. Some little things always tend to slip between the cracks of our sidewalks and our souls."

—*THE LOVE SONG OF J. EDGAR HOOVER*

LiME-AND-CHILI-ROASTED CORN

SERVES 4

4 ears of corn, unshucked
¼ cup extra-virgin olive oil
¼ cup fresh lime juice (about 3 limes)
2 teaspoons chili powder
Salt

1. Preheat the oven to 350 degrees F. Or, preheat a charcoal grill until coals are white hot. If using oven for roasting, oil a medium baking pan. Have ready a large bowl of cold water with ice cubes.

2. Gently pull back the husk on each ear of corn and remove the silk; smooth the husk back into place. Put the corn in the bowl of ice water and let soak for 20 to 30 minutes.

3. In a medium bowl, stir together the olive oil, lime juice, chili powder, and salt until well blended.

4. Drain the corn, pull back the husk on each ear, and brush the kernels with some of the lime-chili oil. Smooth husk back into place. If roasting in the oven, arrange the ears on the baking pan. Roast for 30 minutes, turning ears occasionally and basting the husks with any remaining seasoned oil or pan drippings. If grilling, put the ears on to cook 20 minutes before you plan to serve the main course. Turn the ears occasionally and baste as above. After 20 minutes, test the ears for doneness. The kernels should be soft to the touch. Remove to a platter, turn back the husks so that they can be used as "handles," and serve.

Imagination, of course, is the money of childhood. This is why it is not a surprise that little children have a better understanding of Indians, nature, death, God, animals, the universe, and some truly hard to grasp concepts like the Catholic Church, than most adults.

—ROADKILL

SWEET YAMS CHICAGO

SERVES 4

EQUIPMENT NEEDED: MEDIUM BAKING DISH (10 X 8 X 2 INCHES)

¼ cup sesame oil
½ cup packed light or dark brown sugar
Pinch of chili powder
Salt and freshly ground black pepper
4 medium yams, lightly scrubbed and cut into chunks

1. Preheat the oven to 400 degrees F. Rub the baking dish with flavorless vegetable cooking oil.

2. In a large bowl, stir together the sesame oil, brown sugar, chili powder, and salt and pepper to taste until well blended. Add the yams and toss to coat. Place the yams with any seasoned oil in the baking dish and bake 30 minutes, turning them over halfway through, or until the wedges are crispy and caramelized on the edges.

That's the way it happens, I thought, as I stared into the gaping mouth of an assault rifle that looked like it was ready to say *Ahhh.* You go on a short trip to help a friend and you leave behind your protective good ol' New York paranoia behind. You look for answers and, incredibly enough, you even find them. Then the kraut car closes, then it pulls next to you, then the weapon rises into view like a daydream gone bad, and somewhere between the fun and the sun and the rum and the gun you follow that last airplane picture right up into the sky. A window seat to limbo if the Catholic Church is correct, where you fly a tight, tedious holding pattern through night and fog for at least a thousand years with a small Aryan child kicking the seat behind you, while next to you a fat man from Des Moines is locked in a hideous rictus of eternal vomiting upon the half-completed crossword puzzle that is all of our lives.

—*GOD BLESS JOHN WAYNE*

EAT, DRINK, AND BE KINKY

SCALLION PARSNIP PANCAKES

MAKES APPROXIMATELY TWELVE 3-INCH PANCAKES, SERVING 4 AS
A SIDE DISH

EQUIPMENT NEEDED: FOOD PROCESSOR OR BOX GRATER; MEDIUM
SKILLET

1 pound parsnips, peeled and cut in large pieces
1 tablespoon canola oil, plus ¼ cup for frying
⅔ cup minced scallions (1 bunch large scallions)
2 extra-large egg whites
1 teaspoon grated fresh ginger
½ teaspoon garlic powder
½ teaspoon onion powder
½ teaspoon celery salt
¼ teaspoon freshly ground black pepper
¼ cup all-purpose flour

1. In a medium saucepan, bring the parsnips to a boil in water to cover; boil until tender. Drain, then shred in the food processor fitted with the grating blade or with a box grater.

2. Heat the 1 tablespoon of the oil in the skillet over medium heat. Add the scallions and cook, stirring, for 3 minutes, or until tender. Remove from heat.

3. In a bowl, beat the egg whites until broken, then stir in the shredded parsnips, scallions, ginger, garlic powder, onion powder, celery salt, and pepper. Using a ¼-cup measure, form pancakes about 3 inches wide and ½ inch thick. One at a time, dredge the pancakes, on both sides, in the flour. Shake off the excess.

4. Heat the remaining ¼ cup oil in the skillet over medium heat until hot. Add the pancakes, three at a time, more or less, depending on the size of your skillet, and fry them for 3 to 4 minutes; turn and fry about 2 minutes, until golden. Remove the pancakes to paper towels to drain. Keep them warm in the oven while you cook the next batch. Serve hot.

Nothing ever happens when you expect it, even if you're ready for it. But there is an uncanny timing to certain events on this planet that leads one, if not to believe in the Baby Jesus, at least to realize that somebody's building a lot of time-share condos in hell.

—*MUSICAL CHAIRS*

EAT, DRINK, AND BE KINKY

ZUCCHINI FRITTERS

MAKES 12 TO 14 FRITTERS, ENOUGH FOR 6 (AS A SIDE)

EQUIPMENT NEEDED: BOX GRATER; LARGE NONSTICK OR CAST-
  IRON SKILLET

2 pounds zucchini, trimmed and julienned

4 extra-large egg whites

2 tablespoons nonfat milk

2 tablespoons all-purpose flour

1 teaspoon onion powder

¼ cup julienned fresh mint leaves

1 garlic clove, minced

Salt and freshly ground black pepper

2 tablespoons extra-virgin olive oil

2 tablespoons canola oil

1. Grate the zucchini on the large holes of the box grater. (You should have about 3 cups grated.) Wrap the grated zucchini in paper towels and press out the excess moisture.

2. Preheat the oven to 300 degrees F.

3. In a large bowl, beat together the egg whites, milk, flour, onion powder, mint leaves, garlic, and salt and pepper. Stir in the zucchini. Make patties, about 2 to 2½ inches in diameter, with the batter. (You should have 12 to 14.)

4. Heat the olive and canola oils in the skillet until hot. Fry the fritters, in batches, carefully adding them to the pan, about 3 minutes per side, or until browned to taste. Transfer the fritters to paper towels to drain, then keep them warm in the oven while you cook the next batch. Serve hot.

Wandering around backstage at a Willie Nelson concert is a bit like being the parrot on the shoulder of the guy who's running the ferris wheel. It's not the best seat in the house, but you see enough lights, action, people, and confusion to make you wonder if anybody knows what the hell's really going on. If you're sitting out front, of course, the show rolls along as smoothly as a German train schedule, but as Willie Nelson, like any great magician, would be the first to point out, the real show is never in the center ring.

—*ROADKILL*

SANDWICHES

Sandwiched in between the words of wisdom that come
from the authority figures in our lives, one will usually
find a fair helping of baloney. But as long as one is old
enough to cut the mustard, enjoy a tasty tomato, and earn
a little lettuce, there's still hope. Certainly Kinky and his
cohorts hold to that belief, as these tasty recommendations
will show.

. . . [T]he good thing about Sundays that almost made up for all the other crap was the total, unearthly absence of garbage trucks. You could grind your teeth in peace. You could really get into a hangover. You could cling to the tattered fabric of your dreams.

—*A CASE OF LONE STAR*

PeANUT BUTTeR AND BANANA SANDWICHeS

MAKES 4 SANDWICHES

EQUIPMENT NEEDED: PARCHMENT PAPER

8 slices of brioche or other rich bread, crusts removed
Canola oil, as needed
1 cup chunky peanut butter
2 large bananas, sliced
¼ cup honey, warmed
½ cup nonfat plain yogurt or 1 cup nonfat whipped topping, for serving (optional)

1. Preheat the oven to 425 degrees F. Line a large shallow baking pan with the parchment paper.

2. Brush one side of 4 of the bread slices lightly with oil. Turn the slices over and spread them evenly with half the peanut butter; top with banana slices, then brush the banana slices with the honey.

3. Spread the remaining peanut butter on the remaining untopped slices. Make sandwiches. Brush the top slices lightly with oil and arrange the sandwiches in the prepared baking pan. Bake for 5 minutes, or until golden, turn, and bake for 5 minutes more.

4. Serve the sandwiches with a spoonful of yogurt or whipped topping on top, if desired.

Everybody's got to die sometime, I figured. Either you die suddenly at the hands of strangers near an abandoned warehouse or you die of ennui sitting around your house wondering how you're going to die. I tell you, it's no way to live.

—*THE LOVE SONG OF J. EDGAR HOOVER*

FRIED-EGG SANDWICH A GO-GO

If you are opposed to whole eggs, you can substitute two egg whites for the whole egg that is called for below. The end result won't be the same, but it will be better for you. Of course, when you factor in the bacon, even if it is Canadian, and peanut butter, who knows what the difference a yolk makes? It all tastes great, though.

MAKES 1 SANDWICH

2 slices white bread (any kind you like)
2 slices low-fat Swiss or American cheese
1 whole extra-large egg or 2 extra-large egg whites
3 slices Canadian bacon
2 tablespoons chunky peanut butter (optional)
1 tablespoon blackberry jelly (or what's on hand)
1 scallion, finely chopped

1. Toast the bread slices and while still warm, top each slice with a piece of cheese.

2. In a nonstick skillet (the 9-inch size should do), fry the egg at the same time as you heat the bacon. Put the bacon on one of the cheese-topped slices and top with the fried egg.

3. Spread the peanut butter, if using, over the cheese on the other slice of bread and top with the jelly and scallion. Put the slices together. Serve the sandwich sliced in half on the diagonal, if desired. (Try not to cut into the yolk, if you can.)

If you plumbed deeply enough into the triple-decker sandwich of the mind until you reached that Land of Oz, the subconscious, you'd find that every homosexual was a heterosexual and that every heterosexual was a homosexual. You'd probably also find out that neither group was too fond of Sigmund Freud.

—*GREENWICH KILLING TIME*

EAT, DRINK, AND BE KINKY

TRIPLE-DECKER BACON 'N' EGG BRIOCHE SANDWICH

SERVES 4

EQUIPMENT NEEDED: 2 LARGE SKILLETS, THE LARGEST YOU CAN
GET YOUR HANDS ON

THE MAPLE BUTTER
8 tablespoons (1 stick) unsalted butter, softened
2 tablespoons pure maple syrup

THE CANADIAN BACON
1 tablespoon canola oil
16 slices Canadian bacon

THE FRENCH TOAST
2 tablespoons unsalted butter
2 whole extra-large eggs or 4 extra-large egg whites
¼ cup orange juice
2 tablespoons confectioners' sugar
1 teaspoon ground cinnamon
12 thin slices of brioche or white bakery bread

THE FRIED EGGS
2 tablespoons unsalted butter
4 extra-large eggs

1. Make the maple butter: In a bowl, cream the butter until fluffy, add the maple syrup, and beat to combine. Cover and refrigerate about 10 minutes, until slightly solid.

2. Preheat the oven to 250 degrees F.

3. Make the Canadian bacon: Heat the oil in a large skillet until hot, add the bacon, and cook, turning, about 1 minute per side, until golden. Remove and keep warm in the oven.

4. Make the French toast: Place one of the large skillets over medium heat, add the butter, and let it melt. Meanwhile, in a bowl, whisk the eggs together with the orange juice, sugar, and cinnamon until combined. Dip the bread slices into the egg mixture, coating both sides well, and add in a single layer to the hot skillet. Cook until golden, about 2 to 3 minutes; turn and cook another 2 minutes. Remove and keep warm in the oven. Cook the remaining bread slices, in batches, in the same way.

5. Make the fried eggs: Heat the butter in the other large skillet until melted. Break the eggs, 1 at a time, into the pan and cook until set, about 2 to 3 minutes for sunny side up, or until set and cooked. Remove to a plate.

6. Build the triple deckers: On each serving plate, place a slice of hot French toast and top with a tablespoon of the maple butter and 2 slices of bacon. Top with a slice of French toast. Put a fried egg on the toast and top it with 2 slices of bacon. Top with another slice of French toast. Put a large spoonful of maple butter on last. Keep warm in the oven while making triple deckers with the remaining ingredients. Serve hot.

"It's just possible that all of us are fictional characters in some perverse comedy that never did much box office. Maybe that's why we spend our lives searching for meaning that just isn't there, or for truth that we wouldn't recognize if it was."

—*SPANKING WATSON*

EAT, DRINK, AND BE KINKY

DELI HE-MAN HIGH-ROLLER

SERVES 4

¼ cup extra-virgin olive oil

1 small red onion, finely diced

2 plum tomatoes, peeled, seeded, and finely chopped

1 small cucumber, peeled, seeded, and finely diced

1 tablespoon balsamic or red wine vinegar

1 tablespoon packed light or dark brown sugar

Salt and freshly ground black pepper

¾ cup nonfat mayonnaise

¼ cup sweet and spicy mustard or honey mustard

2 pounds deli meat, such as prosciutto, Parma ham, salami, chorizo, or pastrami), sliced

2 pounds your favorite deli cheese, such as Monterey Jack, Swiss, Cheddar, or gouda, sliced

4 sheets lavash bread (flat bread, available in packages in the deli section of most supermarkets; see note)

8 romaine lettuce leaves

1. Heat the olive oil in a medium skillet over medium heat. Add the onion and sauté, stirring, until soft, about 5 minutes. Add the tomatoes and cucumber and toss to coat. Add the vinegar and sugar, stir to combine, then cook until the liquid all but evaporates. Remove the pan from the heat, season to taste with salt and pepper, taste, and adjust seasonings if necessary.

2. In a small bowl, stir together the mayonnaise and mustard until combined.

3. Divide the deli meats and cheeses into 4 portions. Lay the 4 lavash sheets on the counter. Spread each sheet generously with the mustard mayonnaise. Cover two-thirds of each bread with the romaine, pressing it down flat. Top the lettuce with meats and cheeses, alternating the slices, and a large dollop of the tomato-cucumber mixture. Roll each bread up jelly-roll fashion, using your fingers to keep the filling in place. Secure the seam with a toothpick, if desired. Wrap each roll-up tightly in plastic wrap and refrigerate at least 20 minutes, but no more than 2 hours.

4. To serve, slice the roll-ups, still wrapped in plastic wrap, on the diagonal; remove plastic wrap and toothpicks, if used. Wrap halves in napkins for eating.

NOTE: If you can't find lavash sheets, substitute pita bread. Split it horizontally and use the halves as you would the lavash sheets.

Old friends are ones you may not really like but you're stuck with because you're old friends. You can pick your friends and you can pick your nose, but you can't wipe your friends off on your saddle.

—A CASE OF LONE STAR

ENTRÉES

Why did the chicken cross the road?

KINDERGARTEN TEACHER: To get to the other side.

PLATO: For the greater good.

COLONEL SANDERS: What, ah missed one?

RONALD REAGAN: I forget.

WILLIE NELSON: Because it's the only trip the establishment would let it take.

ERNEST HEMINGWAY: To die. In the rain.

IMUS: Asking the question denies your own chicken nature.

CAPT. JAMES T. KIRK: To boldly go where no chicken has gone before.

F. MURRAY ABRAHAM: And God came down from the Heavens and He said unto the chicken, "Thou shalt cross the road." And the chicken crossed the road, and there was much rejoicing.

RAMBAM: This was an unprovoked act of rebellion and we are quite justified in dropping fifty tons of Tomahawk missiles and nerve gas on it.

JOSEPH HELLER: Because of an excess of phlegm in its pancreas.

MARCIE FRIEDMAN: To see Gregory Peck.

RICHARD NIXON: The chicken did not cross the road. I repeat, the chicken did not cross the road.

JERRY SEINFELD: Why does anyone cross a road? I mean, why doesn't anyone ever think to ask, What the heck was this chicken doing walking around all over the place, anyway?

FREUD: That you are concerned the chicken crossed the road reveals your underlying sexual insecurity.

WILLIAM JEFFERSON CLINTON: Whether the chicken crossed the road or the road moved is dependent on your frame of reference.

RALPH WALDO EMERSON: The chicken did not cross the road, it transcended.

SHAMPOO KING JOHN MCCALL, AFTER SPEAKING WITH A CONSULTANT: Deregulation of the chicken's side of the road was threatening its dominant market position. The chicken was faced with significant challenge to create and develop the competencies required for the newly competitive market. Consulting, in a partnering with the client, helped the chicken by rethinking its physical distribution strategy and implementation processes. Using the Poultry Integration Model (PIM) helped the chicken use all its skills, methodologies, knowledge, capital, and experiences to align the chicken's people, processes, and technology, in support of its overall strategy developed by a diverse cross-spectrum of road analysts and the best minds within a Program Management framework.

The meeting was held in a parklike setting, enabling and creating an environment that was strategically based, industry focused, and built upon a consistent, clear, and united market message and aligned with the chicken's mission, vision, and core values. Consulting helped the chicken change.

"There are, no doubt . . . primitive enclaves on this planet, possibly in the outback of Australia, in New Guinea, in the secret hearts of Africa and South America. But these peoples and places are as fragile and ephemeral as a smile in childhood. Yet they do exist. Cultural and spiritual oases where you may truly escape what we have come to think of as the world . . . In these places you are safe from harm and sheltered from sorrow. If you ever find one of these places, and then leave it, as I have done, you may spend the rest of your life with the better part of your soul living in the shadow of regret."

—ELVIS, JESUS & COCA-COLA

DAGWOOD HERO

¼ cup distilled white vinegar

¼ cup water

2 tablespoons sugar or 3 packets aspartame

½ teaspoon *nuoc mam* (fish sauce, available in Asian markets and some supermarkets)

½ teaspoon chili paste (optional, available in Asian markets)

½ pound carrots, grated

2 baguettes or 4 hero rolls

¼ pound sliced low-salt low-fat roast pork or ham

¼ pound sliced, skinless roast turkey or chicken

2 stalks celery, thinly sliced

Leaves from 1 bunch flat-leafed parsley

¼ cup chili sauce or salsa (p. 119, Beef Fajitas with Salsa)

¼ cup low-fat mayonnaise

¼ pound pâté, sliced thin

1. In a medium bowl, stir together the vinegar, water, sugar, fish sauce, and chili paste, if using, until combined. Add the carrots and stir to coat. Cover and marinate in the refrigerator for 2 hours.

2. Halve the baguettes, then split them open horizontally with a knife. Divide the pork, turkey, celery, and parsley equally and layer them on 4 pieces of the bread. Top with a spoonful of the chili sauce and some of the carrot mixture.

3. Spread the remaining bread with the mayonnaise and top with the pâté. Put the pâté-topped bread on the cheese-and-everything-else-topped pieces, pressing the halves together firmly. Cut the baguettes into pieces for easier serving.

That's just what usually happens when you take in a bird with a broken wing, I thought. Once the wing heals good and strong they beat you to death with it.

—BLAST FROM THE PAST

OUR AMERICA BURGER

SERVES 4 TO 6

EQUIPMENT NEEDED: LARGE CAST-IRON SKILLET

1½ pounds ground round or chuck
1 medium onion, grated
1 teaspoon finely chopped flat-leafed parsley
1 teaspoon freshly ground black pepper
½ teaspoon dried marjoram (see note)
¼ teaspoon sea salt or kosher salt
¼ cup fresh lemon juice
2 tablespoons A-1 Sauce (optional)

1. In a medium bowl, mix together the beef, onion, parsley, pepper, and marjoram (or curry powder) just until combined. Shape into equal patties, 4 large or 6 smaller.

2. Heat the ungreased cast-iron skillet over high heat for 5 minutes. Sprinkle the salt in an even layer into the skillet. Add the patties and cook for 3 minutes per side for medium-rare, or to taste. Transfer the burgers to a serving plate and drizzle with the lemon juice.

3. Remove any fat from the skillet and add the A-1 to the pan juices, if desired; stir. Pour the sauce over the burgers and serve.

NOTE: If you don't have dried marjoram, go for a completely different taste and use ½ teaspoon curry powder instead. It's good, too.

I wished I could say I loved her. I wished I could say I loved anyone. The way I loved the cat [the late Cuddles] and the Bakerman [Kinky's closest pal, the late Tom Baker]. Historically, I thought, cats and dead people had always been cheap dates. Easy to love. Easy to keep in your heart.

—*ELVIS, JESUS & COCA-COLA*

ow to the meat of the subject. Or the chicken. Or the fish. Or the burritos. Whatever your preference, ladies and germs, for your dining pleasure, an entrée to the entrées.

SPINACH PASTA WITH VODKA SAUCE

SERVES 4

EQUIPMENT NEEDED: MEDIUM SAUTÉ PAN (OR HIGH-SIDED SKILLET)

8 ounces dried spinach pasta (see note)

THE VODKA SAUCE
1 tablespoon unsalted butter
8 ounces button mushrooms or cremini mushrooms, sliced
1 can (8.5 ounces) Le Sueur very young small early peas, drained
2 ounces prosciutto, finely chopped
3 shots (3 ounces) vodka
¾ cup whipping cream
1 cup homemade or jarred tomato sauce
2 tablespoons freshly grated Parmesan cheese
Salt and freshly ground black pepper

1. Bring a large pot of salted water to a boil. Add the pasta and cook, according to package directions, until al dente.

2. While the pasta is cooking, make the vodka sauce: Heat the butter in the sauté pan until melted. Add the mushrooms, peas, and prosciutto, and cook, stirring, for 1 minute. Remove the pan from the heat and pour in the vodka. Carefully return the pan to the heat; the vodka will ignite. When the flame subsides, stir in the cream and tomato sauce. Bring the mixture to a boil, stir in the Parmesan and salt and pepper to taste, and simmer, stirring, for 5 minutes.

3. Drain the pasta well. Serve in bowls, topped with some of the vodka sauce.

NOTE: Plain rigatoni goes well with this sauce, too.

There's lots of doors swinging open and closed in this world, I thought. And there's lots of people in our lives leaving and entering doors that we cannot see. All we can hope is that when the Lord closes the door, He opens a little window.

—*BLAST FROM THE PAST*

It was at this time that I began seeing some rather uncanny parallels between my life and the life of Jesus. Both of us, of course, were of the Jewish persuasion. Neither of us ever really had a home to speak of. Neither of us ever married during the course of our lives. Neither of us ever actually held a job during the course of our lives. We both just basically traveled around the countryside irritating people.

—*ELVIS, JESUS & COCA-COLA*

EAT, DRINK, AND BE **KINKY**

LiFE-SAVER PiZZA

SERVES 4

EQUIPMENT NEEDED: DEEP-DISH PIZZA PAN (9 x 1½ INCHES DEEP)

THE DOUGH
1 package (6½ ounces) Betty Crocker Pizza Crust Mix (1-crust Smart Size)
2 tablespoons extra-virgin olive oil

THE TOPPING
2 tablespoons olive oil
1 large onion, chopped
¼ cup tomato sauce
2 garlic cloves, minced
1 can (14½ ounces) Italian-style stewed tomatoes, drained
1 tablespoon finely chopped flat-leafed parsley
1 tablespoon finely chopped fresh basil leaves
1 tablespoon finely chopped fresh oregano
1 teaspoon crushed red pepper flakes, or to taste
Salt and freshly ground black pepper
1 pound sweet or hot Italian sausage, fried and drained of all fat
½ cup shredded low-fat mozzarella cheese
½ cup crumbled goat cheese (optional)

1. Preheat the oven to 425 degrees F. Make deep-dish pizza dough according to the directions on the package. Press the dough into the deep-dish pan and up the sides. Brush the dough with the olive oil and bake 7 minutes. Keep the oven on.

2. Prepare the topping: Heat the olive oil in a medium saucepan until hot. Add the onion and fry slowly, about 15 minutes, until caramelized.

3. Top the dough. First spread it with the tomato sauce. Then sprinkle the onion, garlic, tomatoes, parsley, basil, oregano, pepper flakes, and salt and pepper on top. Scatter the sausage, mozzarella, and goat cheese, if using, evenly over the crust.

4. Return the crust to the oven and bake the pizza for 12 to 15 minutes, or until the crust is golden brown and the cheeses are just beginning to brown.

5. Serve with a romaine lettuce salad and a good dressing, like Ken's Steak House Lite Raspberry Walnut Vinaigrette.

Life itself . . . is very much like the cardboard scenery in a spaghetti western; everybody drives around in Yom Kippur Clippers and they still won't give Jim Thorpe his fucking medals back. No one's ever won the human race but guys like Abbie [Hoffman] sometimes make it fun to watch. Every hamster doesn't ride the wheel.

—BLAST FROM THE PAST

HUEVOS RANCHEROS

SERVES 4

EQUIPMENT NEEDED: 2 LARGE SKILLETS

THE RANCHERO SALSA (MAKES ABOUT 1 CUP)
1 tablespoon extra-virgin olive oil
2 tablespoons minced garlic
1 tablespoon chopped fresh oregano
1 teaspoon cumin seeds, toasted and ground
Salt and freshly ground black pepper
2 pounds plum tomatoes, peeled, seeded, and chopped
½ cup canned tomato sauce
2 tablespoons fresh lime juice
Dash of Tabasco sauce
2 tablespoons chopped cilantro (optional)

THE EGGS
2 tablespoons canola oil
4 corn tortillas
4 whole extra-large eggs
¾ cup sharp cheddar cheese, grated

2 tablespoons chopped cilantro
Sour cream, for serving (optional)
Mexican Guacamole (p. 21, optional)

1. Make the ranchero salsa: Heat the olive oil in the skillet over moderate heat until hot. Add the garlic, oregano, cumin, and salt and pepper to taste and cook, stirring, for 2 minutes. Add the tomatoes, tomato sauce, and lime juice and stir to combine; heat through. Add the Tabasco and adjust the seasonings. Remove the pan from the heat and stir in the cilantro, if using. Set aside.

2. Make the eggs: Heat the canola oil in the other large skillet over moderate heat until hot. Add the tortillas, 2 at a time, and fry on both sides, turning once, about 1 minute. Drain on paper towels. Put the tortillas on a large nonstick baking sheet.

3. Preheat the broiler.

4. In the same skillet, fry the eggs the way you like best. Top each tortilla with a fried egg. Top each egg with a dollop of salsa and some of the cheese. Place the baking sheet under the broiler and broil until the cheese bubbles.

5. To serve: Put 1 tortilla on each plate and sprinkle with some of the cilantro. Spoon on sour cream and guacamole, if desired, and serve immediately.

I'd come to travel the open road with the gypsy king, wild and free. To get away from the city of gray, depressed, worn-out souls. But the unfortunate thing about traveling is that you always have to take yourself with you. If you travel with the gypsies, soon you will learn to leave behind the excess baggage of your life. Then one day you find yourself standing with a paper suitcase on the track of time, smoking your old pipe upside down in the rain, like a knight born out of your time, wondering not who you are or how you got there in the first place, but why people have been drinking ginger ale on airplanes for over two thousand years and if women really fake orgasms because they think men care. The next thing you know you're wandering around lost and looking for your locker at Coconut University.

—*ROADKILL*

SADDLE UP BURRITOS

2 medium red potatoes, diced

4 flour tortillas (7 inches in diameter)

1 tablespoon canola oil

¾ cup chopped scallions (about 5 whole) or 1 large Vidalia onion, finely chopped

1 tomato, seeded and diced

1 can (4 ounces) chopped green chilies, drained, or to taste

Salt and freshly ground black pepper

1 whole extra-large egg, lightly beaten

4 extra-large egg whites, lightly beaten

Yellow food coloring (optional)

2 tablespoons chopped cilantro

Pinch of cayenne pepper (optional)

½ cup Salsa (p. 119, Beef Fajitas with Salsa)

¼ cup grated or shredded low-fat cheddar or Monterey Jack cheese

½ cup nonfat sour cream

1. Preheat the oven to 350 degrees F.

2. Put the potatoes in a medium saucepan, cover with water, and bring the water to a boil. Simmer about 15 minutes, or until tender. Drain.

3. Wrap the tortillas in aluminum foil and heat them in the oven while you make the eggs.

4. Heat the oil in a large skillet over moderate heat until hot. Add ½ cup of the scallions and the potatoes and cook, stirring, 1 minute. Add the tomato and chilies and cook, stirring, 2 minutes. Season to taste with the salt and pepper. Transfer the mixture to a bowl and keep warm.

5. Add the egg, egg whites, and food coloring, if using, to the skillet, along with 1 tablespoon water, and cook, stirring for 2 minutes, until the eggs start to set but are still creamy. Stir in the cilantro and potato-scallion mixture and stir to combine well. Taste and adjust seasonings if necessary, adding a pinch of cayenne, if desired.

6. To serve: Divide the egg mixture among the hot tortillas and roll each up. Top each burrito with a dollop of salsa, some cheese, and sour cream, and a sprinkling of the remaining ¼ cup scallions.

Winnie Katz's lesbian dance class was like God. Mankind never saw it, but you always knew it was there.

. . . I listened to the rhythmic thuddings in the loft above me. I wondered what the hell was really going on up there. If someone's wayward daughter from Coeur d'Alene, Idaho, was being broken down like a double-barreled shotgun, it'd be a hell of a lot of early ballroom lessons gone to waste. On the other hand, what did I know about modern dance?

It was a chilly evening in late January and I was sitting at my desk just sort of waiting for something besides my New Year's resolutions to kick in. If you're patient and you wait long enough, something will usually happen and it'll usually be something you don't like.

—WHEN THE CAT'S AWAY

EAT, DRINK, AND BE **KINKY**

IRISH SNAPPER WITH LIME SAUCE

SERVES 4

EQUIPMENT NEEDED: LARGE SKILLET (FOR WHOLE FISH) OR 2
  LARGE SKILLETS (FOR FILLETS)

2 tablespoons extra-virgin olive oil
One 3- to 4-pound red snapper, cleaned, or 3 pounds red snapper fillets

THE LIME SAUCE
2 tablespoons water
2 tablespoons fresh lime juice
4 tablespoons (½ stick) unsalted butter, in pieces, or canola oil
1 tablespoon chopped fresh mint (or another favorite fresh herb)
Salt and freshly ground black pepper

1. Heat the olive oil in the skillet over moderately high heat until hot. Add the snapper and brown on both sides. Lower the heat to moderate and sauté the fish for 20 minutes, turning it once, until the flesh at the thickest part just flakes when tested. If using snapper fillets, cook them for 5 to 8 minutes, or until the flesh flakes when tested with a fork.

2. Meanwhile, make the lime sauce: In a small saucepan, reduce the water and lime juice over high heat by half. Add the butter and stir until melted, but creamy. Remove the pan from the heat and stir in the mint and salt and pepper to taste. Keep warm, but do not let boil.

3. To serve, put the snapper on a heated platter and pour the lime sauce over it. Serve at once.

n Sydney, where Piers Akerman lives with his lawyer-wife, Suzanne, and Tessa and Pia, their two gorgeous teenage daughters, Kinky is often a guest. And the emphasis is on fresh food, as in things he hauls out of the water near the family digs.

It would not be unusual to see Kinky, in his brontosaurus foreskin cowboy boots, and Piers, in his high-heeled sneakers, swing out on a game boat a dozen miles from shore and pick up a few tuna, dolphin fish, or even a marlin for a home-cooked meal.

"Some people kiss fish and drop them back in the water," Kinky says, "but it's tough to kiss a marlin—their noses get in the way."

The marlin makes steaks not unlike swordfish. Piers marinates marlin steaks for 20 minutes in lime juice and mashed mango, then tosses them on the barbie with a sprinkle of fresh ground pepper.

They'll handle a crisp white wine or red, as Kinky does when he sits down with the Akermans.

When they bag a tuna, Piers slices off fillets and cuts them into bite-sized bits. Add some shredded fresh horseradish, mix in wasabi powder, and place on a platter with a brace of Coopers ales or Tasmanian Boag beer.

Even cowboys who don't like fish come back for more.

Piers says, "If the Kinkster was not a Texan, I suspect he'd like to have been born as Australian. Over the years, he has stayed with me in Newport, Rhode Island, when I covered the America's Cup, and both in Melbourne and Sydney.

"One of the best times was spent aboard a yacht, loaned to me, when we cruised the Whitsunday Islands with Mike McGovern, Kinky's recently widowed father, Tom, and his eighty-year-old compadre Earl Buckelew, a Texan who had never before left the state. Earl was a real cowboy who used to ride the range; his grandfather had been kidnapped by Apaches before they knew they were Native Americans.

"As for animals, none had embodied Opal's qualities. My closest mate now is Max, my dog. He's no Rin Tin Tin, but he has been
around the world [with Piers] two or three times and, the Good Lord
knows, not many mutts from the Sandy Creek Dogs Home can say
that."

TERI AND CHINGA CHAVIN'S OL' BEN LUCAS SWORDFISH STEW

SERVES 4

2 tablespoons extra-virgin olive oil or canola oil

2 large onions (about 8 ounces total), thinly sliced

2 garlic cloves, minced

2 cans (14 ounces each) Italian-style crushed tomatoes

1 can (6 ounces) tomato paste

2 tablespoons chopped fresh thyme, or 2 teaspoons dried

1 teaspoon fennel seeds

1 bay leaf

Grated zest of 1 orange

1½ cups dry white wine

1 pound swordfish (or red snapper, sea bass, or grouper, boned), cut into 1½-inch chunks

1. Heat the olive oil in a large skillet until hot. Add the onions and cook them over low heat, stirring, for 10 minutes, or until browned. Add the garlic and cook until fragrant, about 2 or 3 minutes.

2. Stir in the tomatoes, tomato paste, thyme, fennel seeds, bay leaf, and grated zest until blended. Cook over moderate heat, stirring occasionally, for 10 minutes.

3. Add the wine and fish. Simmer for 5 to 10 minutes, until the fish flakes easily when tested with a fork.

New Year's Eve came around relentless as a tedious housepest. You can coddle a tedious housepest, pretend you like him, ignore him, but he'll still be hanging around like a bad smell unless you get a forklift and get him the hell out of there. New Year's Eve was the same way—unforgivable and unforkliftable. Like Exxon or a twenty-four-hour Chinese restaurant, New Year's Eve didn't care if you sang, danced, or hung yourself from a shower rod. The only remedy was to sleep through the bastard like a bad dream . . .

—*MUSICAL CHAIRS*

JOE HELLER'S BACK-BITING SHRIMP

SERVES 4

EQUIPMENT NEEDED: WELL-SEASONED WOK (OR LARGE NONSTICK
    SKILLET)

3 tablespoons peanut oil
3 whole garlic cloves, or to taste, minced
24 large shrimp, deveined but still in the shell
6 scallions, chopped, including most of the greens
1 tablespoon grated fresh ginger, or to taste
¼ cup low-sodium soy sauce, or to taste

1. Heat the wok over high heat until hot. Add the oil and garlic
and cook, tossing, until golden, about 1 minute.

2. Add the shrimp, scallions, and ginger, and with a Chinese
shovel or large spoon, stir-fry until the shells turn pink and the meat
opaque, several minutes only. Add the soy sauce and toss to coat the
shrimp. Remove the wok from the heat and serve at once, with
steamed brown rice and a crisp green salad.

Home can be a pretty tedious place if you're not far enough away to begin
to start to miss it.

—*SPANKING WATSON*

EAT, DRINK, AND BE KINKY

Cleve's kinky clam sauce
(for pasta)

SERVES 2

2 tablespoons olive oil
2 garlic cloves, minced
1 tablespoon chopped fresh basil
1 teaspoon chopped fresh thyme
¼ cup clam juice
¼ cup dry white wine
¼ teaspoon crushed red pepper flakes or freshly ground black pepper, or more
 to taste
½ cup chopped fresh hard-shelled clams
¼ cup chopped parsley
2 tablespoons fresh lemon juice
2 or 3 jalapeño chili peppers, seeded and chopped (optional)
8 ounces pasta, freshly cooked
Freshly grated Parmesan cheese, for serving

1. Heat the olive oil in a medium skillet until hot. Add the garlic, basil, and thyme, and cook, stirring, 2 minutes.

2. Add the clam juice, wine, pepper flakes, and clams and bring to a simmer. Simmer gently for 5 minutes. Stir in the parsley, lemon juice, and jalapeños, if using, and cook only to heat through, a minute or two.

3. Divide the hot pasta between bowls and top with the clam sauce. Serve at once, with the Parmesan and plenty of freshly ground black pepper.

. . . [F]or those few who find lasting fame within their lifetime, things can sometimes be even more frustrating. If you think it's hard living with who you are, try living with who you've become.

—*ROADKILL*

SOUSED CHICKEN CROSSING THE ROAD

SERVES 2 OR 3

EQUIPMENT NEEDED: LARGE ICE SHAKER; 2 LARGE MARGARITA
    GLASSES; A STOVE OR A GRILL

2 cups tequila

2 cups Triple Sec or Cointreau

½ cup fresh lime juice (about a dozen limes) or pineapple juice

¼ cup cranberry juice

One whole 3½- to 4-pound chicken, soaked in water with 1 tablespoon sea salt
    added for 1 hour at room temperature or overnight in the refrigerator,
    drained, and patted completely dry

3 sprigs fresh thyme

Grated zest of 1 lime

1. In an ice shaker, mix the tequila, Triple Sec, lime juice, and cranberry juice. Pour yourself and a guest a margarita or two—but you'll need to set aside at least 1 cup of the mixture for use in cooking.

2. You can cook the chicken one of two ways: Roast it in the oven, in which case you will want to preheat the oven to 350 degrees F. Then place the thyme and lime zest in the cavity. Put the chicken in a baking dish and pour what remains of the margarita mixture over it. Roast for 60 to 90 minutes, basting with the pan juices, until the juices run clear at the leg joint.

3. Or, you can grill the chicken. You will need to preheat a grill and cut the chicken into 8 serving pieces, including thighs and legs separated. Put the chicken in a container, add the remaining Margarita mixture, and cover. Marinate 2 hours or overnight. (If you decide to marinate it for the longer time, remember that you will need something else for dinner. Then again, you may not want dinner by that point.) If you do, light the grill. When the coals turn ash white, put on the legs and thighs and grill for 7 minutes a side. Add the white meat (the breasts) and cook about 5 to 7 minutes a side, or until done. Baste as it grills with the remaining marinade.

4. Serve—in other words, eat in. Do not drive anywhere.

The fried chicken was still great . . . Eating a fried chicken lunch with a tableful of seven-year-olds will certainly take your mind off weightier matters. Along with the chicken and the mashed potatoes and gravy, the adult world with its ponderous problems just seems to disappear. . . . The subject of girls never even comes up.

—ARMADILLOS & OLD LACE

SAUCED CHICKEN IN A BLANKET

SERVES 4

EQUIPMENT NEEDED: LARGE HEAVY-BOTTOMED SKILLET; BAKING
  DISH OR CASSEROLE (13 x 9 x 2 INCHES)

THE CHICKEN

4 tablespoons extra-virgin olive oil

1 large onion, diced

One 3½- to 4-pound chicken, wing tips discarded, cut into 10 pieces, and skin
  removed

THE BLANKET

1 extra-large whole egg

4 extra-large egg whites

1½ cups nonfat milk

1½ cups all-purpose flour

¼ cup freshly grated Parmigiano-Reggiano cheese

2 tablespoons minced flat-leafed parsley

½ teaspoon sea salt

Freshly ground black pepper

THE SAUCE

1 cup mushroom soup, homemade or canned

½ cup dry white wine

2 tablespoons minced flat-leafed parsley

1 cup thinly sliced fresh white mushrooms

Salt and freshly ground black pepper

1. Make the chicken: Heat 2 tablespoons of the oil in the skillet until hot. Add the onion and sauté, stirring, until browned. Remove to a plate. Add the remaining 2 tablespoons oil to the skillet and add the chicken, in batches, if necessary; cook about 5 minutes per side, until browned. Add salt and pepper to taste and arrange the pieces in the baking dish.

2. Preheat the oven to 350 degrees F.

3. Make the blanket: In a bowl, whisk together the whole egg, egg whites, milk, flour, cheese, parsley, salt, and pepper to taste until well combined and smooth. Pour over the chicken.

4. Bake 1 hour, or until the chicken is tender and the blanket has turned golden brown.

5. While the chicken bakes, make the sauce: Heat the soup, wine, and parsley in a medium saucepan until hot. Add the mushrooms and salt and pepper to taste and cook over moderate heat about 10 minutes, until the mushrooms are tender.

6. Serve the blanketed chicken with the mushroom sauce spooned over the top.

. . . [S]ex is forever overrated, they say. To that I might add that taking a Nixon is forever underrated.

—*BLAST FROM THE PAST*

KINKY'S LAST SUPPER AT JOHN McCALL'S PEDRIGAL IN CABO SAN LUCAS

SERVES 5 OR 6

EQUIPMENT NEEDED: DUTCH OVEN OR BIG POT; BAKING DISH
   (13 x 9 x 2 INCHES); BLENDER OR FOOD PROCESSOR

THE SALSA VERDE (MAKES ABOUT 3 CUPS)
4 poblano chili peppers
16 fresh tomatillos, papery husks removed and coarsely chopped
1 jalapeño chili pepper, seeded and chopped
1 can (14½ ounces) chicken broth
1 small onion, chopped
1 garlic clove, minced
¼ cup chopped cilantro (optional)
1 teaspoon salt

THE ENCHILADAS
4 pounds chicken pieces
6 cups water
1 tablespoon cayenne pepper
1 teaspoon salt, plus additional for seasoning
1 cup chopped onions
2 garlic cloves, chopped
2 jalapeño chili peppers, seeded and chopped
1 tablespoon plus ½ cup canola oil
¼ cup chopped cilantro, or to taste
2 cups shredded part-skim Monterey Jack cheese (an 8-ounce block)
½ cup low-fat or nonfat sour cream
10 corn tortillas

1. Make the salsa verde: Wash and dry the poblano peppers. Char them, either on a fork over a direct flame or under the broiler, turning them often, until blistered all over. Transfer the peppers immediately to a heavy plastic bag or brown paper bag and close it tight. Let the peppers stand in the bag for 10 minutes. Remove, peel off the charred skin, and seed. Coarsely chop the peppers.

2. Parboil the tomatillos in a large saucepan of boiling water to cover for 5 minutes. Drain.

3. In the blender or food processor, combine the poblanos, tomatillos, jalapeño pepper, ½ cup of the chicken broth, onion, garlic, and cilantro, if using, in batches, if necessary, and blend 20 to 30 seconds, stopping once to scrape down the bowl. Transfer the sauce to a saucepan, add the salt, and cook over medium heat, stirring frequently, for 5 minutes, until heated through.

4. Stir in the remaining 1½ cups chicken broth and simmer until the sauce is thickened, about 10 minutes. Remove from the heat and keep warm while making the enchiladas.

5. Make the enchiladas: In the Dutch oven, combine the chicken, water, cayenne, and 1 teaspoon salt and bring to a boil over medium heat. Cover and simmer for 35 minutes, or until the chicken is cooked through but still tender. Remove the chicken and save the broth for another use. Let the chicken cool, skin and bone it, and pull the meat into shreds.

6. In a large skillet, cook the onions, garlic, and the jalapeño peppers in 1 tablespoon of the oil, stirring often, about 5 minutes, or until softened. Remove the pan from the heat, add the chicken and cilantro, and combine. Stir in 1 cup of the shredded cheese and the sour cream; combine well and add salt to taste, if desired.

7. Heat the remaining canola oil in a medium skillet until hot. Fry the tortillas, 1 at a time, for 3 to 5 seconds a side. Drain on paper towels.

8. Preheat the oven to 400 degrees F.

9. To assemble the dish: Dip each tortilla into the salsa verde, coating both sides. Place ⅓ to ½ cup of the chicken filling across the lower third of each tortilla and roll it up. Place, seam side down, in the baking dish. Repeat with the remaining tortillas and filling. Top the rolled tortillas with the remaining sauce, spreading it to cover them. Sprinkle with the remaining 1 cup cheese. Cover the dish tightly with foil and bake for 30 minutes.

. . . I probably could've done without the "look of ecstasy" Rambam had described in Stephanie's eyes when the redhead [a fellow student in Winnie Katz's dance class] was helping her adjust her leg on the ballet bar. She was playing a part, I reminded myself, but had the look of ecstasy really been necessary? I knew Stephanie better than almost anybody and I'd only seen a look of ecstasy in her eyes on one occasion. That had been the night at McGovern's several years back. We'd just finished eating a killer-bee Chicken McGovern and we'd found an old recipe from a dead gangster named Leaning Jesus, which had turned out to be a map that would supposedly lead us to Al Capone's buried treasure. We were walking back home through the glittering streets of the Village when Stephanie'd grabbed me by the lapels of my jacket and shouted: "And I get a third, right?" It was when I said "Yes" that the look of ecstasy had come into her eyes.

In this life, I reflected, it's probably better not to look too deeply into people's eyes or into their motivations. Take any look of ecstasy you can get and don't ask questions. The answers are bound to eventually come whether you want them or not.

—*SPANKING WATSON*

EAT, DRINK, AND BE KINKY

SON OF CHICKEN McGOVERN

SERVES 3 (AND DOUBLES EASILY)

EQUIPMENT NEEDED: LARGE HEAVY-BOTTOMED SKILLET; DEEP-FAT
THERMOMETER

THE BUTTERMILK SOAK
1 cup low-fat or fat-free buttermilk
¼ cup whole-grain mustard
2 large garlic cloves, minced
½ teaspoon Worcestershire sauce
½ teaspoon hot pepper sauce, or to taste
½ teaspoon sea salt
¼ teaspoon white pepper

One 3-pound chicken, cut into 8 pieces, separating thighs and legs

THE SEASONED FLOUR
1 cup all-purpose flour
1 teaspoon celery salt
1 teaspoon cayenne
1 teaspoon paprika
1 teaspoon garlic powder
1 teaspoon onion powder
1 teaspoon poultry seasoning
½ teaspoon white pepper
½ teaspoon lemon pepper

½ cup canola oil

1. Make the buttermilk soak: In a medium bowl, combine the buttermilk, mustard, garlic, Worcestershire, hot pepper sauce, salt, and pepper until blended. Arrange the chicken pieces in a shallow dish. Pour the buttermilk soak over it, and turn to coat. Cover and marinate in the refrigerator for at least 2 hours or overnight. Drain.

2. Make the seasoned flour: In a large plastic bag, combine the flour, celery salt, cayenne, paprika, garlic powder, onion powder, poultry seasoning, and peppers.

3. Add the chicken, a few pieces at a time, to the seasoned flour, and coat well.

4. Preheat the oven to 350 degrees F.

5. Heat the canola oil in the skillet until the deep-fat thermometer reaches 375 degrees F. Carefully add the chicken to the skillet, a few pieces at a time, and fry, turning it, until golden and crusty all over, about 5 minutes. Transfer to the paper towels to drain. Cook the second batch.

6. Arrange the fried chicken on a baking pan and bake for 20 to 25 minutes, or until cooked and crispy. Serve and watch the pieces disappear.

To be totally fair to McGovern, he had many rare, human, almost Christlike qualities. How a guy like that ever wound up in New York was another question. . . . McGovern was there when you needed him. Unfortunately, McGovern was also there when you didn't need him.

—*THE LOVE SONG OF J. EDGAR HOOVER*

CORONATION CURRIED CHICKEN SALAD WITH YOGURT SAUCE

SERVES 6

EQUIPMENT NEEDED: PARCHMENT PAPER

THE CHICKEN

¼ cup peanut oil

Juice of 1 lime

2 tablespoons curry powder, or to taste

1 tablespoon chili powder

2 garlic cloves, smashed and minced

1 chunk (1 inch) fresh ginger, peeled and minced

Salt and freshly ground black pepper

2 pounds chicken tenders or 2 large whole chicken breasts, cut into thumb-sized slivers, skinned, and boned

YOGURT SAUCE

1½ cups nonfat plain yogurt

½ cup nonfat mayonnaise

½ cup curried fruit chutney, such as curried peach, mango, or lime (available in Indian markets and some supermarkets)

1 tablespoon chopped cilantro

Grated zest of 2 limes, plus the juice of 1 lime

Salt and freshly ground black pepper

SALAD

1 head romaine, broken into bite-size pieces

2 stalks celery or 1 celery heart, chopped

1 small red onion, diced

1 orange, peeled, pith removed, and sectioned

1 Granny Smith or Fuji apple, cored and sliced

1 cup chopped cilantro, or to taste (optional)

1. Preheat the oven to 375 degrees F. Line a shallow baking pan with the parchment paper.

2. Prepare the chicken: In a small bowl, combine the peanut oil, lime juice, curry powder, chili powder, garlic, ginger, and salt and pepper to taste until it is a paste. Coat the chicken pieces with the paste and place on the prepared baking pan. Bake 15 minutes, or until the juices run clear when tested. Remove and let cool. If using breasts, slice into 1-inch-wide strips.

3. While the chicken cooks, make the yogurt sauce: In a small bowl, blend together the yogurt, mayonnaise, chutney, cilantro, and lime zest and juice. Season with salt and pepper. Pour half of the sauce into a squeeze bottle and set aside.

4. Make the salad: On a serving platter, gently toss together the romaine, celery, onion, orange, and apple.

5. To serve, spoon a little of the yogurt sauce over the salad greens; top with the chicken and spoon the remaining sauce over it. Garnish with the cilantro, if using. Serve.

A trail may be old and a trail may be cold, but any trail at all beats wandering around this Grand Central Station of a world with a busted valise searching for someone who's never there.

—BLAST FROM THE PAST

EAT, DRINK, AND BE KINKY

CAJUN CHICKEN NUGGET SALAD

MAKES 60 PIECES

EQUIPMENT NEEDED: NONSTICK BAKING PAN (13 x 9 x 2 INCHES); BLENDER

Vegetable cooking spray (for pan)
1 envelope (1 ounce) onion soup mix or onion-mushroom soup mix (.9 ounce)
½ cup bread crumbs (Panko, if available)
1½ teaspoons chili powder
1 teaspoon cumin seeds, toasted and ground
1 teaspoon fresh thyme leaves
¼ teaspoon cayenne pepper
2 pounds skinless boneless chicken breasts or thighs, or both, cut into chunks
3 tablespoons canola oil
1 head romaine lettuce, torn into large pieces
Assorted mustards, for serving

1. Preheat the oven to 350 degrees F. Lightly spray the baking pan with vegetable cooking spray.

2. In the blender, blend the soup mix, bread crumbs, chili powder, cumin, thyme, and cayenne until combined well. Pour onto a sheet of waxed paper or a plate.

3. Roll the chicken, a few pieces at a time, on all sides in the seasoned crumbs and place in a single layer on the prepared baking pan. Drizzle with the oil. Bake 20 minutes, or until just cooked through.

4. Meanwhile, line a platter with the romaine, put the hot chicken nuggets on top, and serve with the mustards.

You don't see people's testicles hanging out of their bathing suits much anymore. Styles have changed, people have changed, the world's a different kind of place, they say. Instead of looking up at things we now spend most of our time looking down on them. Another reason we don't have Danny Rosenthal's testicle to kick around anymore is that people don't appear to have any balls these days. Balls, like imagination, seem to shrivel with age.

—*ROADKILL*

EAT, DRINK, AND BE KINKY

DWIGHT YOAKAM'S STEWED SQUIRREL WITH GRAVY AND FRIED APPLES

SERVES 2

EQUIPMENT NEEDED: SOURCE FOR DRESSED SQUIRREL; STEWPOT;
   LARGE CAST-IRON SKILLET

2 squirrels, dressed and cut into pieces (see note)
1 large onion, chopped
½ teaspoon salt
Freshly ground black pepper

THE FRIED APPLES
1 tablespoon extra-virgin olive oil or unsalted butter
6 McIntosh or Winesap apples, peeled, cored, and quartered
⅓ cup pure maple syrup or honey

THE GRAVY
3 tablespoons all-purpose flour
2½ cups nonfat milk
Salt and freshly ground black pepper

1. In the stewpot, combine the squirrels, onion, 2 cups of water, salt, and pepper to taste. Bring the water to a boil and simmer 1 hour, or until the meat is tender.

2. While the meat is stewing, make the fried apples: Heat the oil in the skillet over moderate heat until hot. Add the apples, turning to coat them, cover the skillet, and cook for 5 minutes. Pour in the maple syrup, stir to coat, and cook the apples, turning them occasionally, for 10 minutes. Keep warm.

3. Make the gravy: Remove the squirrel meat from the pot and keep warm, covered, on a platter. In a cup, stir the flour and ½ cup of the milk into a paste. Bring the cooking liquid in the stewpot back to a boil, add the remaining 2 cups of milk and the flour paste, and cook, stirring constantly, until the gravy is thickened to the desired consistency.

4. Serve the squirrel with the gravy and fried apples and mashed potatoes (see Mashed Potato Topping, p. 114, Shepherd's Pie).

NOTE: If you don't have an immediate source for dressed squirrel, try making this with rabbit pieces instead. Rabbit will be a lot easier to find. It even comes frozen.

"Hello," she said very briskly. Sounded like she was in a hurry to set up a tripod. Like she had to rush to catch something before it went away. I was used to that. All photographers sounded that way. Except the ones who worked for the morgue. . . .

"Who is this?" she asked. I wasn't Professor Higgins, but her accent sounded good to me.

"F. Stop Fitzgerald," I said. Thought I'd try a lighthearted approach.

—*A CASE OF LONE STAR*

WILL HOOVER'S BACHELOR'S DELIGHT, WASHED DOWN WITH TROPICAL PEACHY (AKA KINKY COLADA)

SERVES 1 MISBEGOTTEN SOUL

BACHELOR'S DELIGHT
1 can Campbell's Pork and Beans
Squirt catsup
Onion powder
Garlic powder
1 hot dog

1. Open can of beans. Add catsup and onion and garlic powders.

2. Stick hot dog in middle of beans, in can. Place can directly on stove burner.

3. Heat for 2 minutes, no more. Cool can so that you can handle it. Eat directly from can.

TROPICAL PEACHY

EQUIPMENT NEEDED: BLENDER

2 just-ripened medium peaches, peeled and pitted
1 apple, peeled, cored, and cut into chunks
1 banana, cut into chunks
½ cup chopped peeled ripe mango
1 can (6 ounces) frozen passion fruit concentrate or frozen pink lemonade
  concentrate
3 jiggers (6 ounces) vodka (optional)
1 jigger (2 ounces) rum, Palo Viejo, if possible
1 jigger (2 ounces) Triple Sec
1 cup crushed ice

In the blender, combine the peaches, apple, banana, mango, and concentrate and blend until pureed. Add the vodka, if using, rum, Triple Sec, and ice and blend for 1 minute. Do not overblend. Pour into the biggest Tom Collins glass you can find.

At Big Wong's all the waiters kept asking me, "Where Ratso?" I told them, "He turned gay." They all laughed and said, "Chee-Chee! Chee-Chee!" This, indeed, lent some degree of credence to the theory that they believed Ratso and I were homosexual lovers. What Chinese waiters, lesbian dancers, Nazis in Canada, or anybody else might think should never bother you too much. It is, however, just another good reason to keep your tailbone curved under.

—*SPANKING WATSON*

EAT, DRINK, AND BE KINKY

LARRY ("RATSO") SLOMAN'S BIG WONG DREAM

EQUIPMENT NEEDED: CHOPSTICKS, OR STURDY FORK

4 tablespoons green Big Wong ginger sauce
1 order Big Wong wonton soup
2-liter bottle Diet Cherry Coke
1 order Big Wong spareribs (lean, if available)
1 tablespoon Chinese mustard
1 container Big Wong Roast Pork with Scrambled Egg, with white rice
1 copy Daniel Ortega's 1986 speech on the Sandinista economy

1. Unholster chopsticks. Place green sauce in small bowl, soup in a second large bowl, clean, if available. Pour Coke over ice, keep at the ready.

2. Spear wonton soup noodles, dip into mustard or green sauce. Open mouth, insert. When noodles are finished, bring bowl to mouth, slurp noisily.

3. Dab ribs into mustard before eating.

4. Empty container of roast pork with scrambled egg on clean plate. Mix with white rice. Use remaining mustard to taste.

It is a troubling but true phenomenon of life that people who, for whatever the reason, possibly through no fault of their own, have assumed animal names, invariably find them impossible to shed for all eternity. So if you are indeed saddled with one of these names, you may consort with the Rockefellers, but you will forever be a Ratso.

—*GOD BLESS JOHN WAYNE*

SpIced Roast pork Tenderloin with Sweet Corn Cream Sauce

SERVES 6

EQUIPMENT NEEDED: BROILER PAN WITH RACK; BLENDER

THE SPICE PASTE

4 large garlic cloves, minced

2 tablespoons chopped fresh oregano

2 tablespoons chopped flat-leafed parsley

2 tablespoons finely ground coffee grounds

2 teaspoons ground cinnamon

1 teaspoon ground allspice

1 teaspoon freshly ground black pepper

1 teaspoon cayenne

1 teaspoon sea salt

2 pork tenderloins, ¾ to 1 pound each, trimmed of fat and silver skin removed

THE SALAD

1 tablespoon fresh orange juice

1 tablespoon extra-virgin olive oil

1 tablespoon white wine vinegar

2 oranges, peel, white pith removed, and diced

1 medium red onion, diced

¼ teaspoon crushed red pepper flakes, or to taste

THE SWEET CORN CREAM SAUCE

2 tablespoons canola oil or unsalted butter

½ Vidalia or other sweet onion, finely chopped

1 large garlic clove, minced

1 carrot, peeled and diced

1 celery stalk, diced

1½ cups fresh corn kernels stripped from the cobs (about 3 large) or frozen corn, thawed

Pinch of saffron (optional)

1 small thyme sprig, stem trimmed

¼ cup minced flat-leafed parsley
2 cups half-and-half or whole milk
Salt and freshly ground black pepper

1. Make the spice paste: In a small bowl, blend the garlic, oregano, parsley, coffee, cinnamon, allspice, black pepper, cayenne, and salt into a paste. Rub the paste all over both pork tenderloins, wrap in plastic wrap, and refrigerate at least 2 hours or overnight.

2. Preheat the oven to 350 degrees F.

3. Place the tenderloins on the rack of the broiler pan and roast 45 to 50 minutes, or until a meat thermometer inserted in the thickest part of the meat reaches 170 degrees F. Transfer the tenderloins to a platter and let stand, loosely covered, 10 minutes.

4. While the pork is roasting, make the salad and sweet corn cream sauce: In a medium bowl, combine the orange juice, oil, vinegar, oranges, onion, and pepper flakes. Cover and let stand at room temperature.

5. Make the sweet corn cream sauce: Heat the oil in a medium saucepan over moderate heat until hot. Add the onion, garlic, carrot, and celery, and cook, stirring, about 5 minutes, or until softened. Lower the heat to moderately low and add the corn and saffron, if using. Stir in the thyme, parsley, and half-and-half and heat until hot. Transfer the mixture to a blender and puree. Add salt and pepper to taste and reheat, if necessary.

6. To serve: Slice the tenderloins across the grain. Serve topped with the sweet corn cream sauce and a little of the salad as a garnish on the side.

Lenny Bruce possibly lived his life in the truest imitation of Christ the world has ever seen. He was skinny, he was Jewish, he was misunderstood, and he fully grasped the nobility of suffering. In death, as well as life, Lenny continued his conscious campaign to be cryptically Christ-like. Jesus died nailed to a cross between Dismas and Barabbas, two thieves. Bruce died on a toilet with a needle in his arm. Between the gutter and the stars, the windmill and the world, the commode and the cross, there has never been a noticeably significant spiritual difference.

—SPANKING WATSON

CRIMSON BABY BACK RIBS

MAKES 4 LARGE MAIN-COURSE SERVINGS

EQUIPMENT NEEDED: LARGE BAKING PAN WITH RACK

THE RIBS
4 pounds baby back ribs, with membrane that runs across back of ribs removed

¼ cup soy sauce

Freshly ground black pepper

THE SAUCE
1 cup Alizé Red Passion (a liqueur of cognac, passion fruit, and cranberries, available in most liquor stores)

1 cup orange juice

½ cup honey

¼ cup fresh lemon juice (about 2 lemons)

¼ cup red wine vinegar

¼ cup extra-virgin olive oil

3 garlic cloves, chopped

1 medium onion, diced

1 cinnamon stick

Salt and freshly ground black pepper

1. Preheat the oven to 350 degrees F.

2. Make the ribs: Put the ribs in a large pot; cover them with water, and bring to a boil. Parboil for 5 minutes. Drain and let stand until cool enough to handle. Rub the ribs with the soy sauce and pepper to taste and put on the rack in the baking pan. Bake for 60 to 90 minutes until fork-tender.

3. While the ribs are baking, make the sauce: In a medium saucepan, combine the Alizé Red Passion, orange juice, honey, lemon juice, vinegar, olive oil, garlic, onion, cinnamon stick, and salt and pepper to taste. Bring to a boil and simmer 15 minutes. Remove the cinnamon stick.

4. To serve: Transfer the sauce to a serving bowl, and put the ribs on a platter. Serve the ribs topped with the sauce.

Like an unfulfilled, lonely housewife, I began clearing away the glasses and dishes and the general detritus of other people's happy experiences. I offered the cat a portion of a half-eaten pork pie that had been part of a large feast Pete Myers had apparently catered from his British gourmet shop, Myers of Keswick on Hudson Street. With a slight mew of distaste, the cat demurred. Cat's realize that, of all man's many follies, the notion that there may exist such a thing as British gourmet cooking rises right to the top of the litter.

—*ROADKILL*

EAT, DRINK, AND BE **KINKY**

MICK BRENNAN'S TOAD IN THE HOLE

SERVES 2

1 pound pork sausage links (preferably Myers of Keswick's)
2 teaspoons canola oil
1 medium onion, diced
¼ cup all-purpose flour
¼ teaspoon salt
¼ teaspoon freshly ground black pepper
½ cup milk
½ cup water
2 large egg whites

1. Prick the sausage links with a fork, then cook them in a medium ovenproof skillet over medium-high heat, turning, until lightly browned all over, about 5 minutes. Transfer to paper towels to drain.

2. Wipe the fat out of the skillet. Add the canola oil and heat until hot. Add the onion and cook, stirring occasionally, until softened and golden in color. Remove the pan from the heat.

3. Preheat the oven to 400 degrees F.

4. In a medium bowl, combine the flour, salt, and pepper and make a well in the mixture. In a small bowl, combine the milk and water; add the liquid to the flour mixture, right in the well, and stir with a fork until a batter forms.

5. In another bowl, beat the egg whites until soft peaks form. Fold the egg whites into the batter.

6. Return the cooked sausages to the skillet and pour in the batter. Bake for 20 minutes, or until nicely browned and puffy. Serve at once.

When there's no cards left to play, . . . even destiny can't shuffle the deck.

—*GOD BLESS JOHN WAYNE*

ROAST PORK BURRITOS

SERVES 4

EQUIPMENT NEEDED: LARGE NONSTICK SKILLET

THE ROAST PORK

3 large garlic cloves, minced

1 tablespoon chopped fresh thyme or 2 teaspoons dried

1 tablespoon chopped fresh oregano or 2 teaspoons dried, crushed

2 tablespoons packed light or dark brown sugar

1½ teaspoons chili powder

1 teaspoon cumin seeds, toasted and ground

¼ cup fresh lime juice (about 3 limes)

Sea salt and freshly ground black pepper

1 pound pork tenderloin, trimmed of fat and silver skin, if any, removed

THE BURRITOS

4 fat-free flour tortillas

8 whole extra-large eggs or 12 extra-large egg whites and 2 whole extra-large
  eggs

Sea salt and freshly ground black pepper

1 teaspoon cumin seeds, toasted and ground (optional)

Pinch of chili powder (optional)

1 cup Ranchero Salsa (p. 77)

1 cup grated low-fat jalapeño Jack or other grating cheese

¼ cup chopped cilantro

1. Preheat the oven to 350 degrees F. Oil a medium shallow baking dish.

2. Make the roast pork: In a small bowl, stir together the garlic, thyme, oregano, sugar, chili powder, cumin, lime juice, and salt and pepper to taste. Rub the mixture over the pork. Tie the loin with kitchen twine, cover, and refrigerate 20 minutes. Put the pork loin in the prepared baking dish and roast 25 minutes, or until a meat thermometer reaches an internal temperature of 170 degrees F. Remove and let stand for 15 minutes. Cut into strips, then dice. Cover and keep warm.

3. Make the burritos: Warm the tortillas in the oven or in a large skillet until lightly speckled but still soft and pliable.

4. Meanwhile, in the large nonstick skillet, scramble the eggs with the salt and pepper and cumin and chili powder, if desired, over low heat. Keep warm.

5. To assemble: Place a warm tortilla on each plate. Top with a dollop, about a ¼ cup, of the salsa. Add one quarter of the scrambled eggs and pork. Sprinkle the cheese on top. Roll up the tortilla and top with more cheese, if desired, and some cilantro. Serve.

I wondered if I'd always be a party of one. I wondered if I'd be an old man with a bow tie sitting alone on New Year's Eve looking out the window of some little restaurant at two dogs hosing on the sidewalk. That was certainly something to look forward to.

—FREQUENT FLYER

SHepHerd's Pie

SERVES 8

EQUIPMENT NEEDED: LARGE HEAVY-BOTTOMED SKILLET; 2-QUART
   BAKING DISH

THE FILLING

2 pounds lean ground lamb

1 large white onion, chopped

2 garlic cloves, minced

2 carrots, peeled, julienned, then diced

2 tablespoons chopped fresh oregano or 1 tablespoon dried

2 tablespoons chopped fresh thyme or 1 tablespoon dried

2 tablespoons chopped flat-leafed parsley

Salt and freshly ground black pepper

½ cup all-purpose flour

2 tablespoons dry red wine

1 tablespoon balsamic vinegar

2 cups lamb stock if you happen to have some on hand, otherwise use chicken
   stock

½ cup tomato paste

2 tablespoons Worcestershire sauce

2 cups fresh or frozen small peas

THE MASHED POTATO TOPPING

4 medium Yukon gold or russet potatoes (1½ pounds), peeled and cut into
   chunks

1 teaspoon salt, or to taste

4 tablespoons (½ stick) unsalted butter, softened, or canola oil

1 cup nonfat milk

2 tablespoons freshly grated Parmigiano-Reggiano cheese

1. Make the filling: In the large skillet, without any oil at all, cook
the lamb over moderate heat, in batches if necessary, breaking up the
lumps with the side of a wooden spoon, until browned, about 7 minutes. Drain the lamb in a colander set over a bowl. Defat the meat
juices; discard the fat and reserve the cooking juices. Without wiping
out the skillet, return it to the heat and sauté the onion, garlic, and

carrots with the oregano, thyme, and parsley, stirring, for 3 or 4 minutes, until the vegetables are softened.

2. Add the cooked lamb and defatted juices to the skillet. Season to taste with salt and pepper. When the cooking juices have all but evaporated, add the flour, stirring constantly to incorporate. Add the wine, vinegar, and stock, stirring to blend. When the sauce thickens, stir in the tomato paste and Worcestershire sauce; reduce the heat to low and cook slowly, tasting and adjusting the seasonings, for 15 minutes.

3. Remove the skillet from the heat and add the peas. Cover and keep warm.

4. Make the topping: Put the potatoes in a large saucepan and cover them with cold water. Bring to a boil, add the salt, and reduce the heat to moderate. Boil the potatoes gently, about 15 minutes, until they can be easily pierced with a fork. Drain and return to the pan. Add 2 tablespoons of the butter and the milk and mash the potatoes with a potato masher.

5. Preheat the oven to 350 degrees F. Lightly oil the baking dish. Melt the remaining 2 tablespoons butter.

6. Ladle the lamb mixture into the prepared baking dish. Using a spatula, spread the mashed potatoes over the filling to cover it in an even layer. Brush the potatoes with the melted butter and sprinkle with the cheese. Bake 1 hour, or until top is golden and crusty. Let stand 10 minutes before serving.

I'd been reading the *Houston Chronicle* while eating a prime rib. Flipping the pages, I saw a small head of Kirk Douglas, a small head of the football player The Boz, and then suddenly a big head of myself. This, as you can imagine, gave me rather a big head myself, and I quickly swallowed a large piece of prime rib in my excitement to show the pic to Rambam.

As I looked admiringly at the big head of Kinky I could feel the meat lodge firmly in my throat in such a way that I couldn't speak, or gurgle, or even make the usual choking sounds. When you can't make choking sounds it's a pretty good bet you're choking to death. My first thought, of course, was of Mama Cass. My second was that choking to death because you got so excited when you looked in a newspaper and saw that your own head was bigger than Kirk Douglas's or Brian Bosworth's could trap you in your vanity forever and become the thing you were forever known for, as it had, undoubtedly, with Mama Cass eating a ham sandwich, or Nelson Rockefeller hosing his secretary. People rarely give a damn who you are or what kind of a life you've lived, but if you choke to death celebrating the fact that a photo of your head is bigger than Kirk Douglas's or Brian Bosworth's, that's the kind of news folks can really get their teeth into.

—*SPANKING WATSON*

PeTe MeYeRS'S ROAST BeeF WiTH PeARL ONiONS AND SPUDS AND MeRLOT SAUCe

SERVES 6

EQUIPMENT NEEDED: DEEP-FAT THERMOMETER

THE PEARL ONIONS AND SPUDS
12 pearl onions

2 cups canola oil, plus additional for brushing potatoes

4 large baking potatoes, scrubbed

2 tablespoons Dijon mustard

1 teaspoon caraway seeds, toasted and chopped

Salt and freshly ground black pepper

THE ROAST BEEF
One 4- to 5-pound boneless sirloin tri-tip roast (also known as a silver tip roast)

2 tablespoons Lawry's Seasoned Salt

Freshly ground black pepper

THE MERLOT SAUCE
¼ cup sugar

¼ cup water

¼ cup red wine vinegar

1 tablespoon canola oil

1 medium onion, diced (about 1 cup diced)

2 cups Merlot

2 cups chicken stock

1. Preheat the oven to 425 degrees F.

2. Blanch the onions in a small saucepan of boiling salted water for about 3 minutes. Drain, cool, and peel, leaving the skin at root ends intact. Pat the onions dry.

3. Heat the 2 cups of oil in a heavy saucepan over moderately high heat to 375 degrees F on the deep-fat thermometer. Carefully add the onions, in batches, to the hot oil and fry them until crisp and brown, about 3 minutes. Remove to paper towels and drain.

4. Slice the potatoes lengthwise into ½-inch pieces. Brush generously with the canola oil, then with the mustard. Sprinkle with the caraway seeds and salt and pepper to taste. Arrange the pieces in a single layer on a baking pan and roast, turning once, about 35 minutes, or until golden brown. Remove and keep warm, loosely covered.

5. Reduce the oven temperature to 350 degrees F.

6. Prepare the roast beef: Rub the roast all over with the seasoned salt and pepper to taste. Place on a rack in a roasting pan and add enough water to the pan to just touch the bottom of the roast. Roast 20 minutes per pound—80 to 100 minutes, depending upon the size— plus another 20 minutes for medium rare. Meat thermometer inserted in thickest part of beef should read 140 degrees F. Remove and let stand about 10 minutes, loosely covered.

7. Make the Merlot sauce: In a heavy small saucepan, combine the sugar with the water; bring to a boil and boil 5 minutes. Remove the pan from the heat and very carefully pour the vinegar down the side of the pan. Return the pan to the heat and cook over moderate heat about 5 minutes. Set aside.

8. Heat the oil in a heavy medium saucepan until hot. Add the onion and cook, stirring, about 5 minutes, or until golden brown. Add the wine and simmer until it is reduced to 1 cup. Stir in the stock and simmer over high heat about 10 minutes, until the sauce is reduced to about 2 cups. Remove the pan from the heat and stir in the caramel-vinegar mixture until combined. Pour the sauce through a sieve into a bowl for serving. The sauce may be made one day ahead, cooled, and stored, covered, in the refrigerator. Reheat over moderate heat before serving.

9. While the sauce is reducing, reheat the onions and potatoes in a preheated 300 degree F. oven for 10 minutes or so. Slice the beef. Make sure the Merlot sauce is well heated. Serve this swell dinner.

There is, of course, a very thin line between laughing and choking to death. . . . The only difference is that if you're only laughing you'll eventually stop, but if you're truly choking to death, you'll go on laughing forever.

—ARMADILLOS & OLD LACE

EAT, DRINK, AND BE KINKY

BEEF FAJITAS WITH SALSA

SERVES 2

THE SALSA
¾ pound plum tomatoes (about 5), diced
3 tablespoons chopped cilantro or flat-leafed parsley
1 large garlic clove, minced
1 tablespoon balsamic vinegar
Pinch of crushed red pepper flakes

THE FAJITAS
6 ounces flank steak or sirloin steak, trimmed and cut into strips about 1½
    inches long and ¼ inch thick
1⅔ cups sliced onion (about 1 large)
1 teaspoon ground cumin
4 cups chopped red and yellow bell peppers (about 4 medium)
Salt and freshly ground black pepper
4 fat-free tortillas, preferably whole wheat, or plain (7 inches in diameter)
½ cup plain nonfat yogurt
¼ cup chopped ripe avocado

1. Make the salsa: In a glass bowl, combine the tomatoes, cilantro, garlic, vinegar, and pepper flakes. Cover and set aside at room temperature for 1 hour.

2. Preheat the oven to 350 degrees F.

3. Make the fajitas: In a large nonstick skillet, without any oil at all, sear the beef over high heat, tossing, for about 4 minutes. Add the onion, cumin, and peppers and cook, tossing, until the vegetables are soft but crunchy, about 3 to 4 minutes. Add salt and pepper to taste.

4. While the filling is cooking, wrap the tortillas in aluminum foil and heat them for about 10 minutes, until warmed.

5. To serve: Spoon about a quarter of the beef filling over each hot tortilla. Add a quarter of the yogurt and avocado to each and top with a big dollop of the salsa. Roll up the tortillas and serve. Serve the remaining salsa on the side.

There are times when you feel close to God and times when you don't and there are times when the two of you need to get away from each other for a while.

—*THE LOVE SONG OF J. EDGAR HOOVER*

EAT, DRINK, AND BE KINKY

WATSON'S BEEF SATAYS WITH KINKY PEANUT SAUCE

SERVES 4

EQUIPMENT NEEDED: 4 SKEWERS; BROILER PAN

KINKY PEANUT SAUCE (MAKES ABOUT 1 CUP)

3 tablespoons hoisin sauce

2 tablespoons peanut butter (preferably chunky)

1 tablespoon honey (preferably Tupelo) or aspartame

1 tablespoon peanut oil

2 tablespoons minced garlic

3 tablespoons coconut milk

¼ cup roughly crushed roasted peanuts

1 teaspoon chili sauce (available in Asian markets), or to taste (optional)

THE SATAYS

1½ pounds boneless well-trimmed sirloin, cut into 1-inch cubes

1 tablespoon freshly grated lemon zest

2 teaspoons ground turmeric

2 teaspoons ground cumin

2 teaspoons fennel seeds, ground

1 teaspoon salt

1. Make Kinky peanut sauce: In a small bowl, stir together the hoisin sauce, peanut butter, honey, and 3 tablespoons water until combined. Heat the oil in a small saucepan over moderate heat until hot, add the garlic, and cook it, stirring, for 1 minute. Do not let burn. Add the hoisin mixture, stirring, until combined, and cook about 1 minute. Reduce the heat to low and stir in the coconut milk. Stir in the peanuts and chili sauce, if using; cover and keep the sauce warm.

2. Preheat the broiler.

3. Prepare the satays: Put the beef in a medium bowl. In a small bowl, combine the zest, turmeric, cumin, fennel seeds, and salt. Rub the spice mixture onto the cubes of beef.

4. If using wooden skewers, soak covered in water for 20 minutes. Thread the beef evenly among the skewers. Place on the broiler pan and broil for 5 to 6 minutes, turning once or twice, to brown on all sides, or until cooked to desired doneness.

5. Serve at once, with the warm peanut sauce spooned over the top.

Whether your destination is heaven or hell, first you have to change planes in Dallas–Fort Worth.

—ARMADILLOS & OLD LACE

MEAT LOAF

SERVES 6 TO 8

EQUIPMENT NEEDED: GLASS OR METAL LOAF PAN (9 x 5 x 3
  INCHES)

3 tablespoons extra-virgin olive oil
1 large Vidalia onion, finely chopped
3 garlic cloves, minced
2 whole scallions, chopped (include some of the green)
1½ pounds lean ground veal
½ pound pork sausage (in bulk)
2 extra-large egg whites
3 tablespoons ketchup
1 cup low-fat or fat-free buttermilk
1 cup bread crumbs (Panko, if available)
¼ cup finely chopped flat-leafed parsley

1. Preheat the oven to 350 degrees F.

2. Heat the olive oil in a small skillet until hot. Add the onion, garlic, and scallions and sauté until softened. Let cool.

3. In a large bowl, work together gently the veal, sausage, onion mixture, egg whites, ketchup, buttermilk, bread crumbs, and parsley until combined. Do not overmix. Put the mixture in the loaf pan, smooth the top, and bake 1 hour, or until the juices run clear. Let stand 10 to 15 minutes before slicing.

f you ever find your sleeping arrangements organized by Uncle Sam, if, say, you're summering at the Federal Correctional Institution at Lompoc (California), your biggest problem may be mind-numbing boredom.

To fight this creeping ennui, keep busy reading and writing. Also get a hot plate for your cell.

Cooking will help fill up some of your empty time. And any deviation from the biological warfare experiments they call prison meals will be welcomed.

Jailhouse chili is a tradition in most federal prisons south of the Big House in Lewisburg, Pennsylvania. It's easy to prepare, with easy-to-find ingredients. No small consideration when your grocer is named Fingers.

Also, a good diet will help you keep up your strength for those first few stabs at the group showering experience.

For this recipe, if possible, don't cut corners, unless you're in lockdown.

First-class chili ingredients are worth those few extra packs of smokes the kitchen staff will charge you.

—Steve Rambam

STEVE RAMBAM'S
JAILHOUSE CHILI

SERVES 3 OR 4 FELONS

EQUIPMENT NEEDED: HOT PLATE

3 or 4 pounds beef, chopped or ground, or whatever ground meat is available, turkey or chicken

1 or 2 beers, bottles or cans (12 ounces each)

¼ cup canola or other vegetable oil

1 or 2 onions, finely chopped

5 garlic cloves, minced, or 1 tablespoon garlic powder

2 to 4 jalapeño chili peppers (or 2 tablespoons chili powder)

2 tablespoons dried oregano, or 3 tablespoons chopped fresh (optional)

2 tablespoons cumin seeds, toasted and ground

1 or 2 tablespoons paprika

1 teaspoon cayenne, or to taste

Salt and pepper

2 chicken bouillon cubes

2 cans (15½ ounces each) pinto beans

1. Trim the beef of fat, and cut into thumb-sized pieces. If you don't have any thumbs, use your neighbor's for measuring purposes.

2. Marinate the beef in the beer for at least 2 hours. Do not drink the marinade. If there's no beer available and no one is willing to risk bringing it in—you can get two weeks in the Hole if caught with alcohol—use any alcoholic beverage, such as homemade applejack, from your nearest in-house brewery. (If Château de Bubba brewed up a batch of jack with the usual standbys, such as peaches in heavy syrup, adjust the recipe by adding a few extra jalapeños to help neutralize the sweetness of Bubba's Peach Jack.)

3. In a skillet on the hot plate, brown the beef on all sides in the oil. If the meat was gray when you started, try for new meat and start over. Some jailhouse cooks, especially in Texas, like to throw in finely chopped onion while browning the meat. Also, in New York City's

Metropolitan Correctional Center, some of the old-time Guidos drop in garlic here.

4. The appropriate quantities of the ingredients will be determined by experimentation, by your personal taste. For mild chili, use 2 jalapeño peppers; for three-alarm chili, use 4 jalapeños per pound of meat.

5. If a blender is available, put in the peppers and 2 cups of water and puree. If no blender is available, mince the peppers as finely as possible.

6. In a large pot, combine the browned meat, pureed peppers, and the marinade. Bring to a boil and simmer for 45 minutes.

7. Remove the pot from the hot plate and let cool. Begin adding the spices (cumin, paprika, cayenne) when you like—whether to add oregano and how much is your call. Too much and the chili will taste like marinara sauce. Unless your neighbors, like Vinnie the Hook and No-Knuckles Sal, are expected for dinner, go light on the oregano.

8. Return the pot to the hot plate and bring to a boil. Add the bouillon cubes and simmer for 1 hour, or until the meat is tender and the sauce is the consistency you prefer. (If chili is allowed to cool, the fat will rise to the top. If you are a health nut, spoon it off and toss the grease. Frankly, for the best taste, leave it alone. If you want health food, eat a freakin' salad.)

(Tomatoes or tomato sauce help to thicken and extend the chili: Way, way down in Texas or in the Deep South, some cooks like to add corn flour to the chili. I think it makes it taste like a burrito. If you're determined to use this method and you don't have corn flour, Kellogg's Corn Flakes crushed into powder will do the trick.)

9. Drain and rinse the pinto beans. Add to pot.

Remember, before eating, always wash your hands and say your prayers because God and germs are everywhere.

Serve with rice or corn bread, or both.

EAT, DRINK, AND BE KINKY

I called Rambam, a friend of mine in Brooklyn who was a private investigator and a couple of other things. Rambam knew the kind of people most folks only watch on the late-night movies. I liked to think of him as a rather militant Jewish Jim Rockford. He was charming and likable, but there were aspects of his life you didn't want to know about. Could land you in a hospital bed.

—WHEN THE CAT'S AWAY

FRANKIE LASAGNA

SERVES 6

EQUIPMENT NEEDED: BAKING DISH OR LASAGNA PAN (13 x 9 x 2
  INCHES)

10 ounces lean ground beef

4 tablespoons extra-virgin olive oil

8 ounces roasted red peppers (homemade or store bought), chopped

1 large red onion, diced

4 garlic cloves, minced

1 to 2 tablespoons dried oregano, or to taste

1 to 2 tablespoons dried basil, or to taste

2 tablespoons chopped flat-leafed parsley

Salt and freshly ground black pepper

½ cup plus about 1 tablespoon balsamic vinegar

2 pounds plum tomatoes, diced

2 cups homemade or canned tomato sauce

1 container (15 ounces) low-fat ricotta cheese

4 ounces goat cheese

¼ cup nonfat milk

2 pounds mozzarella cheese, grated

1 cup freshly grated Parmigiano-Reggiano cheese

1 package (1 pound) precooked lasagna noodles

1. In a large skillet, without any oil at all, brown the beef over moderate heat, breaking up the lumps with the side of a wooden spoon, for 5 minutes. Drain the beef in a colander set over a bowl. Defat the meat juices; discard the fat and reserve the cooking juices.

2. Add 2 tablespoons of the oil to the skillet and heat until hot. Add the red peppers and half of the onion and cook until softened. Return the beef to the skillet with the reserved cooking juices. Add the garlic, oregano, basil, parsley, salt and pepper to taste, and the ½ cup vinegar and simmer, stirring occasionally, 20 minutes. Transfer to a large bowl and set aside.

3. Heat the remaining 2 tablespoons oil in the skillet and add the remaining onion; cook until softened, about 3 minutes. Add the tomatoes, tomato sauce, and a splash, about 1 tablespoon, more vinegar, and simmer, stirring occasionally, 20 minutes. Stir the tomato mixture into the bowl with the meat until combined.

4. Preheat the oven to 350 degrees F. Oil the baking dish.

5. In a small bowl, stir together the ricotta and goat cheese, and moisten further with the milk. In another small bowl, stir together the mozzarella and Parmesan.

6. Assemble the lasagna: Spread a dollop of the ricotta mixture over the bottom of the prepared baking dish. Arrange a layer of the lasagna noodles on top to cover the bottom of the baking dish. Cover with a layer of the meat mixture. Top with a layer of the ricotta mixture and sprinkle it with a layer of the grated cheese. Repeat the layering, ending with a layer of cheese. (You should have 3 layers.) Bake the lasagna 1 hour, until bubbly and brown on the top. Remove from the oven and let stand 15 to 20 minutes before cutting into squares.

The death of someone close to you is never as much fun as it's cracked up to be. I should know. I've been to that rodeo on a handful of occasions and every time you get thrown it gets a little bit harder for you to pick up your hat and dust it off.

—GOD BLESS JOHN WAYNE

RATSO'S WHITE
CASTLE OMELET

SERVES 6

EQUIPMENT NEEDED: 9-INCH PIE PLATE

2 boxes (9.5 ounces each; or 6 to a box) frozen White Castle burgers with buns,
    thawed
6 slices bacon, cooked until crisp, then crumbled
1 cup shredded low-fat Cheddar or mozzarella cheese
2 whole extra-large eggs
4 extra-large egg whites
1 cup low-fat milk

1. Preheat oven to 350 degrees F. Oil the pie plate.

2. Remove a total of 10 burgers from the boxes; reserve the burgers that remain for eating. Remove the buns on 5 of the burgers, discard the buns, and put 1 of the burgers that remains on top of the patty in each of the remaining burgers. Replace the buns. You now have 10 "double burgers." Quarter each burger; press the pieces into the prepared pie plate to cover the bottom. Sprinkle the bacon and cheese evenly on top.

3. In a medium bowl, whisk together the whole eggs, egg whites, and milk until combined. Pour over the burgers, bacon, and cheese in the pie plate. Bake 35 to 40 minutes, or until set in the middle. Let stand 10 minutes before cutting into wedges and serving.

May I remind you, . . . of the words Naomi Judd told her children as they were growing up: "Wash your hands and say your prayers, 'cause germs and Jesus are everywhere."

—*ELVIS, JESUS & COCA-COLA*

SCALLION SAUCE

MAKES A GENEROUS 1½ CUPS

EQUIPMENT NEEDED: BLENDER

1 cup canola oil, or more, as needed
2 tablespoons Dijon mustard
2 tablespoons fresh lemon juice
1 tablespoon white wine vinegar
2 cups sliced scallions (about 2 bunches)
2 garlic cloves, chopped
½ cup drained capers
2 tablespoons chopped fresh dill
Salt and freshly ground black pepper

1. Combine the oil, mustard, lemon juice, vinegar, scallions, garlic, capers, dill, and salt and pepper to taste in the blender and blend until pureed. Pour the sauce into a bowl and add additional oil to thin it to the desired consistency, if necessary.

2. Serve with grilled ham steaks, chicken, or fish, or as a dipping sauce for artichokes.

"Well, I hate to be the one to take the flyswatter to Tinker Bell, but . . . "

—GREENWICH KILLING TIME

BREADS

As mentor to his kneady fellowmen (and fellowwomen)—
even those who loaf about (**especially** those who loaf
about)—Kinky Friedman has been known, on more than
one occasion, to be the dispenser of bread, sometimes hand-
ing out more dough than a chef in a French bakery. But
whether it's French or Italian, or, if you're so inclined,
Greek you crave, look no further, for on these pages are
displayed a veritable Wonder-ment of breaded delights,
guaranteed to get a rise out of even the most unleavened
among you.

It is a fact of life today that New Yorkers are fast moving out of New York to live in other parts of the country, and, upon arrival in Buttocks, Texas, or Plymouth Rock, . . . they never stop bitching about the absence of things that they never gave a damn about when they lived in New York. While this does not endear them to the locals, it does make people begin to wonder what they might be missing by living in Buttocks, Texas. So they try to accommodate. The result is that today you can get a bagel in Texas, but you can't really get a *bagel* in Texas.

—*FREQUENT FLYER*

BUTTERMILK BISCUITS

MAKES 8 BISCUITS

EQUIPMENT NEEDED: BAKING SHEET

Vegetable cooking spray (for baking sheet)
1½ cups all-purpose flour, plus additional for rolling and cutting
2 teaspoons sugar
2 teaspoons baking powder
½ teaspoon baking soda
½ teaspoon salt
⅔ cup low-fat or fat-free buttermilk
¼ cup canola or corn oil

1. Preheat the oven to 425 degrees F. Spray the baking sheet with vegetable cooking spray.

2. In a large bowl, stir together the flour, sugar, baking powder, baking soda, and salt. Add the buttermilk and oil and stir just until the mixture clears the sides of the bowl. (The mixture will be lumpy.) Do not overmix.

3. Turn the dough out onto a lightly floured surface. With floured hands, pat the dough into a round 6 to 7 inches in diameter and ½ inch thick. With a 2¾-inch biscuit or cookie cutter or the floured rim of an inverted glass, cut out biscuits and put them on the prepared baking sheet, 2 inches apart. Reroll the scraps and cut out more biscuits, flouring the cutter as needed.

4. Bake the biscuits about 10 minutes, or until lightly golden on the top. Serve hot.

When all was said and done, life was very probably a stalemate, I reflected. Like winning or losing a game of chess as you're moving through somebody else's time and space.

—ROADKILL

Beer Bread

You can substitute a 12-ounce bottle of seltzer for the beer if you like.
Of course, it will no longer be beer bread—just a simple,
plain-tasting, likable loaf.

MAKES 1 LOAF

EQUIPMENT NEEDED: LOAF PAN (9 X 5 X 3 INCHES)

3 cups self-rising cake flour
3 tablespoons sugar
1 can (12 ounces) beer
8 tablespoons (1 stick) unsalted butter, melted and divided into thirds

1. Preheat the oven to 375 degrees F. Oil the loaf pan.

2. In a large bowl, whisk together the flour and sugar. Add the beer and beat with a wooden spoon until just lumpy. Do not overmix.

3. Spoon the dough into the prepared pan and smooth the top. Pour one-third of the melted butter over the dough and bake the loaf for 40 minutes. Pour another third of the butter over the dough and bake 10 minutes. Pour the remaining butter over the loaf and bake another 10 minutes. Transfer the pan to a wire rack and let the bread cool for 30 minutes before serving warm.

ulitzer Prize–winning author Frank McCourt was an early Kinky fan. The shy, soft-spoken English teacher had been a faculty member of the besieged New York school system in 1985 when Kinky published his first book, *Greenwich Killing Time*.

At the same time, Frank was just beginning to write his modern classic, *Angela's Ashes*. Like Kinky, Frank was changing horses midstream. After twenty-seven years of riding the range of teaching, Frank was finally putting to paper the stories of his Irish childhood that had so delighted his students.

McCourt won Kinky's attention and affection with stories of his tender youth, and like Kinky, celebrated the pleasures of food in his writing.

Frank McCourt's Food Secrets of the McCourt Blatherhood
(handed down from mother to oldest son)

IRISH TOAST
(a welcome alternative to French Toast and English Muffins)

It is important that the cook-chef/provider observe diligently the
most frequently and most heavily emphasized cooking step here:
Set Aside. To ignore a single "Set Aside" is to court disaster
for this ancient recipe.

EQUIPMENT NEEDED: 8-OUNCE GLASS, 1 SHALLOW GLASS DISH

1 loaf rye bread
1 bottle Irish Whiskey

Place 4 slices of rye toast in toaster.

Toast toasting toast with 2 ounces of the whiskey.

Remove toast from toaster.

Set aside.

Toast the toasted toast with 2 ounces of the whiskey. (This is a separate step. Toasting the toasted toast is not the same as toasting the
toasting toast.)

Take glass and set aside.

In shallow dish, place the 4 slices of toast.

Set aside.

Into the glass pour 4 ounces of the whiskey.

Taste to ensure authenticity.

Set bottle aside.

Gently pour whiskey from the glass over the toast.

Shake gently to ensure the slices are equally saturated. (An un-
saturated morsel will destroy the whole effect.)

Set aside.

In the glass replace the 4 ounces of whiskey. Taste.

Set aside.

Pour additional whiskey from the bottle over the toast. Rock gently to ensure saturation.

Set aside.

Taste whiskey in glass to ensure what was ensured previously.

Set aside.

Place shallow dish with marinating toast in refrigerator.

Gently close refrigerator door.

Set aside.

What?

The refrigerator.

Drink whiskey remaining in glass.

Drink whiskey remaining in bottle.

Retire.

After 12 hours take shallow marinating dish from refrigerator.

With a spatula remove each slice of marinated toast from dish.

Squeeze marinade from toast into glass.

Set aside.

Drink.

Send squeezed marinated slices of toast to a nursing home.

Lick shallow dish.

Set aside.

—Frank McCourt

There's a special way to talk to a beautiful woman, and if you don't know the way, you can be in for an awkward and rather painful experience. You've got to show her that, while you're aware of her obvious beauty, there are other aspects of life that have fascinated you so completely that they've made you the kind of person that you are. You do not live because of her beauty, but yet, you're able to appreciate it. You live to become the first man to circumnavigate Lake Stupid, or to get a government grant to sculpt a skyscraper-sized scrotum, or to shoot and kill one of every kind of animal in the world and stuff their heads with your dreams, or to become a stand-up tragedy, or to write the great Armenian novel, or to wander off into the wilderness or the suburbs until you cease to exist or have to get dressed up to take out the trash, which is pretty much the same thing, or to bake Amish friendship bread or to win many wars and football games for Jesus.

—*SPANKING WATSON*

EAT, DRINK, AND BE KINKY

F. MURRAY ABRAHAM'S JALAPEÑO AND CHEDDAR CORN BREAD

MAKES NINE 3-INCH SQUARES

EQUIPMENT NEEDED: 9-INCH SQUARE BAKING PAN

1 cup yellow cornmeal

2 teaspoons baking soda

1 teaspoon salt

2 whole extra-large eggs or 4 extra-large egg whites, beaten lightly

1 cup nonfat milk or low-fat buttermilk

½ cup canola oil

2 cups fresh corn kernels or 1 can (8 ounces) creamed corn

2 cups shredded low-fat Monterey Jack or sharp Cheddar cheese

1 large red onion, finely diced

About ½ can (2 ounces) chopped canned green chilies (preferably Old El Paso brand)

1. Preheat the oven to 350 degrees F. Lightly oil the baking pan.

2. In a medium bowl, stir together the cornmeal, baking soda, and salt. Add the eggs, milk, oil, corn, cheese, onion, and chilies and combine well.

3. Scrape the batter into the prepared pan, spreading it evenly, and bake 1 hour, or until set. Let stand in the pan on a wire rack for 10 minutes before cutting into 3-inch squares.

New York is like a lady standing in the fog. From one angle she looks like a beautiful young girl. From another, she's a weatherbeaten old whore.

—*FREQUENT FLYER*

BANANA BREAD

MAKES 1 LOAF

EQUIPMENT NEEDED: LOAF PAN (9 X 5 X 3 INCHES)

2 cups all-purpose flour

2 teaspoons baking powder

½ teaspoon salt, or to taste

8 tablespoons unsalted butter (1 stick), softened

1 cup firmly packed light brown sugar

4 extra-large egg whites

1 teaspoon coconut extract

1½ cups mashed ripe bananas (about 3 medium)

1 tablespoon fresh lemon juice

1 cup chopped walnuts or pecans, toasted

8 ounces ripe Brie, at room temperature, for serving (optional)

1. Preheat the oven to 350 degrees F. Butter or oil the loaf pan.

2. In a medium bowl, stir together the flour, baking powder, and salt.

3. In another medium bowl, cream together the butter and brown sugar until fluffy. Add the egg whites and coconut extract and stir until mixed. Stir in the bananas and lemon juice. Add the flour mixture, stirring just until combined. Stir in the nuts.

4. Spoon the batter into the prepared pan, level the top, and bake 45 to 60 minutes, or until a cake tester inserted in the center comes out clean. Transfer the pan to a wire rack and let stand 10 minutes. Remove the loaf from the pan to cool on the rack.

5. Cut the bread into slices. Top with thin slices of Brie, if desired.

"Actually, I have a great many friends," I said, "and they come from all walks of life. If you're a very nice, pleasant person and you always think of others, then if you have a lot of friends, it's practically meaningless. But if you're an eccentric, self-directed sort like I am who voyages through the dark and troubled waters of life and doesn't give a damn about anybody and you still have a lot of friends in spite of all that, that could be seen as a sort of tribute to you."

—*GREENWICH KILLING TIME*

DESSERTS

As the great obese one, Jackie Gleason, used to say, "How sweet it is!" And despite his having stepped on a rainbow and gone to the land of cream puffs and floating meringues, how sweet it remains, for wherever there are overeaters ready to indulge their fancies for desserts, there are pastry chefs and doting mothers ready to tickle them.

Something was eatin' all of us pretty bad, I thought, and we didn't want to admit it either. It was a little thing called life and it probably wasn't going to stop eating us until there was nothing left but a cat pissing on the post-card you left in the secret pocket of your childhood. Yes, ma'am, life was going to eat us all alive, all right. Then it was going to order a crème brûlée and maybe an afterdinner drink. Then it was going to walk the check.

—*ROADKILL*

CINNAMON COFFEE CAKE

MAKES ONE 9-INCH CAKE

EQUIPMENT NEEDED: 9-INCH SPRINGFORM PAN; ELECTRIC MIXER

THE FILLING AND TOPPING
¾ cup chopped walnuts
½ cup packed light brown sugar
½ cup sweetened flaked coconut

THE CAKE
2 cups all-purpose flour
1 teaspoon baking soda
½ cup canola oil
½ cup white sugar or 12 packets aspartame
¼ cup brown sugar
4 extra-large egg whites
8 ounces nonfat sour cream
1 teaspoon vanilla extract
1 teaspoon coconut extract
1 teaspoon ground cinnamon

1. Preheat the oven to 350 degrees F. Lightly oil the springform pan. Cut a round of waxed paper to fit the bottom of the pan, line the pan with it, and oil the paper.

2. Make the filling and topping: Toast the nuts on a small baking sheet for 10 minutes. In a bowl, combine the nuts, brown sugar, and coconut.

3. Make the cake: On a sheet of waxed paper, combine the flour and baking soda. In a medium bowl, with an electric mixer, beat the oil with the white and brown sugars until combined. Add the egg whites, sour cream, extracts, and cinnamon and combine well. Stir in the dry ingredients until blended.

4. Spread half of the batter in the prepared pan. Sprinkle half of the filling over the batter. Top with the remaining batter and sprinkle it with the remaining topping. Bake the cake 65 minutes, or until the edges pull away from the side of the pan. Cool in the pan on a wire rack for 10 minutes. Remove the sides of the pan and cool completely.

Cigars, like love, are often better the second time around.

—*MUSICAL CHAIRS*

EAT, DRINK, AND BE KINKY

Martin Persson's Ginger Pound Cake with Tangerine Sauce

SERVES 8 TO 10

EQUIPMENT NEEDED: LOAF PAN (9 x 5 x 3 INCHES)

THE TANGERINE SAUCE

½ cup sugar or aspartame

2 cups water

1 vanilla bean

1 star anise

½ stick Ceylon cinnamon or 1 to 2 sticks regular cinnamon, or 1 teaspoon ground cinnamon

Pinch of saffron

8 tangerines, preferably seedless, peeled, pith removed, and separated into sections

THE GINGER POUND CAKE

2 tablespoons fine bread crumbs (Panko, if available), for the pan

8 tablespoons (1 stick) unsalted butter, softened, or ½ cup canola oil, plus extra for the pan

1 cup packed dark brown sugar

4 large egg whites

¾ cup low-fat or nonfat sour cream

1¼ cups all-purpose flour

1 tablespoon ground cinnamon

½ teaspoon ground ginger

½ teaspoon ground cloves

1 ripe medium banana, mashed

1 teaspoon baking soda

Vanilla ice cream, for serving

1. Make the tangerine sauce: In a medium saucepan, bring the sugar and water to a boil. Meanwhile, split the vanilla bean lengthwise; with a sharp knife, scrape the seeds in the bean into the sugar syrup. Add the star anise, cinnamon stick, and saffron and simmer for 5 minutes. Let the sauce cool.

2. Pour the cooled sauce over the tangerine segments in a medium bowl. Cover and refrigerate at least 4 hours, or preferably overnight.

3. Make the ginger cake: Preheat the oven to 350 degrees F. Oil the loaf pan and dust with the bread crumbs; shake out the excess.

4. In a large bowl, blend the butter and brown sugar until well combined.

5. In a medium bowl, beat the egg whites until frothy. Add the egg whites to the butter mixture with the sour cream, stirring until incorporated. Stir in the flour, ground cinnamon, ginger, cloves, mashed banana, and baking soda and combine well.

6. Pour the batter into the prepared pan and bake for 50 to 60 minutes, until a bamboo tester inserted in the middle of the loaf comes out clean. Transfer the pan to a wire rack and let cool 20 minutes before serving.

7. Remove the spices from the tangerine sauce. Serve the cake in slices topped with tangerine sauce, with a scoop or two of vanilla ice cream alongside.

"So many ladies," I said to the cat, "so little time."
The cat, of course, said nothing. She was not a Catholic. Too much dogma.
—*SPANKING WATSON*

PINEAPPLE UPSIDE-DOWN CAKE

SERVES 8

EQUIPMENT NEEDED: 9-INCH SPRINGFORM PAN; ELECTRIC
MIXER

THE TOPPING

1 can (20 ounces) crushed pineapple in unsweetened pineapple juice, drained,
reserving ⅓ cup of the juice

1 cup packed dark brown sugar

⅓ cup canola oil

THE CAKE

1¼ cups all-purpose flour

⅔ cup sugar or 16 packets aspartame

2 teaspoons baking soda

1 teaspoon baking powder

½ teaspoon salt

2 extra-large egg whites

½ cup nonfat milk

⅓ cup canola oil or unsalted butter, softened

1 teaspoon vanilla extract

½ teaspoon coconut extract

¼ teaspoon freshly ground mace

1. Preheat the oven to 350 degrees F. Lightly oil the springform pan. Cut a round of waxed paper to fit inside the bottom of the pan; line the pan with the round and oil the round.

2. Make the topping: In a bowl, stir together the pineapple, sugar, and oil. Spread the mixture over the bottom of the pan, distributing the pineapple evenly in the sugar mixture.

3. Make the cake: In a large bowl, stir together the flour, sugar, baking soda, baking powder, and salt.

4. In a medium bowl, stir together the reserved ⅓ cup pineapple juice, egg whites, milk, oil, extracts, and mace. With the electric mixer on low speed, beat the juice mixture into the dry ingredients, beating for 30 seconds. Increase the speed of the mixer to high, and beat for 2 minutes.

5. Pour the batter evenly over the topping in the pan, spreading it evenly, without disturbing the topping. Bake the cake for 50 minutes, or until a cake tester inserted in the cake only comes out clean. Let the cake cool in the pan for 15 minutes. Place a cake plate over the pan and carefully invert the pan. Let the cake settle a minute or two, then release the springform catch. Remove the sides and bottom (now top) of the pan and paper liner, if necessary. Let the cake cool completely on the plate, then serve.

There is something about beautiful, unhappy women that seems to make them particularly soulful as travelling companions. Since life is a journey, not a destination, who rides with you in the Dusty of your dreams can be of lasting, even lingering, importance. Of course, the only woman who might've been more soulful than Bobbie Nelson was Bobby McGee, whom Kris Kristofferson lost on the road in a song. In a vain effort to make up for this enormous spiritual loss, Kris proceeded in the years immediately following to hose everything that moved in the state of California. He was quite successful and among his many conquests, reportedly, was the young Farrah Fawcett, about whom Kris was said to have remarked: "Just enough butt to keep my balls off the bed." But he never found Bobby McGee again. Nobody else ever found her again either. Wherever she is, all we can do is hope that she's happy or, at least, that she never has to do an interview with Barbara Walters.

—ROADKILL

CRUNCHY COCONUT BANANA CAKE

MAKES 1 CAKE

EQUIPMENT NEEDED: BAKING PAN (13 x 9 x 2 INCHES)

THE CAKE
½ cup canola oil
1 cup sweetened flaked coconut
1 cup quick-cooking rolled oats
¾ cup packed dark brown sugar
½ cup all-purpose flour
½ cup chopped nuts, such as walnuts or pecans, toasted
1½ cups mashed ripe bananas (about 3 medium)
½ cup nonfat sour cream
1 whole extra-large egg
6 extra-large egg whites
1 teaspoon vanilla extract
1 teaspoon coconut extract
1 box (18.25 ounces) Betty Crocker or Duncan Hines cake mix for chocolate, yellow, or French vanilla cake

THE FROSTING
3 tablespoons canola oil
3 tablespoons good-quality unsweetened cocoa powder
1½ cups confectioners' sugar
1 teaspoon vanilla extract

1. Preheat the oven to 350 degrees F. Oil and lightly flour the baking pan.

2. Make the cake: In a medium bowl, stir together the oil, coconut, oats, brown sugar, flour, and nuts until combined.

3. In a large bowl, with an electric mixer, beat the bananas, sour cream, whole egg, and egg whites until well blended. Stir in the extracts until combined. Add the cake mix and beat on high for 2 minutes.

4. Spread one-third of the batter in the prepared pan; sprinkle with one-third of the coconut-nut mixture. Repeat layers, ending with a layer of the coconut-nut mixture. Tamp the top layer of coconut gently down into the batter with the back of a metal spatula. Bake the cake for 50 to 60 minutes, or until a cake tester inserted near the center comes out clean.

5. While the cake is baking, make the frosting: In a medium saucepan, combine the oil, 3 tablespoons water, and cocoa powder over low heat, stirring, until the mixture thickens, about 1 minute. Remove the pan from the heat and add the sugar and extract, stirring until smooth. If frosting is too syrupy, add more confectioner's sugar.

6. Remove the cake from the oven and let stand in the pan on a wire rack for 15 minutes.

7. While the frosting is still warm, spread it over the top of the warm cake. Let set and serve.

"Foodies are serious folk," explains Kinky, "but it's okay to have fun with your food, like Albert Finney in *Tom Jones*."

Sandy Wolfmueller remembers Kinky's love of fun with his food *and* his women.

Sandy and her husband, Jon, own and operate Pampell's soda fountain at the foot of Water Street (formerly Ichoupitoulos Street), on the beautiful Guadeloupe River, set down among the hulking hills of Kerrville, Texas.

For more than ninety years, the "thing to do" in Kerrville was "to meet your friends at Pampell's, the sweetest corner in town."

Their soda fountain is considered part of the Western culture. Discovered by the store's founder, John L. Pampell, and his wife, Annie, at the World's Fair in St. Louis in 1904, they hauled it back to Water Street, where it set the stage of a simple, but enchanted world. The soda jerk only had to pull a handle to create sweet, fizzy life out of shapeless matter.

Black Cows (root beer, chocolate syrup, and vanilla ice cream), Brown Cows (Coke, chocolate syrup, and chocolate ice cream), even Purple Cows (grape juice, carbonated water, and vanilla ice cream) lined up in the shimmering Texas sun with Frosty (two scoops of your favorite ice cream blended with your favorite soda), in pastures of Banana or Pineapple Smoothies. Green Rivers and Red Cream sodas flowed along with the perky Dr Pepper.

By Gary Cooper time, Kinky had soaped off the creeping ennui and boarded ol' trusty Dusty, a talking convertible inherited from his mother Min, after she died in May 1985, for the serpentine twenty-two-mile slam-dunk, roller-coaster jaunt over the two-lane seventy-mile-per-hour blacktop that runs from the ranch to town.

At Pampell's Kinky perched on a soda fountain stool, the suburban cowboy at his best, and ordered his favorite—one Banana Split, Kinky-style: One large scoop of Bluebell vanilla ice cream, with a generous dollop of pineapple topping; one large scoop of Bluebell

Chocolate, topped with chocolate sauce; one large scoop of Blue-bell strawberry ice cream, slathered by fresh strawberry topping; and one banana sliced lengthwise to sandwich the ice cream.

"Kinky-style" meant a single dollop of whipped cream on the middle ball of ice cream only. A sprinkle of toasted, crushed pecans covered the boat. Each creamy scoop was finished off with a fire-engine red cherry, stemmed of course.

The Wolfmueller's new best hand, Erin Bailey, stepped up and took Kinky's order, blissfully unaware of what constituted a "Kinky-style" banana split.

Scoop! Splash! Whoosh! Three squirts of mouthwatering whipped cream topped the creation.

You could almost hear a Gene Krupa solo playing out as the triple-dealing Ms. Bailey set out the dish before the single-minded visitor.

Sandy Wolfmueller explains. "Kinky looked down and immediately proceeded to scoop off the excess topping and plop it on the counter while Erin looked on in total disbelief.

"Kinky said to Ms. Bailey, 'Whassamatter, you never seen a rich man eat?' "

Maria Krieger's Peanut-Butter Chocolate-Chip Cheesecake

SERVES 8 TO 10

EQUIPMENT NEEDED: 9-INCH SPRINGFORM PAN; BLENDER OR FOOD
   PROCESSOR

THE CRUST
1 box (12 ounces) vanilla wafers, broken into pieces
½ cup sugar or 12 packets aspartame
2 tablespoons butter, melted, or canola oil, plus additional for pan

THE FILLING
16 ounces (2 cups) nonfat or low-fat cream cheese, at room temperature
1½ cups sugar or aspartame
1 jar (6 ounces) low-fat peanut butter, creamy or chunky
1 whole large egg
8 large egg whites
½ cup nonfat sour cream
2 teaspoons fresh lemon juice
¾ cup semisweet chocolate chips

THE TOPPING
1 cup nonfat sour cream
⅔ cup semisweet chocolate chips, melted
½ cup sugar or aspartame

1. Preheat the oven to 350 degrees F. Lightly oil the bottom and sides of the springform pan.

2. Make the crust: In a blender or food processor, process the vanilla wafers with the sugar and butter until ground into crumbs. Press the crust over the bottom and up the sides of the prepared springform pan.

3. Make the filling: Wash out and dry the blender. In the blender or food processor, combine the cream cheese, sugar, peanut butter, egg, egg whites, sour cream, and lemon juice and blend until smooth.

Add the chocolate chips and pulse the machine for 15 seconds, until the chips are slightly broken up.

4. Pour the filling into the crust and bake until the filling is firm in the center, about 70 minutes. Remove the pan to a wire rack and let stand at room temperature for 15 minutes. Do not turn off the oven.

5. Make the topping: In a medium bowl, stir together the sour cream, melted chocolate chips, and sugar until combined.

6. Spread the topping evenly over the cheesecake and return the cake to the oven; bake 10 minutes. Cool the cake on the wire rack for 20 minutes, then refrigerate for at least 3 hours before serving. Remove the side of the pan before serving.

. . . my kinky little head disappeared in a blue cloud of protective cigar smoke.

—*GOD BLESS JOHN WAYNE*

Einstein and Davy Crockett did not understand women, and there was no particular reason why I should either. No man really knew what went on between the earrings.

—*ELVIS, JESUS & COCA-COLA*

Becky Priour's Buttermilk Pie

MAKES ONE 9-INCH PIE, SERVING 8

EQUIPMENT NEEDED: 9-INCH PIE PLATE

THE CRUST

1⅓ cups all-purpose flour

½ teaspoon salt

⅓ cup canola oil, plus additional if needed

¼ cup low-fat or fat-free buttermilk, chilled

Grated zest of 1 lemon

THE FILLING

4 extra-large eggs

1½ cups sugar or aspartame

2 tablespoons all-purpose flour

½ cup low-fat or fat-free buttermilk, at room temperature

½ cup canola oil

2 teaspoons vanilla extract

1 teaspoon coconut extract

1 teaspoon freshly grated lemon zest

1. Preheat the oven to 425 degrees F.

2. Make the crust: In a large bowl, stir together the flour and salt. Using a fork, stir in the oil, buttermilk, and zest, tossing until a dough forms. (You may need to add additional oil, a teaspoon at a time, to achieve the right consistency.) Shape the dough into a ball. Place the dough between 2 large sheets of waxed paper and roll it into a 12-inch round. Remove the top sheet of waxed paper, then invert the round over pie plate. Center the crust in the plate, if necessary; remove the waxed paper, and press the dough into the plate. Crimp the edge decoratively. Prick the bottom and sides of the crust with a fork. Bake the shell 10 minutes, until golden. Remove the plate to a wire rack and let cool.

3. Make the filling: In a large bowl, with an electric mixer, beat the eggs and sugar until frothy, about 3 minutes. Stir in the flour and but-

termilk until combined. Drizzle in the oil and beat well to incorporate. Stir in the extracts and lemon zest. Pour the filling into the prebaked shell.

4. Bake the pie 10 minutes. Lower the oven temperature to 350 degrees F and bake the pie 45 minutes, or until the filling is just set and turns a deep golden brown. You may need to cover the edges of the crust loosely with strips of aluminum foil to prevent them from browning. Cool the pie on a wire rack. Serve at room temperature. Or refrigerate and serve well chilled.

I was sitting in my loft the day after Christmas smoking a cigar and killing a medicinal shot of Jameson's Irish whiskey when I found myself vaguely wishing I was a Young Republican. I never liked Young Republicans much but I'd never seen an unhappy Young Republican and I kind of wondered what their secret was. I wasn't really feeling sorry for myself but I wasn't feeling much of anything else, either.

I stroked the cat, poured another shot, and looked at the calendar. I'd sort of penciled in a New Year's date with Winnie Katz, the girl who ran the lesbian dance class in the loft above me. Of course, with a lesbian, you never really know how things stood, or lay, as the case may be. There was some fine, slightly twisted silk machinery in their minds that no man would ever be able to observe intimately. It was hard enough understanding normal broads which, in itself, was about as likely as making eye contact with a unicorn.

—*MUSICAL CHAIRS*

PUMPKIN PIE

MAKES ONE 8½-INCH PIE, SERVING 9

EQUIPMENT NEEDED: 8½-INCH PIE PLATE

THE CRUST
1⅓ cups all-purpose flour
⅓ cup canola oil
¼ cup nonfat milk
1 tablespoon sugar
Grated zest of 1 lemon

THE FILLING
1 can (15 ounces) pumpkin (not pie filling)
1 can (14 ounces) nonfat sweetened condensed skimmed milk (not condensed milk)
4 extra-large egg whites
1 teaspoon ground cinnamon
½ teaspoon ground ginger
½ teaspoon ground cloves
½ teaspoon nutmeg
½ teaspoon salt

Nonfat whipped cream or ice cream, for serving

1. Preheat the oven to 350 degrees F. Lightly oil the pie plate.

2. Make the crust: In a large bowl, combine the flour, oil, milk, sugar, and zest until a dough forms. Press the crust evenly into the pie plate and form a decorative edge. Bake 10 minutes, until golden. Set aside on a wire rack to cool.

3. Increase the oven to 425 degrees F.

4. Make the filling: In a medium bowl, combine the pumpkin, milk, egg whites, cinnamon, ginger, cloves, nutmeg, and salt until well combined. Pour the filling into the shell.

5. Bake the pie for 15 minutes. Reduce the oven temperature to 350 degrees F and bake the pie for 25 to 30 minutes longer, or until a knife inserted 1 inch from the edge comes out clean. If, during the second half of baking, the edges of the crust start to overbrown, cover loosely with strips of aluminum foil. Remove the pie to a wire rack and let cool completely. Serve with nonfat whipped cream or your favorite ice cream, if desired.

... [E]ver since I was thirty-seven years old, I haven't been the kind of person who looks under his bed. I believe so much weird stuff that can mess up your life happens *in* the bed that anything happening underneath is going to need all the help it can get.

—*FREQUENT FLYER*

EAT, DRINK, AND **KINKY**

WILLIE NELSON'S SURPRISE BROWNIES

MAKES NINE 3-INCH SQUARES

EQUIPMENT NEEDED: 9-INCH SQUARE NONSTICK BAKING PAN

THE BROWNIES
Vegetable cooking spray

4 extra-large egg whites

½ cup canola oil or 8 tablespoons (1 stick) unsalted butter, melted

1 cup sugar or aspartame

½ cup Nutella

½ cup all-purpose flour

½ cup nuts, such as hazelnuts, walnuts, or pecans, toasted and coarsely chopped

THE FROSTING
2 tablespoons canola oil or unsalted butter

2 tablespoons unsweetened cocoa powder

1 cup confectioners' sugar

1 teaspoon vanilla extract

1. Preheat the oven to 350 degrees F. Spray the baking pan with the cooking spray.

2. Make the brownies: In a medium bowl, beat the egg whites, oil, sugar, and Nutella until combined. Stir in the flour. Pour the batter into the prepared pan, spread it evenly, then sprinkle the nuts on top. Press them lightly into the batter.

3. Bake the brownies for 30 minutes, or until a cake tester inserted in the center comes out clean. Do not overbake. Transfer to a wire rack and let cool.

4. Make the frosting: In a medium saucepan, combine the oil, 2 tablespoons water, and cocoa powder over low heat, stirring, until combined. Remove the pan from the heat and stir in the sugar and extract; stir until the frosting reaches the consistency of soft butter.

5. Spread the frosting over the cooled brownies, let set, then cut into 3-inch squares.

Piers's Bickies

Piers Akerman always welcomes houseguests (or house pests as the Kinkster refers to them) who drop in when they want to drop out.

But it's probable that of all those who dropped in, Piers's favorite was Opal.

A gentle soul, with wonderfully lustrous brown eyes, Opal loved her soft gray fur, loved to caress it with her delicate slender artist's fingers which in another life could have made her a decent living as a piano player. She had a three-octave reach.

Opal was a Gibbon ape. She came into Piers's bachelor life as most females did in the sixties—after a few drinks at Los Angeles's famed Troubador down on Santa Monica Boulevard. The joint catered to stars on the rise and those who simply wanted a place to perform, and to drink until dawn.

As the sun lightened the eastern sky one morning, an acquaintance who once designed instrument panels for the F-14 Tomcat and other fighter aircraft but was now customizing backboards for pinball wizards asked whether I enjoyed the company of animals.

Knowing that Piers counted several beasts among his friends in the press corps, the designer produced Opal and introduced the two soon-to-be fast friends. Soon Opal was being carried across Piers's threshold.

His pad was in a nearby complex, hard by Sunset Boulevard, managed by Lucius Foster, Jodie's estranged father.

The complex was home to a cast who looked like they walked from the pages of *Day of the Locust.*

Opal fit in without a murmur. She spent her days like many of the young wannabe actresses Piers knew, watching the soaps and, by her shiny eyes, imagining herself in prime roles. Opal, to her credit however, was not as self-focused as most.

She answered the door when it rang, could find a beer in the fridge, and loved cruising Sunset in the car.

When answering nature's call, she took herself into the clump of palm growing by the complex's pool and clambered up a tree. Holding herself by one hand and one pedal extremity, she swung out the other foot and . . .

As hostess of the Akerman's home, Opal was generous with my beer and a good listener to the many misbegotten souls of the day who washed up on Sunset's bereft shores, including Kinky.

Opal and Piers rode to L.A. International Airport to surprise Kinky when he hit town with a battered guitar case in one hand and a major stogie in the other.

Kinky loved Opal's habit of popping beer cans with a toe.

To keep up their strength—and to contribute to their daily fiber diet—I made oatmeal cookies. Opal loved them, but at first they weren't high on Kinky's menu of Jewish cuisine.

PIERS AKERMAN'S AUSSIE OAT BISCUITS

MAKES 12 TO 16 BISCUITS

EQUIPMENT NEEDED: LARGE COOKIE SHEET

8 tablespoons (1 stick) butter, melted, or canola oil
¾ cup sugar or 18 packets aspartame
2 large egg whites
2 cups quick-cooking rolled oats
½ cup all-purpose flour
1 teaspoon baking powder

1. Preheat the oven to 350 degrees F. Lightly oil the cookie sheet.

2. In a large bowl, beat together the melted butter and sugar until blended. Add the egg whites and beat well. Stir in the oats, flour, and baking powder until combined.

3. Drop the batter by tablespoons, 2 inches apart, onto the prepared cookie sheet. Bake 10 minutes, or until the edges of the biscuits begin to brown.

The only things that came out of all the time and effort I expended there were a large harvest of tedium, a tattoo, a handful of friends I'll probably never see again, two blowpipes gathering cobwebs on the wall, and an occasional late-night craving for monkey brains. Some would say that's pretty good for eleven cents an hour.

"Monkey brains," I said to the cat, as I drew my second cup of espresso, "are considered quite a delicacy by the Punan tribe of Borneo."

The cat wrinkled her nose slightly in a moue of distaste. She followed this patrician behavior with a barely audible *mew* of distaste. Like many cats, and many Republicans, she was extremely ethnocentric. Her attitude toward the Punan tribe of Borneo might be effectively summed up as: "Let them eat monkey brains."

—*SPANKING WATSON*

GORILLA COOKIES

MAKES 2 DOZEN COOKIES

EQUIPMENT NEEDED: ELECTRIC MIXER

1½ cups all-purpose flour, plus additional as needed
½ cup canola oil
½ cup confectioners' sugar
½ cup walnuts, toasted and finely ground
¼ teaspoon salt

1. Preheat the oven to 375 degrees F.

2. In a medium bowl, with the electric mixer, beat the flour with the oil until the mixture resembles bread crumbs. Blend in the sugar, nuts, and salt, beating until a dough forms. If the dough is too sticky, add more flour, a tablespoon at a time, until the dough can be handled. Form the dough into a ball. With your hands, pinch off walnut-sized pieces of the dough and place on an ungreased cookie sheet; form into crescent shapes, leaving 1 inch between cookies.

3. Bake the cookies about 10 minutes, until lightly golden. Transfer the cookies to a wire rack and let them cool and crisp up, preferably overnight, if your accomplices will let you.

Later that night, down in the open-air pub with drunken Aussies throwing darts across the bridges of our noses, McGovern and I were drinking Cascade beer from Tassie (Tasmania) and listening to a British tourist bellyaching about his bad luck. He'd hit a kangaroo in his Land Rover and, not wanting to miss a photo op for the folks back home, had taken the dead body, dressed it up in his jacket, knapsack, and sunglasses, and leaned it against a nearby gum tree. He was taking the kangaroo's photo when the animal, apparently only stunned, suddenly bounded away with all his money and his passport.

"Now I'm stuck here broke and getting bitten to death by the bloody flies," he complained.

"Serves you right, mate," said one of the locals. "First thing, you run down one of our 'roos. Next thing, you'll be swattin' our flies."

—KINKY FRIEDMAN, *AMERICAN WAY* MAGAZINE

CHOCOLATE ALMOND TASSIES

MAKES 12 MINIATURE TARTS

EQUIPMENT NEEDED: 12-CUP MINIATURE NONSTICK MUFFIN PAN

Vegetable cooking spray
½ cup canola oil
1 package (8 ounces) fat-free cream cheese, softened
1 cup all-purpose flour
⅓ cup Nutella
½ cup chopped blanched almonds, toasted until golden
⅓ cup semisweet chocolate chips
2 extra-large egg whites
½ cup packed dark brown sugar
1 teaspoon vanilla extract

1. Preheat the oven to 350 degrees F. Spray the muffin cups with cooking spray.

2. In a medium bowl, stir together the oil, cream cheese, and flour until a dough forms. Shape into a ball. Pinch off 1-inch pieces of dough and press into each of the prepared muffin cups to line them evenly.

3. Into each muffin cup, spoon a dollop of Nutella. Top with a few nut pieces and some chocolate chips.

4. In a small bowl, beat together the egg whites, brown sugar, and vanilla. Using a tablespoon, spoon enough of the egg-white mixture into each cup to nearly fill it.

5. Bake the tassies for 35 minutes, or until dark and crunchy. While the tassies are still warm, run a thin knife around the sides of them to loosen them and to loosen any filling that may have bubbled up onto the top of the muffin pan. Then let cool completely in the pan.

The period between Christmas and New Year's can be a rather lonely time for those of us married to the wind. Old people living alone tend to leap from their top-floor balconies in greatly increased numbers, sometimes taking until Purim to hit the pavement. Young people who feel alone see the holiday season as a pretty good time to end it all before it begins. They hang themselves while listening to albums by Whitesnake, overdose on St. Joseph's baby aspirins, or just wander away, having always dreamed of someday seeing themselves on milk cartons.

—*MUSICAL CHAIRS*

LOTTIE COTTON'S
DROP-DEAD COOKIES

MAKES ABOUT 30 COOKIES (2 INCHES EACH)

EQUIPMENT NEEDED: LARGE COOKIE SHEET

1⅓ cups all-purpose flour

¾ teaspoon baking soda

½ teaspoon salt

½ cup canola oil

½ cup packed light or dark brown sugar

½ cup sugar or 12 packets aspartame

2 extra-large egg whites

1 teaspoon vanilla extract

1 teaspoon coconut extract

½ cup walnuts, toasted and coarsely chopped

½ cup semisweet chocolate chips

2 squares (2 ounces) semisweet chocolate, chopped

1. Preheat the oven to 350 degrees F. Lightly oil the cookie sheet.

2. In a bowl, stir together the flour, baking soda, and salt.

3. In another bowl, stir together the oil, brown sugar, sugar, egg whites, and extracts until well combined. Stir in the nuts and chocolate chips. Then fold into flour mixture, combining thoroughly.

4. Drop the batter by rounded tablespoons, leaving 2 inches in between, onto the prepared cookie sheet. Dip your fingertips into water and pat down each mound until flat. Bake the cookies 10 to 15 minutes, or until brown around the edges. If you like your cookies crisper, bake a few minutes more. Remove with a metal spatula to brown paper bags to cool.

"You never see a luggage rack on a hearse," I said.

—WHEN THE CAT'S AWAY

JACK DANIEL'S TIRAMISU

SERVES 8

EQUIPMENT NEEDED: ELECTRIC MIXER; 3-QUART SERVING BOWL

4 packages (8 ounces each) mascarpone (low fat, if available), or low-fat or
   nonfat Philadelphia cream cheese, at room temperature

1 cup plus 2 teaspoons sugar or 25 packets aspartame

½ cup half-and-half

2 tablespoons Jack Daniel's, or a lot more, to taste

1 teaspoon vanilla extract

½ teaspoon orange extract

1½ cups strong espresso (decaffeinated, if preferred), cooled

1 package (14 ounces) ladyfingers (48 in package)

8 ounces milk chocolate or semisweet chocolate, if preferred, grated or very
   finely chopped

1. In a large bowl, with the electric mixer, beat the cheese until light and fluffy. Add the 1 cup sugar or 24 packets aspartame, half-and-half, 1 tablespoon of the Jack Daniel's, and vanilla and orange extracts and beat for 1 minute, until well combined.

2. Place espresso, remaining 2 teaspoons sugar or 1 packet aspartame, and remaining 1 tablespoon Jack Daniel's (or more to taste) in a 2-cup measuring cup or bowl and stir until the sweetener is dissolved.

3. Dip enough of the ladyfingers, one at a time, quickly into the coffee mixture and use them to cover the bottom and line the sides of the 3-quart serving bowl. Spoon half of the cheese mixture over them in an even layer. Sprinkle with half of the grated chocolate.

4. Make another layer of ladyfingers and cheese, dunking the ladyfingers quickly to prevent them from becoming soggy. Top with the remaining chocolate. If you are a coffee lover, drizzle with a small amount of the coffee mixture. Cover the bowl and refrigerate for at least 2 hours.

5. Spoon the tiramisu onto dessert plates or into bowls to serve.

There were no cabs. Cabs, apparently, thought I was dead. So I ankled it through the slush in my brontosaurus foreskin cowboy boots and I counted maître d's to keep my brain stem at least active enough not to turn into a toxic icicle.

—*GOD BLESS JOHN WAYNE*

HOT FUDGE SAUCE

MAKES 1½ CUPS

EQUIPMENT NEEDED: HEAVY-BOTTOMED MEDIUM SAUCEPAN

1 cup semisweet chocolate chips
½ cup nonfat evaporated milk (not condensed milk) or whipping cream
¼ cup sugar or 6 packets aspartame
1 tablespoon unsalted butter or canola oil

Melt the chocolate chips in the saucepan with the milk, sugar, and butter over low heat, stirring occasionally, until smooth. Serve hot, over brownies, cake, frozen yogurt, or other desserts. Store any left over covered in the refrigerator. Reheat in a small saucepan of warm water until smooth.

There are more people, pigeons, and potholes in New York than cross-ties on the railroad or stars in the skies, and there's no elbow room for Daniel Boone. But people in this city have something else. They all feel that it means something just to be here. For example, a mugger in New York knows that he's at the top of his profession. Child molesters, hit men, killer fags, all smile a secret little smile to themselves in New York. They know they are the best that they can be.

—*FREQUENT FLYER*

WHITE CHOCOLATE SAUCE

MAKES 1¼ CUPS

EQUIPMENT NEEDED: HEAVY-BOTTOMED MEDIUM SAUCEPAN

12 ounces white chocolate (made with cocoa butter, not palm oil), coarsely
   chopped
1 cup nonfat evaporated milk or whipping cream
1 teaspoon coconut extract
½ teaspoon almond extract

Melt the chocolate in the saucepan with the milk over low heat until the mixture is smooth. Remove from the heat and stir in the extracts. Serve warm. Store any left over covered in the refrigerator. Reheat in a small pan of warm water until smooth.

"Money may buy you a fine dog," I said to the cat, "but only love can make it wag its tail."

—BLAST FROM THE PAST

LAURIE HUTTON'S
POTATO CANDY

1 medium-to-large russet potato, peeled and cut into chunks
1 cup confectioners' sugar
¼ teaspoon vanilla extract
¼ to ½ cup smooth or chunky peanut butter

1. Put the potato in a saucepan and cover with cold water. Bring to a boil, then simmer 10 to 15 minutes, until the potato is fork-tender. Drain. Return the potato to the pan and mash; slowly add the sugar, stirring it in, until the mixture is the consistency of pie dough. Stir in the vanilla.

2. Roll the potato mixture out on a piece of waxed paper until ⅛-inch thick. Spread peanut butter over the surface. Using the paper as a guide, roll up jelly-roll fashion. Wrap the roll in plastic wrap and refrigerate until firm.

3. Slice to serve, if desired.

They say if you're looking for trouble you'll find it, but the truth is, if you look too hard for anything you probably won't find it. The way you find stuff is not to look for it. You might even try praying for things you don't want. Run in a little reverse psychology on God. You could get lucky.

—*FREQUENT FLYER*

DRINKS AND LIBATIONS

After pondering the derivation of the word **libation**—and deciding it must have to do with an increased libido—Kinky once proposed a toast to his entourage of friends and supplicants. Looking about him and realizing just how fatal life really is, he lifted his bullhorn full of Jameson's and said, "Eat, drink, and be Kinky, for tomorrow will come, and then where will you be?"

Once you've been a country singer on the road for a while, there's not a lot of things that you'd think of as tough. Maybe ordering from a wine list.

—*WHEN THE CAT'S AWAY*

ICED TEA

SERVES 8

10 tea bags or ¼ cup loose black tea leaves (my favorite is Hill & Brooks Tea,
   available at specialty food shops)
¼ teaspoon spearmint extract
2 cups sugar or aspartame, or to taste
Lemon slices, for serving (optional)

1. Bring 3 quarts water to a boil in a large pot. Put the tea bags or tea in a stainless steel bowl. Pour in the boiling water and let the tea steep for 10 minutes. Stir in the mint extract and sweeten the tea to taste. Strain into a pitcher and let cool, then cover and refrigerate until cold.

2. Serve in tall glasses over ice, with lemon slices, if desired.

Maybe we'll all have our fifteen minutes of fame. But time, of course, is the money of fame. And time, as Albert Einstein observed when he wasn't busy looking for his bicycle in Princeton, New Jersey, is relative. Therefore, my fellow members of the slide-rule club, my fellow passengers on this ship of fools, we are forced to draw the following conclusion: We may all have our fifteen minutes of fame, but Edith Piaf's fifteen minutes is likely to run on a little longer than Vanilla Ice's fifteen minutes. Nevertheless, when everybody's time and fame has all run out and lovely Rita Meter Maid, Former Miss Texas 1987, finally waltzes up and embraces us at the end of the troubled dream, we will all die alone in hopeless, courageous oblivion like Gauguin or Tiny Tim. And when the end comes at last, each and every one of us will have at least one comforting thought as we fall through that timeless trapdoor: Albert Einstein is still probably out there somewhere looking for his fucking bicycle.

—ROADKILL

ICED LEMON LATTE

MAKES 2 DRINKS

EQUIPMENT NEEDED: BLENDER

2 tablespoons instant espresso granules
3 tablespoons hot water
1½ cups nonfat milk
2 tablespoons sugar or aspartame
3 cups crushed ice or small ice cubes
Lemon slices, for garnish

1. In a small cup, dissolve the espresso granules in the water.

2. In the blender, combine the coffee, milk, sugar, and ice until blended. Pour into tall glasses and garnish each with a lemon slice.

I reasoned that it wasn't the kind of case one would like to drink nor the kind one might possibly obtain from any recent unsavory sexualis.

—*GREENWICH KILLING TIME*

owboys love Indians. It's the modern code of the real Kinky West. The last time Willie Nelson stopped to help just one Native American, the living legend was compelled to shell out millions of dollars and endure years of hard times by U.S. government agents.

Willie's amigo, artist-and-screenwriter Doug Holloway, picks up the tale. "The last time Willie said 'Sure' like that was when Kris Kristofferson asked him in the fall of '85 to lend his name to a fund-raising concert on behalf of an Indian trouble. Willie was completely unaware of any political implication with that 'Yes.' Willie had never heard the name Peltier before."

So what does the U.S. Tokemaster General say when Kinky Friedman asks for help?

"I told him, 'Find another sucker,'" Willie says, with a belly laugh.

Kinky says, "In truth, Willie gave me a lot of his time, allowed me to use his name for commercial porpoises and spent days, if not weeks, helping promote my book."

The book was Kinky's 1997 bestselling thriller, *Roadkill.*

Willie can't help laughing out loud when remembering the whole Kinky story. "When we first talked about his new book back in '96, Kinky asked me if I could help out and I said, 'Sure.'"

Willie says: "Kinky also asked me to help when the book was being published in September '97. To start in New York and help with the promotion."

"Willie likes New York, anyway," Kinky says. "But, I must confess, it was a helluva pace he put up with, getting up in the middle of the night and whatnot, all in the name of friendship."

"I come to New York, as agreed," Willie explains. "Then he tells me I've got to be up by 4:30 in the morning, and that we're doing about one thousand shows and book signings all in one day."

"Jesus Christ!" said Willie.

"I'll see that Jesus and raise you a Peter," I said.

—*MUSICAL CHAIRS*

EAT, DRINK, AND BE KINKY

ther New York lovers along for the Manhattan media tour were Bob Dylan's fabled guitarist Larry Campbell, and Willie's manager, Mark Rothbaum, who'd also managed Miles Davis, Emmylou Harris, Roger Miller, and Delbert McClinton, Don Imus's second-favorite singer. Kinky, Willie, and Campbell were kept alive for the day by Willie's beloved long-time chauffeur, Mikey, who has since stepped on a rainbow.

"The first thing we did was to stop for a show with Charlie Rose," says Willie. "And all Kinky wanted to do was talk about my deal with the FBI and the Indian."

What deal?

"Oooooh," said Willie, pausing to decide how much to reveal, "many years ago I had a run-in, and Kinky wanted to talk about that."

Willie burst into laughter and took a father-to-son tone, "I said to Kinky, 'This is your deal, not mine.' Let's talk about the fuckin' book."

Trying to stifle his own laughter, Willie adds, "An hour later, we were doing Imus and Kinky starts trashing Mother Teresa. She'd just died. I thought he was finally gonna talk about the book. But here he is on Imus, with a nationwide audience of—what does Imus say?—ten million—talking about Mother Teresa.

"I say to myself, What the fuck is this guy crowing about so early in the morning?

"Kinky was hilarious. I was just enjoying watching him shoot hisself in the foot, no, both feet. You see why I was a little worried. Imus got mad; he realized Kinky was screwing up the whole interview (with me). Wasting a lot of time, and pissing off a lot of Catholics, too.

"For what reason, I don't know. What did Mother Teresa ever do to Kinky?"

Kinky explains. "The argument was Princess Di versus Mother

Teresa. I saw Mother Teresa as a mouthpiece for the Vatican, or as she was known, the Ghoul of Calcutta. Imus was putting down Princess Di. So I said Mother Teresa only wanted a big score for saving souls, but didn't care about actually helping people who'd sought her out; she'd wanted a big score so she'd get to Heaven and be saved. I said Di's love for the masses was purer because she wanted to help end their suffering."

After escaping Imus's wrath, Kinky and Willie rolled over to the Barnes & Noble bookstore on Fifth Avenue in midtown Manhattan.

The Kinky-Willie combo proved irresistible for thousands of book buyers who tied up traffic for hours. It was the store's second largest crowd ever, the first being the historic whopper turnout for shock jock Howard Stern's literary effort.

Besides the Kinky book lovers, the Kinky-Willie throng included dozens of Willie-loving cops, firemen, and city sanitation workers.

"That's when Willie said, 'Find a new sucker.' So I called Dwight Yoakam. Dwight, I understand, laughed at my sucker line—the first time he heard it."

Kinky adds, "Oh yes, Willie also asked me not to use the *M* word anymore."

BLOOD RED LEMONADE

MAKES 2 DRINKS

EQUIPMENT NEEDED: BLENDER

2 lemons, peeled, seeded, and quartered, plus 2 lemon slices, for garnish
1 tablespoon sugar or 2 packets aspartame, or to taste
3 cups crushed ice or small ice cubes
Maraschino cherry juice, plus 2 cherries, for garnish

1. Put the lemons, sugar, and ice in the blender; blend until the lemons are completely pulverized.

2. In a glass, add enough cherry juice to 1 cup water to color it blood red; add to the lemonade and combine. Serve the lemonade in tall glasses and garnish each with a lemon slice and cherry.

Beauty's all in the eye of the beerholder.

—THE LOVE SONG OF J. EDGAR HOOVER

DREAMSICLE SHAKE

MAKES 2 BIG DRINKS

EQUIPMENT NEEDED: BLENDER

4 scoops nonfat vanilla ice cream or frozen yogurt
2 scoops orange sherbet
⅔ cup nonfat milk
1 teaspoon orange extract or Grand Marnier
Splash fresh orange juice
Fresh mint sprigs, for garnish (optional)

In the blender, combine the ice cream, sherbet, milk, extract, and orange juice and blend until smooth. Serve over ice in tall glasses and garnish each with a mint sprig, if using.

One of the mild little ironies of crime solving, not to mention life, is that if you want to be a good guy you've got to be able to think like a bad guy. There's never existed a good little church-worker with the God-given talent to casually crawl inside the criminal mind. God gives good little church-workers other things: grief, guilt, absolution, moral superiority, blissful ignorance, the ability to see the world the way it never was and never will be. If all of this fails to add up to any semblance of true happiness, it's not really surprising. That's why when you look back over the fleeting yet inescapably tedious history of mankind, you'll always find more criminals than church-workers.

—*BLAST FROM THE PAST*

EAT, DRINK, AND BE KINKY

ORANGE CHALLENGER

MAKES 2 DRINKS

EQUIPMENT NEEDED: BLENDER

1 cup orange juice

6 tablespoons (3 ounces) nonfat milk

2 tablespoons sugar or aspartame, or to taste

4 ice cubes

2 slices blood orange with rind, for garnish (optional)

In the blender, combine the orange juice, milk, sugar, and ice cubes and blend until smooth. Serve in tall glasses and garnish each with an orange slice, if using.

Always let the woman choose the wine. Makes you look sensitive, innocent. Maybe a little vulnerable. It's also usually cheaper because the woman is trying to protect you because she thinks you're so vulnerable.

—*A CASE OF LONE STAR*

If everybody drank enough sambuca we could probably solve all the major problems of the world. Religious conflicts and ethnic violence would no doubt disappear. National boundaries would disintegrate and the world would at last realize John Lennon's dream in the song "Imagine." Such is the power of sambuca. Of course, before all this happened, it might be a good idea, just in case, to buy up a large quantity of coffee bean futures.

—*ELVIS, JESUS & COCA-COLA*

STRAWBERRY WONDER

MAKES 2 DRINKS

EQUIPMENT NEEDED: BLENDER

½ pint strawberries, hulled and sliced (about 1 cup)
1 cup nonfat milk or water
2 tablespoons sugar or 4 packets aspartame, or to taste
4 ice cubes

In the blender, combine the strawberries, milk, sugar, and ice cubes and blend until smooth. Serve in tall glasses.

PEACHY CREAM

MAKES 2 DRINKS

EQUIPMENT NEEDED: BLENDER

1 cup canned peach nectar

2 ripe peaches, peeled, pitted, and quartered

2 tablespoons sugar or 4 packets aspartame, or to taste

3 cups crushed ice or small ice cubes

Frozen whipped topping and 2 maraschino cherries, for garnish

In the blender, combine the peach nectar, peaches, sugar, and ice and blend until smooth. Pour into tall glasses and garnish each with whipped topping and a cherry on top.

For a guy who had the mind of a modern-day Sherlock Holmes, I figured it was definitely time for me to start using my head for something other than a hat rack.

. . . The love of my life was already smoke from the Vatican. . . . Smoke that blinds your cowboy heart to everything but the campfires of the past.

—*BLAST FROM THE PAST*

'NANA SMOOTHIE

MAKES 1 SMOOTHIE

EQUIPMENT NEEDED: BLENDER OR FOOD PROCESSOR

1 large banana
¼ cantaloupe, seeds and rind removed, flesh cut into chunks
½ cup plain nonfat yogurt
2 tablespoons skim milk powder
2 tablespoons thawed orange juice concentrate
2 teaspoons honey

Slice the banana into the blender or food processor. Add the cantaloupe, yogurt, milk powder, orange juice concentrate, and honey and blend until smooth. Serve immediately, in a tall glass.

The road could've ended anywhere, but it didn't. So you keep driving life's lonely DeSoto, looking ahead into the rain and darkness with the windshield wipers coming down like reaper's blades just missing your dreams. And you don't stop till you're damn well ready. Till you come to the right place. Till you come to the right face. The place may be New York or Texas or it may be somewhere painted with the colors Negroes use in their neon lights.

The face will be smiling. So you take the key out of the ignition and you see if it opens her heart.

—WHEN THE CAT'S AWAY

EAT, DRINK, AND BE KINKY

BANANA SHAKE

MAKES 2 BIG DRINKS

EQUIPMENT NEEDED: BLENDER

1 large ripe banana
6 scoops nonfat banana ice cream or frozen yogurt
1 cup nonfat milk

Slice the banana into the blender and add the ice cream and milk.
Blend until smooth. Serve at once in tall glasses, with or without ice.

There's a little bit of Nazi, I thought, and a little bit of Jew in all of us. How
we deal with these diverse parts of our being will have a lot to do with what
kind of lives we will eventually lead and what kind of world we'll be able to
make for our children and our kittens.

—*FREQUENT FLYER*

CHOCOLATE EGG CREAM

MAKES 1 DRINK

3 tablespoons low-fat chocolate syrup
3 tablespoons ice-cold nonfat milk
1 cup ice-cold sodium-free seltzer

Pour the chocolate syrup and milk into a 16-ounce glass. Add enough of the seltzer to come halfway up the glass and stir vigorously to blend in the syrup. Holding it about 12 inches from the top of the glass, pour in the remaining seltzer. (Pouring the seltzer from a distance, it turns out, promotes a good frothy foam.)

Sometimes you can see things more clearly when they're not there. Most of the great books about human freedom, for instance, were written in prison. From my own personal experience, I have put a black pill of opium into a cup of coffee, drunk it down, stood at the edge of the Borneo jungle staring out across the South China Sea, and seen America more lucidly than at any time in my life. This was made possible partly by the drug, but mostly, I believe, by the physical absence of America.

—*FREQUENT FLYER*

EGGNOG

This first-rate version of eggnog calls for, not surprisingly, raw
eggs. Eating raw eggs has become, however, somewhat hazardous
of late because of the increase in the incidence of salmonella that
has been traced back to the ingestion of uncooked whites and/or
yolks. The very young, the very old, and anyone with a
compromised immune system should not eat foods
containing raw eggs. (Unlike certain other
recipes, there is no immediate solution
here because cooking eggs for eggnog is unthinkable.) That said,
I've enjoyed this nog for years,
and I'm still standing. But
forewarned is forearmed.

MAKES 2 GENEROUS QUARTS

EQUIPMENT NEEDED: BLENDER; IMMERSION BLENDER

THE NOG
1 pint nonfat vanilla frozen yogurt
1 pint nonfat milk
½ cup extra-large egg whites or ½ cup egg substitute
2 teaspoons vanilla extract
Pinch of freshly grated nutmeg

THE TOPPING
2 cups ice-cold nonfat milk
2 tablespoons sugar or 4 packets aspartame
Splash of cognac or rum

1. Make the nog: In the blender, combine the yogurt, milk, egg
whites, vanilla, and nutmeg and blend until well combined. Pour into
a punch bowl.

2. Make the topping: In a bowl, with the immersion blender, beat
the milk and sugar until frothy. Add the cognac or rum and beat to
combine and whip.

3. Spoon the topping over the nog. Serve and enjoy.

Teaching a queer a lesson is something that very few big macho men can resist. This is because they fear all fagolas, fear all the people with the holes in the middle, fear that they secretly might be one or the other of them, fear their fathers, fear their mothers, fear their God, and fear that when they were growing up they might've mistakenly read too much Oscar Wilde. In Texas, of course, we consider anyone a queer who likes girls more than he likes football.

—*ROADKILL*

MINT JULEP

MAKES 4 DRINKS

EQUIPMENT NEEDED: SMALL SAUCEPAN; 4 CHILLED TUMBLERS,
  FOR SERVING

½ cup sugar or 12 packets aspartame
½ cup finely chopped mint, plus 4 sprigs, for garnish
Crushed ice (about 2 cups)
1 cup (8 ounces or 8 shots) Kentucky bourbon, or to taste

1. In the saucepan, combine ½ cup water and the sugar and bring
to a boil; simmer 3 minutes. Remove the pan from the heat and stir in
the mint. Let cool. Strain the syrup into a cup.

2. Divide the crushed ice among the 4 chilled tumblers. Divide the
bourbon among them evenly. Stir 2 tablespoons mint syrup into each
glass and garnish each with a mint sprig.

We drove a number of miles farther down 16, then took a left and rolled in
a cloud of dust across a cattle guard, down a country road, and into the
sunset toward Echo Hill. The ranch was set back about two and a half miles
from the scenic little highway, but ever since we passed Pipe Creek we'd
been in a world that most New Yorkers never got to see. They believed the
deer, the jackrabbits, the raccoons, the sun setting the sky on fire in the
west, the cypress trees bathing their knees in the little creek, the pale
moon shyly peeking over the mountain—they believed these things only
really existed in a Disney movie or a children's storybook. I closed my
eyes for a moment, turned a page in my mind. When I opened my eyes
again everything was still there. Only New York was gone.

—*ARMADILLOS & OLD LACE*

Die BY THe
WaTeRMeLoN SLuSH

MAKES 4 TALL DRINKS

EQUIPMENT NEEDED: BLENDER

1 medium-large seedless watermelon, halved
Ice cubes
⅓ cup fresh lime juice (about 4 limes)
¼ cup chopped fresh mint leaves
1 jigger (2 ounces) vodka, or to taste

1. Cutting horizontally, slice a piece off one of the watermelon halves for garnish; reserve. Cut the remaining watermelon into chunks and remove the rind.

2. In the blender, combine watermelon chunks with ice cubes until the blender is filled. Blend until mixture turns creamy pink in color, adding more melon as needed. Add the lime juice and mint and blend again. Pour in the vodka and stir.

3. To serve, pour into tall clear glasses and garnish each with a wedge of the reserved melon.

I glanced quickly at the cat, who was now sitting on the counter staring at me. I thought I detected something akin to a form of feline empathy in her eyes. It was also possible that the cockroach had now crawled up the wall behind me.

"So Robert Louis Stevenson," I said, "had been a great friend of a Samoan chieftain named Mataafa, and once he personally arranged to release many of Mataafa's followers from a wrongful imprisonment. The Samoans, quite reasonably, hated manual labor. But once the prisoners were released, they set about building a road from the town of Apia to Stevenson's house. The road, which still stands today in Samoa, was called 'The Road of the Loving Hearts.'"

A short while later, the cat [fell] asleep.

—*GOD BLESS JOHN WAYNE*

MONTEGO BAY PIÑA COLADA

MAKES 3 DRINKS

EQUIPMENT NEEDED: BLENDER

1½ cups (12 ounces) unsweetened pineapple juice
¾ cup (6 ounces) coconut milk or cream of coconut (see note)
¾ cup (6 ounces—about 3 double shots) light rum
1½ teaspoons sugar or 2 packets aspartame
Ice cubes (about 2 cups)

In the blender, combine the pineapple juice, coconut milk, rum, and sugar and blend well. Fill 3 highball glasses with ice and pour in the piña colada mix, dividing it equally.

NOTE: Piña colada aficionados know that the classic mix is made with cream of coconut. I've used coconut milk as a way of lightening it, but if you want to go with the classic by all means do. In that event, you will also have to adjust the sugar to your own taste.

But getting back to Jesus, as we all find ourselves doing now and then, it must be noted that being King of the Jews, along with all the obvious perks, also requires a rather tedious amount of personal responsibility. Sometimes this becomes too much even for self-effacing types like Jesus and provokes minor outbursts such as the one immediately following the Last Supper, when Jesus is reported to have yelled at the waiter: "Separate checks, please."

—*SPANKING WATSON*

EAT, DRINK, AND BE KINKY

INDEX

Huevos Rancheros, 77–78
Hutton, Laurie, 176

Iced Lemon Latte, 180
Iced Tea, 179
"Imagine," 187
Imus, Don, 23, 67, 183, 184
Irish Snapper with Lime Sauce, 81
Irish Toast, 138–39

Jack Daniel's Tiramisu, 172
Joe Heller's Back-Biting Shrimp, 86
John, Elton, 31
Judd, Naomi, 130

Katz, Robbie, 43
Katz, Winnie, 80, 160
Kinky's Last Supper at John
    McCall's Pedrigal in Cabo San
    Lucas, 92–93
Kirk, James T., 68
Krieger, Maria, 157
Kristofferson, Kris, 152, 181
Krupa, Gene, 156

Larry ("Ratso") Sloman's Big Wong
    Dream, 105
Lasagna, Frankie, 128–29
Laurie Hutton's Potato Candy, 176
Lemons:
    Blood Red Lemonade, 185
    Iced Lemon Latte, 180
Lennon, John, 187
Life-Saver Pizza, 75–76
Limes:
    -and-Chili-Roasted Corn, 53
    Irish Snapper with Lime Sauce,
    81
Lottie Cotton's Drop-Dead Cookies,
    171
Love Song of J. Edgar Hoover, The,
    20, 47, 49, 52, 61, 96, 120, 185

Maid, Rita Meter, 179
Mama Cass, 116
Mango Soup, Chilled Avocado and,
    36
Maple Syrup and Balsamic Salad
    Dressing, Robbie Katz's, 43
Maria Krieger's Peanut-Butter
    Chocolate-Chip Cheesecake,
    157–58
Martin Persson's Ginger Pound
    Cake with Tangerine Sauce,
    149–50
McCall, John, 68–69, 92
McClinton, Delbert, 183

McCourt, Frank, 137, 138–39
McGee, Bobby, 152
McGovern, Mike, 82, 94, 95, 96
Meat:
    Beef Fajitas with Salsa, 119
    Crimson Baby Back Ribs, 109
    Dagwood Hero, 70
    Deli He-Man High-Roller, 65–66
    Dwight Yoakam's Stewed Squir-
        rel with Gravy and Fried Ap-
        ples, 101–2
    Frankie Lasagna, 128–29
    Larry ("Ratso") Sloman's Big
        Wong Dream, 105
    Meat Loaf, 123
    Mick Brennan's Toad in the Hole,
        111
    Our America Burger, 71
    Pete Meyers's Roast Beef with
        Pearl Onions and Spuds and
        Merlot Sauce, 117–18
    Ratso's White Castle Omelet, 130
    Roast Pork Burritos, 112–13
    Shepherd's Pie, 114–15
    Spiced Roast Pork Tenderloin
        with Sweet Corn Cream Sauce,
        106–7
    Steve Rambam's Jailhouse Chili,
        125–26
    Watson's Beef Satays with Kinky
        Peanut Sauce, 121–22
    See also Poultry; specific meat
        type
Meat Loaf, 123
Merlot Sauce, 117
Mexican Guacamole, 21
Mick Brennan's Toad in the Hole,
    111
Miller, Roger, 183
Mint Julep, 195
Montego Bay Piña Colada, 198
Mother Teresa, 38, 183–84
Mushroom Pâté, Stephanie
    DuPont's Oyster-, 24
Musical Chairs, 31, 42, 56, 85,
    148, 160, 170, 182
Myers, Pete, 110, 117

'Nana Smoothie, 190
Nelson, Bobbie, 152
Nelson, Willie, 49, 58, 67, 163,
    181, 183, 184
Nixon, Richard, 68, 91
Nuts:
    Abound, 20
    Cajun, 19
    Chocolate Almond Tassies, 169